KNOX

CHECK YOUR TRIGGERS

Your mental health and emotional well-being matters to me. You can find a list of possible triggers on the book's page on my website katerandallauthor.com or by scanning the QR code below.
Xoxo

For my husband, Matt. Always.

CONTENTS

CHAPTER ONE
KNOX

This last year has been a cluster fuck of epic proportions. The only thing that's kept my head on straight has been being able to take my bike out. It feels like we've barely had a chance to breathe—especially between dealing with the Italians, helping the Irish clean up their mess, and keeping our own businesses running smoothly. I've been looking forward to the day I can ride with my brothers and not have to worry about what shit show tomorrow is going to bring.

The snow has finally melted in Shine, but it's still cold as hell as my brother and I wind through the tree-lined roads leading back into town. The first signs of spring are in the air, and the barren trees are starting to sprout new leaves. Guess that's a sign of new beginnings or some shit. We sure as hell could use it after the last year.

When we reach the city limits, Linc pulls into Maple Street Diner—the little restaurant we've been coming to since we were kids—and parks his bike off to the side of the brick building just like we do every time we stop here.

"I'm fucking freezing," he says when I turn the engine of my Harley off. "Let's get some coffee."

"You should have worn more than just a flannel, dumbass," I say, swinging my leg over the seat.

"Fuck off. It didn't feel this cold when we left."

"Damn, little brother. You kiss our mother with that mouth?" I ask with a smirk.

"Hey, you started it. And leave our poor saintly mother out of it."

We both laugh as we walk through the front door. Our mother is many things, but saintly isn't one of them. Tanya Anderson is one tough cookie. Hell, she had to be—raising me on her own after being kicked out of her house for a teenage pregnancy required strength, that's for sure. When she met Linc's dad, she thought her luck finally turned around. We packed up and moved from Tennessee to Nebraska. I was too young to remember much about Tennessee, but I sure as hell remember Nebraska.

It took a couple years for her new husband to show his true colors after Linc was born. Then it turned into years of him getting drunk and beating on me and my mom. He usually left Linc alone, content with raging at the two of us. When he lost his job, my mom finally kicked his sorry ass out. Then he showed up one night, looking for money or a punching bag, probably both. He attacked our mom, and when I tried to get him off her, he turned his wrath on me. If Linc hadn't hit him over the head with a frying pan, who knows if I'd be here today. We took off that night and didn't stop until we landed in Shine, Massachusetts, where my mom found a good job at the bike shop owned by the Black Roses MC—and an even better man in Trick, the former Black Roses president.

"Saint Tanya would have told you the same thing. Next time you want to take a ride, wear a damn jacket, or at least a sweatshirt so you don't freeze your balls off," I say as we have a seat in the red vinyl booth.

The plastic-covered menus are on the table, and Florence, the waitress who's been here since I was a kid, comes over with two cups of steaming-hot coffee.

"You boys look like you need a warm-up," Florence says when she sets the coffee mugs on the table. "How's your mom?"

Everyone in town knows our mom. After moving to Shine, she threw herself into volunteering for anything the town needed. Whether it's the women's shelter or the various parades and festivals the town hosts throughout the year, Tanya is front and center—directing and squeezing donations from business owners for charity raffles. Hell, maybe there is a touch of saint in her, after all. I don't think she'll be nominated for sainthood just yet—she quite enjoys wringing money from the pockets of rich business owners around town who think they're better than us.

"She's good. Busy getting everything together for the Spring Fling next month," I reply, giving the woman a polite smile.

"Tell her I'm making a few things for her raffle."

I nod with a smile. "Will do."

Florence leaves to go check on her other tables, and Linc leans back in the booth, taking a sip of the hot coffee.

"I can't believe that's coming up already. It doesn't seem like it's been a year since we were out there at the ass crack of dawn setting up all the booths and shit for her," he says.

That's another thing about our mom. Being the old lady of the former MC prez still gives her a lot of sway in the club, not that any of us would ever tell her no to begin with. When she heads the town festivals, all of us get roped into helping. Well, except Trick; his arthritis has gotten so bad he can barely hold a hammer. He's more than happy to sit back and sip coffee while directing us to do Tanya's bidding.

"It'll be nice, especially after this past year, to do something that doesn't involve the Italian and Irish and their bullshit," I say.

"Yeah, I'm all for lending a helping hand, but I think I've made enough trips out to the pig farm to last a lifetime." Linc releases an overdramatic shudder.

"You went once," I say before taking a long drink of the hot coffee. "I had to be there every time."

"Exactly, and once was more than enough for me."

"Pussy."

"Sorry, man, but the way those damn things snort and get excited when we pull up is the stuff of nightmares." Linc's face twists in disgust.

The night Carlo Cataldi was taken out, I introduced Eoghan Monaghan, Finn's brother, to the farmer. He wore a similar look to the one Linc has now.

We've worked with the Monaghan family—the Irish Mob who runs Boston and now pretty much all of Massachusetts—for years, mostly running guns for them. Through the years, our business arrangement has turned into a friendship and has been strengthened with family ties that none of us saw coming. When shit goes down, we have their back like they've had ours. We could all use a little downtime after the chaos of the last few years.

Carlo Cataldi, the *former* head of one of the Italian families in Boston, had been a thorn in our sides for almost a year. He was taken out by Finn Monaghan's cousin who also happened to be Cataldi's new brother-in-law. Though our club had a plenty big bone to pick with Cataldi, our prez, Ozzy, agreed to let the Monaghans take the lead—and that's exactly what they did. We were fortunate enough to help them out with it, and from what I hear, Ozzy got a few licks in. I was stuck in the truck making sure none of the rats scattered, which is a shame because I'd have loved to get a few punches in myself after the shit he put my brothers through. But I go where my prez needs me, and that's all there is to it.

A few months ago, that brought us to the home of Massimo Farina, the head of the other Italian family who had a nice little setup here in Massachusetts, key word being *had*. He decided to take up where Cataldi left off with the skin trade, and just like Cataldi, it didn't end well for him. That was a whole other mess that landed us at the pig farm by the time we were through, but it also brought Nova Reed into our lives. Her brother was a prospect for the club who was killed while trying to protect Jude's old lady, Lucy, from the cult fucks who abused her from the day she was born and wanted her back.

Thinking about Cooper always sends a twinge of grief coupled with guilt through me. As the vice president of the Black Roses MC, the safety and lives of my brothers and the prospects are my responsibility just as much as Ozzy's. Cooper's death wasn't in vain, though, and we got bloody revenge for our fallen brother.

"Hey, where'd you go?" Linc asks, pulling me out of the memories surrounding the night we stormed the cult compound with the help of Jude's brother, Liam, and his team to rescue Lucy and put down as many of those assholes as we could.

It was a good night. For us anyways.

"Nowhere, brother."

It's been a hell of a year, and we could all do with some peace and quiet.

The front door opens and Linc's face lights up, which means only one thing.

"Hey, Charlie Pie," Linc says as his old lady slides into the booth next to him.

"We saw your bikes and decided to stop in and say hi," Charlie says after her lips have disconnected from my brother's in a not-for-public-consumption kiss.

"Where's Jude?" I ask Lucy as she slides in next to me.

"Meeting us here," she answers. "He was putting some finishing touches on his bike before we take it out tomorrow."

Looks like the little excursion with my brother is about to turn into a double date. I don't begrudge Linc and Jude for finding what they have with their old ladies. Hell, I don't even begrudge Ozzy and Freya, and those two have had each other in knots since we were seniors in high school. But I'd be lying if I didn't sometimes feel like a fifth wheel.

"We have drinks with Mia tomorrow after you get off work," Charlie reminds Lucy. My ears may or may not perk up at the mention of the school librarian who came back to town right after Charlie and Lucy got here.

"Maizie wants to work a double. Says Colby wants to start baseball, and she needs the extra cash. So I have the afternoon off."

Fuck. I remember my mom scrimping together money for me and Linc to be able to play sports when we were kids. Trick always made sure there was enough in her check to cover the costs.

"Does Wyatt know?" I ask. Our club secretary has had moon eyes for the bartender at Thorn and Thistle, the bar the club owns, for as long as she's worked there.

"Why would he care?" Linc asks, and Lucy snickers beside me.

Jesus, my brother can be dumb as a box of rocks sometimes.

Wyatt's been pining for Maizie for years now, though the kid is too chicken shit to act on anything.

"I'll make sure there's extra in her check this week. Maybe make sure a few of the guys go in thirsty and generous with their tips," I offer.

"Thanks, Knox," Lucy says as Jude walks over to our table.

"Hey, Lucifer." Jude bends down and gives his woman a typical rough kiss on the mouth.

Jesus, these guys still haven't figured out that they don't need to pee a circle around their women. There's not a soul in town who isn't aware of who Charlie and Lucy belong to and, in turn, who Linc and Jude belong to.

"How's Mia been? We haven't seen her around much," Linc says.

"She's been good. Just busy with work and getting things set up for the Spring Fling. Her new vice principal said that a good portion of the money raised could potentially go toward funding for the library, so she's been drafting proposals and all that shit to make sure it happens," Lucy answers.

When Mia moved back just over a year ago, she met Lucy and Charlie at Thorn and Thistle and the three have been friends since. I remember her from high school, but she was a few years younger and we didn't exactly run in the same circles. She's been out to the clubhouse a few times, but I have a feeling she's not particularly comfortable around bikers. Or maybe it's just me.

When some shit went down with Lucy and that fucking cult that tried to take her, I made it perfectly clear Mia was to remember things exactly the way we needed her to. Maybe I came on a little strong, but there was no doubt things were going to get real fucking violent real fucking fast, and I needed to make sure she understood her version of events matched ours.

Now the girl barely talks to me and is uptight as hell any time I'm around. Just as well. There's no denying there was a spark of attraction on my end when she came back to town. But Mia is too sweet, too *good*. Not only have I decided she's off limits for me, but I also made damn sure every asshole in the club knew she was off limits for them, too.

Here's the thing—Charlie, Lucy, and even Freya are made of pretty fucking tough stock. Life has thrown them all a bunch of shit at one time or another, and they're stronger for it. Strong enough to handle this life. Mia, on the other hand? She's soft, too soft to take on the role of an old lady in a criminal motorcycle club. And I could tell, from the moment I laid eyes on her, that she's the type who would need all or nothing—so nothing it is. It has to be. At least that's what I keep telling myself.

"Is she coming to Knox's birthday party?" my brother asks with a shit-eating grin directed at me.

The man could be dense as hell at times, but he caught a few lingering looks from me toward Mia and likes to rib me about it. He's not so much of an asshole to call me out in front of everyone, but the little fucker likes to see if he can make me squirm.

Spoiler alert—he can't.

"I'm not sure. She really isn't one for parties," Charlie answers.

Mia's been out to the clubhouse for a few of the family dinners my mom hosts, but big parties are a different story. I've considered skipping my birthday entirely. It's not like the club needs much of a reason to party, and the guest of honor not showing up wouldn't stop a bunch of bikers from getting drunk and eating a shit ton of food.

"Don't even think about it, brother," Linc pipes up.

"What are you talking about?" I ask.

My little brother shakes his head. "No, no. I see the wheels turning in your head. You're going to be there."

Fucking asshole.

I roll my eyes and let out a very manly huff of annoyance. "It's just a party. We can have one for any reason. The reason doesn't need to revolve around my birthday."

"Except our dear mother wants to do something for you, and Trick talked to Ozzy, and Ozzy gave him his word that you'd be there. You want to make a liar out of our prez and break Mom's heart in the process?"

"That's a bit dramatic," I reply.

"That's life." The little shit gives a self-satisfied shrug as though he has it all figured out. Not that he doesn't. There's no way in hell I'd be willing to do any of that, and he damn well knows it.

"I'll be there," I concede. "You have my word."

"With a smile on your face," Linc adds.

"Don't push it." I tap Lucy on the shoulder and indicate to her I need to get up.

Linc looks at me with a grin. "Leaving me with the check?"

"Yup." I stand and zip up the jacket I have under my cut.

"Where you heading?" he asks.

"For a ride."

"We just got back from one."

"And now I'm going on another one. By myself."

I'm not necessarily annoyed, but after thinking about the Irish, the shit with the Italians, Cooper, hell, all of it, I'm feeling a little antsy sitting here with everyone.

"Suit yourself," Linc says.

"Catch you assholes later," I say, and Jude throws up a middle finger before sliding into the booth I just vacated.

When I reach the front of the diner, Florence is standing behind the counter and I toss a couple twenties in front of her.

"It's only a few cups of coffee, Knox," she says, looking from the cash, then back to me.

I give her a smile and nod. "I know."

Looking back over at the table, I catch my brother giving his woman a sweet kiss on the head and Lucy smacking Jude on the shoulder while she rolls her eyes at some asinine comment I'm sure he just made. I'm fucking happy as hell that my brother and Jude found those two. I've never seen any of them as happy as they've been over the last year and some change. All the bullshit they had to deal with to get here has been worth it. And now that this shit with the Irish and Italians is over, Massachusetts has a new criminal empire running the show. One we happen to be thick as thieves with. I hope like hell it can stay as peaceful as it is now. Or at the very least, let us enjoy the downtime for a little while.

Chapter Two
Mia

One more hour. That's what I'm giving myself to finish this damn proposal. I've rewritten and triple-checked this thing within an inch of its life. I'm sick of being stuck inside the four beige walls of my office. I swear this proposal is going to be the death of me, but this is my first chance to really prove to the board that they made the right choice in hiring me. Not just because my family has been in this town for generations or because the former librarian retired and they were desperate for someone right away. Though both probably had something to do with me getting the position when I needed it. Either way, the *why* doesn't matter. Shine may be a small town, but these kids deserve the best I can give them, and I didn't spend years studying my ass off to coast through this job.

If Leonard, the vice principal of Shine High, doesn't approve this to go in front of the school board, then...well, I don't know what I'll do other than cry into a glass of wine with Lucy and Charlie. Charlie will be the good friend she always is. I can already picture her rubbing my back and offering me sweet treats. Lucy would probably think of inventive ways to get back at him—like putting dog shit under his car door handle or using his work email to sign him up for a bunch of erectile dysfunction websites. She's already come up with a few in the year that I've had to deal with him.

To say my boss is an asshole is an understatement. He's a misogynist who has zero respect for women...even the young girls in our high school.

My first run-in with him was when two kids were caught making out in the back of the library. Listen, teenage kids have raging hormones, and sometimes those pesky chemicals running rampant through their bodies take over the part of their brains responsible for making decisions. Case in point—having a heavy make-out session where anyone could wander in, which is exactly what happened. Leonard was walking around the library—which I already find odd, but whatever. It's his school, as he likes to remind me, even though he's only the vice principal.

He came upon two kids making out in the stacks, which I'm sure isn't the most scandalous thing to happen in that library to begin with. He pulled them into his office—me included since it happened in the library and that's my domain. Leonard read the poor girl the riot act with some choice words for me and how I run my department. But, of course, the boy got nothing more than a light scolding about time and place. Fucking asshole. Should I have taken it above him? Probably, but I was brand new, and even though Leonard had only started a little bit before me, I was scared to cause problems. I'm a fixer. I put my head down and do everything that's expected of me, and I do it without complaint.

And that's what landed me back in Shine.

My parents decided that someone needed to stay close to my grandmother. They lived here when my brother and I were in high school but moved to Boston when I graduated and left for Phoenix to go to college. There was no way my grandmother was willing to relocate from the town she spent her entire life in. She absolutely refuses to go to any sort of retirement home—not when she has a huge house on several acres and a little cottage I stay in now. Honestly, it's not as though she needs to move. Sure, she's a bit older and doesn't like to drive any longer, but the woman is as fiercely independent as she's been my entire life. Even the driving thing is her choice. It's not because she can't, it's that she would rather not. And you know what? Good for her. I wish I could afford to have someone else drive me everywhere I need to go.

They wanted to hire an in-home nurse for her, which she thought was just as ridiculous as I did, so instead, they offered to have me move back home and live on the property. Naturally, they didn't bother to ask me first, and they conveniently left that little detail out when they broached the subject with her. She told them I was welcome to live in the cottage if I ever wanted to come home, and they told me that she requested that I live on the property. At least Nolan, my older brother, comes by his manipulation tactics honestly.

It was the same shit when my brother was getting into trouble here. They decided that Nolan needed a change of scenery and sent him to live with me in Phoenix. Telling me that he wanted out of Shine and to start a life free from the messes he was getting into around here. They told him I missed my family and was hoping he would come out to Phoenix to be close to me. I should have fucking known. They've been pulling this shit for as long as I can remember, but generally not on the scale of making people move across the country. Should I have confronted them and told them manipulation was not an acceptable form of parenting or, you know, a way they should be treating people in general? Probably, but again, I'm going to do what's needed and not make waves.

Some could call me a pushover—Lucy may have mentioned a time or two—but I look at it as doing what needs to be done regardless of the reasons surrounding the situation. That's just me. I'm the problem solver, the handler. The one everyone knows they can come to. I'll always make sure things are sorted and taken care of. I'm not necessarily a control *freak*, but I'm always in control.

I have to be.

Unfortunately, that doesn't translate well into my love life. I've had a total of two serious relationships. Apparently, men don't like feeling mothered—or smothered, as one of my exes put it when he ended things with me. But it's not exactly easy to compartmentalize the years of making sure my brother, and to some extent, my parents, were where they needed to be. I was the one who had to make all the appointments for my brother, and I had to make sure my parents were aware of whatever school functions were happening. They weren't bad parents. They weren't neglectful or abusive. They just had better things to do rather than make sure my brother was signed up for football or remember the date for parent-teacher conferences—or even know when I had to perform for band competitions. It was my responsibility to keep the family calendar updated with everything or it would fall through the cracks.

God, that sounds terrible.

My parents always made sure we were provided for, but having kids was more about optics than the actual parenting. Some probably thought we came from a rich, spoiled family, and that was true...to an extent. We were given anything we asked for, but we were far from the type of family who sat around the dinner table talking about our day.

My father was usually at some sort of business dinner in the city, and my mother always accompanied him. Or he'd be on a call or business trip. Again, with my mom by his side. She kept him organized and in line, and she considered it my responsibility to do the same for my brother and me. It's not as though they didn't show up for us. They always showed their faces at school events and such. When you handled the portfolios of Shine's wealthiest residents, you made damn sure to look like the involved, loving family man that the others were. Or maybe, like everyone pretended they were.

Wouldn't that just be a kick in the pants? What if all of them were pretending to care about their children's lives in front of the other parents when they were all really as self-involved as the next? It's not like I ever asked any of my friends if they were in charge of the family calendar that hung in their kitchen or if they had to send reminder texts to their parents about the schedule. I never asked if their parents left signed checks to be filled out for the fees of the various activities their kids were in—because chances were, when the due date came, their parents were out of town. Maybe if I had, I'd have realized it was far from a normal upbringing. But as usual, I kept my mouth shut and took care of it. It's not as though we were being abused or anything, just overlooked.

I shake my head at the thought. *Just overlooked.* Jesus, I've become way too good at cosigning other people's bullshit.

The phone sitting beside me vibrates with a text. Glancing down, I realize an hour has passed since I've been staring at the proposal in front of me and taking a sad little walk down memory lane.

Lucy: *Okay lady, I have a drink sitting in front of me with your name on it.*

She's attached a picture of a whiskey on the rocks with a splash of 7UP—just how I like it.

She knows me so well.

Me: *Be there in ten.*

Her reply is a thumbs-up, and I begin packing up my things to get out of the small office, which is about the size of a broom closet, and head through the library to make sure everything is in order before I leave. My gaze travels across the displays that are set up throughout the space. Displays I poured my heart and soul into to make each and every one perfect. I stop for a moment, taking in the particular smell of all the books around me. A smile stretches across my face as I make my way through the front doors and into the parking lot. A sense of pride fills me as I walk to my car. God, I love the space I've created here. I may have arrived back in Shine under dubious pretenses, but I've created a life I'm beyond happy with—and I'm a kick-ass librarian, if I do say so myself.

"Where are you off to in a hurry?" a voice calls from behind me.

I nearly jump out of my skin, almost dropping the computer tucked under my arm, but I only lose my grip on my travel mug filled with cold tea. When it hits the ground, the lid pops off, splattering tea on my bare leg while the rest puddles on the black concrete.

Leonard bends down to pick up the mug and attempts to wipe the tea from my skin with his hand before I step away.

"I got it, thanks," I say, a tad weirded out that he thought that was in any way, shape, or form appropriate.

He straightens and hands the mug back to me. "Didn't mean to scare you," he says with a smirk on his face. *Yeah, you look real sorry, buddy.*

"Just startled. Not scared." The need to clarify that seems important at the moment for some reason. "I'm meeting some friends, and I'm late." The fact that people are expecting me also seems like a point that needs to be made. This guy is a prick, and I don't want to be stuck talking to him longer than I have to.

"Going out on a school night? Do you think that's wise? I still haven't received that new library proposal."

"I was under the impression I had until next week to get it to you."

"Well, technically. But I can't exactly hand something to the board without having a firm understanding of what you have in mind. We should probably set up a meeting after school before you officially turn it in so I can be sure you aren't wasting your time with something that I don't think will pass muster."

"I can check my schedule tomorrow and set up a time," I reply, more than slightly offended that he has the gall to suggest I don't know how to write up a proposal for some school funding. Jesus, I do actually know what I'm doing. That is if the degree from Arizona State is anything to go by. But what do I know?

"We could do it now. Unless going out with your friends is more important than getting the funding for whatever little library programs you were thinking of implementing."

Little library programs? The man is lucky my hands are full, or I'd be hard-pressed not to punch him in the throat.

Shit, I've been hanging out with Lucy too much.

My spine straightens as I clear my throat and look the asshole dead in the eye. "Like I said, Leonard, I'll check tomorrow. Now, if you don't mind, I need to get going. Thank you for your concern over my proposal." I plaster a tight smile on my face as Leonard looks at me with a clenched jaw.

"I prefer my employees to call me Mr. Miller."

"That's fine with me, Mr. Miller. I'll speak to you tomorrow." I hold his stare with my own, though the smile remains brittle on my face. If he thinks he's going to be able to bring any attitude issues to our principal, he has another thing coming. *I'm smiling, goddammit.*

Leonard turns on his heels, and I watch him walk to his car and unlock his door. He gets in the driver's seat and starts his engine before I turn and take the final steps to my car. After I unload everything in my arms into the back seat, I get in my car and take a couple deep breaths to calm my frayed nerves.

Who the hell does that man think he is? First, the snide remarks about me having a social life on a school night. Then, he insinuates that I need his help on a proposal. I've spent the better part of two weeks working on it to make sure every *i* is dotted and *t* crossed. I'm damn dedicated to my job, and the last thing I need is *his* help.

My phone vibrates, and I look down, seeing a message from Lucy.

Lucy: *Where are you?*

Lucy: *I drank the cocktail I ordered for you. Didn't want you to start the night with a watered-down drink.*

She sends me a picture of the glass with nothing left except some ice cubes, and I laugh.

Me: *Thanks for looking out to make sure I have the highest quality cocktail experience. I'm on my way. I hope you ordered me another one...I need it.*

Lucy: *On it.*

Starting my engine, I pull out of my parking spot in the faculty lot. A shiver runs down my spine, and I look at Leonard's car. His taillights are illuminated, so I know the car is running. I may be overreacting after that weird and annoying-as-hell interaction, but I get this sudden feeling he's sitting in his car watching me. It's not like I can see inside his car, but if I pointed my headlights at his back window, I'm ninety-nine point nine percent sure I'd see him staring at me through his rearview mirror.

Knock it off, Mia.

He might be a little weird and a huge asshole, but you're making him out to be some creepy stalker. Prick—yes. Stalker is reaching, though.

I pull out and see him do the same, turning in the other direction. It's more likely he was waiting for me to leave to make sure I got out okay since we were the only two left. Maybe he does have some manners, after all.

But he's still a dick.

"He said *what*?" Lucy asks, eyes narrowed as I recount the story of running into Leonard in the parking lot.

"Basically that I'm nothing more than a stupid little girl who didn't bust her ass in college, and I'm more interested in hanging out with friends than doing my job. Yeah, you heard all of that right."

"Mr. Miller, my *ass*." Lucy leans around me and looks at Charlie, who's sitting on the other side of me at the long, dark oak bar top. "You know what we should do—"

I lean forward and cut off her view of Charlie. "Nothing. No one is going to do anything. I can handle it."

Charlie lets out a soft laugh. "Good luck with that, Mia. You know how she is when she gets a bee in her bonnet. And nothing puts one there faster than someone messing with one of her nearest and dearest."

Though I don't love the threat of Lucy taking out her anger on Leonard—even though he probably deserves it—my heart warms at Charlie referring to me as one of Lucy's close friends. There were a few girls in band who I hung out with in high school, but we weren't really that close. I was too busy keeping everyone in my family in line, and honestly, my brother used to tease me relentlessly about being a band geek. I never invited anyone to my house because I was afraid of what he would say in front of them. Then, when I went to college, we all kind of lost touch.

When I walked into Thorn and Thistle right after moving back to town and starting at Shine High, Maizie was working, and she immediately introduced me to Charlie and Lucy. Maizie and I were in band together, and she made fast friends with the two women sitting on either side of me. It took hardly any time at all for them to welcome me into the fold. Now, I can confidently say these women have turned into the best friends any girl could dream of. Lucy has even tried to give our group a nickname over the last year I've been here. Thankfully, Charlie has shot all her ideas down.

"Listen, he's just a bully. Hell, he was probably bullied in high school, and now he takes it out on the rest of the world. I can deal with his bullshit. Besides, aside from this proposal that I'll be presenting, we have very little interaction. Well, other than having to deal with horny teenagers making out in the stacks."

"Did you ever make out in the library? Get hot and heavy with a guy?" Charlie asks, dramatically wiggling her eyebrows.

"I most certainly did not." I cover my chest with my hand, feigning as though the very idea of what she said is the most scandalous thing I've ever heard.

"I'm sure there were a couple guys you wished would have felt you up under that bulky band jacket, though," Lucy says, laughing at her own joke.

"We didn't wear those to school," I reply.

"Did you have a boyfriend in high school? I don't remember ever seeing you with anyone or talking about a guy you liked," Maizie says from the other side of the bar.

There was one guy who I had a major crush on from the time I was fourteen and saw him on the football field.

"Maybe Knox would be up for indulging some of your library fantasies," Lucy says, taking a sip of her cocktail while she slowly and deliberately blinks in my direction.

"Shut up." I laugh and smack her in the arm. "He didn't know I existed back then, and he doesn't now. And I didn't have library fantasies."

At least none that I'm willing to admit to.

Lucy sets her drink on the bar and pins me with her gaze. "Trust me when I say this, babe. I don't know what you were like in high school, but grown-up Mia is hot as fuck. If he doesn't see that, he's an idiot. And if you don't think he's noticed, you're just as big of an idiot."

"Well, high school Mia was nothing to write home about," I grumble.

"I'm sure you were as pretty then as you are now. Too good for any stupid high school boy," Charlie encouragingly chimes in.

"Did you ever see that movie about the girl who's a reporter and goes back to her high school pretending to be a student for some undercover story?" I ask.

Charlie nods.

"Remember the flashback scenes of her *actually* in high school?"

Charlie nods again, this time with a slight wince on her face.

"Yeah, that was me."

I know I'm not bad-looking now. Lucy may be in much better shape than I am, and I don't have that natural waif thing Charlie has going on, but it's not as though I think of myself as some sort of troll. I'm what you would consider cute, not beautiful.

After high school, I discovered hair products and hair tools and learned how to style my thick auburn locks that have always set off my light-brown eyes. My pale skin and freckles make me look much younger than my age, which was a pain in the ass in college when I would try to go to bars. Every bouncer would scrutinize my ID, not believing I was legally allowed to drink. Once I got my braces off, I was definitely much more confident and started smiling more. But catching the eye of a six-foot-three biker—who is somehow even hotter in leather than I could have imagined when I used to see him on the field in his football uniform—is an entirely different story.

And I'm totally fine with that.

The man barely talks to me or looks in my direction. Not that I give him much reason to. I may be more confident in myself now than back in our high school days, but the second Knox comes around, I clam up like a lovestruck teenager. It's honestly embarrassing, which is why I tend to avoid him at all costs.

"I'm sure most of us have embarrassing high school pictures. It just means you hadn't peaked, and thank God for that. Trust me, I see plenty of guys who peaked in high school come in here, and the cliff they fell off afterward was none too kind," Maizie says, pouring another drink for Lucy. "Want one?" she asks, pointing to my glass.

"No, I'm taking it easy tonight. I need to show up to work tomorrow bright-eyed and bushy-tailed. Otherwise, Leonard will probably say something about me being hungover and not taking my job seriously." I roll my eyes and slouch against my seat.

"Seriously, fuck that douche," Lucy says. "If you want him taken care of, you let me know. Maybe I could send Jude to have a little word with him—"

"Don't even think about it," I interject before she breathes too much life into that thought. "I can say, with the utmost certainty, that would only make things harder on me. Plenty of people in this town appreciate the MC and everything they do for Shine, but there're still some who don't, and they sit on the school board. One word from Leonard about being harassed by a biker, and my life at work will be *infinitely* more difficult."

My family's legacy may have played a role in me getting my job, but that doesn't mean I'm untouchable.

Lucy shakes her head. "Fucking small-town bullshit."

"You don't know the half of it, sister," Maizie says.

Getting pregnant by some unknown man in a town the size of Shine can't have been easy for Maizie. When all of her friends were starting careers, she was changing diapers and trying to figure out how to support a child as a single parent. Adding in the rumors and whispers from the assholes around town made it an unnecessarily rough few years. I'm happy as hell she works for the Black Roses. They've taken her under their wings, and now I haven't seen even a judgmental glance in her direction from anyone since I've moved back.

An hour passes, and I'm sipping from the glass of water that I switched to after my second drink. When the front door opens, four bikers saunter inside like they own the place. Well, I suppose technically they do.

"Hey, Charlie Bear," Linc says, coming to his girlfriend's side before leaning down and kissing her on the cheek. "Having fun?"

Charlie nods enthusiastically—she has *not* stuck to a two-drink minimum—and Linc gives her a lovingly indulgent smile.

"Hey, Lucifer," Jude says as he sits next to Lucy, and Wyatt takes a seat next to him.

"Hey there, buttercup," she replies with a drunk giggle tacked onto the end.

Jude's eyebrows lift nearly to his hairline as he looks from Lucy to me. "How many drinks has she had?"

I laugh and shake my head. "More than me, that's for sure."

"Hey," Lucy interjects. "I'm trying something sweet. Thought you would prefer it over 'asshole.'"

Jude leans in and gives her a hard kiss on the mouth. "I like it. Since you're feeling sweeter today, maybe when we get home, you let me put—"

Lucy covers his mouth with her hand. "Don't push your luck." She quickly jerks it back, looks down at her palm, then back to Jude. "Did you just lick my hand?"

Jude shrugs. "If it's on my face, I'm going to lick it."

Linc groans next to Charlie. "You two have a weird-ass idea of foreplay."

I turn in my seat at the bar and see Cash sitting at a table behind us. He holds up two fingers.

Wait...who else is coming?

Knox walks through the door with his phone to his ear before saying a quick goodbye to whoever he's talking to and slipping his phone in the pocket of his jeans.

God, he looks good. His cheeks are pink, probably from the cold wind while he was riding. His distinct scent of cedar and leather tickles my nose even from where I'm sitting several feet away. I can appreciate a man whose jeans mold to his body, not because they're tight, but because his muscular legs fill them out so well. Couple that with the dark hoodie he's wearing under his leather cut, and I'm practically drooling. He runs a hand through his dark-blond hair in that cool, confident way that reminds me of those silly teen movies I loved growing up. It's fitting since I always thought he was far cuter than the actors in said movies. When his bright-blue eyes scan the bar, my cheeks heat as I abruptly turn back around and face the liquor-lined wall on the other side of the bar top.

Lifting the glass to my lips, I realize there's nothing left except ice cubes, which I gladly start chewing as though it was my intention all along. Maizie shoots me a look, and I pray my smile doesn't make me look as nervous as I feel. When I'm not prepared to see Knox, it's as though I'm looking into the sun.

Jesus, get a grip, Mia. The sun?

But Knox has always had this effect on me, and seeing as I'm nearly thirty years old, it's probably even more juvenile and ridiculous than it was when I was fourteen.

"You want another water?" Maizie asks.

I quickly shake my head and set my glass down. "No. I should actually get going."

She shrugs and sets a beer in front of Wyatt, which he accepts with a small smile tilting the corner of his mouth. That man has it bad. I've been around the club enough in the last year or so to know *that* particular smile is one he reserves only for our gorgeous bartender.

"Fuck that guy," Lucy pipes up. "You better not be leaving because of what he said earlier."

Suddenly, I feel a large presence at my back, and that cedar scent is stronger than it was moments before.

"Who said what to you?" Knox asks, although it comes out as more of a growl.

"Her boss is an asshole. Made some comment about her being out on a school night," Lucy oh so helpfully explains.

I shoot her a glare, but she doesn't catch it. You know who does though? Knox, because he's standing right behind me, staring at me through the mirror behind the bar.

"It's not a big deal. He seems to have a problem with women, and I'm..." I wave my hand over my body, indicating that I am, in fact, a woman.

"Does he make you feel uncomfortable?" Jude asks.

"No, he makes me irritated, but that's really nothing new. It's honestly fine. It's not like this is the first guy I've ever come across who didn't get enough hugs from his mom or some shit."

"If it becomes a problem, let me know," Knox says, and I swear I can feel the rumble of his words in my chest even though he's far from touching me.

"I got it," I reply, and Knox's eyes darken with some sort of emotion that he quickly shuts down.

Grabbing my purse from where it's hanging on my chair, I get up and pat the seat. "All yours," I say to Knox, giving him a double thumbs-up. He looks at me, clearly confused. A *thumbs-up? Really, Mia?*

After an awkward laugh, with my cheeks feeling as though they're on fire with embarrassment, I head over to Charlie and give her a hug, then turn and give one to Lucy, whispering in her ear, "You just couldn't keep your damn trap shut, could you?"

Her response is a loud giggle, and when I stand straight, I give her my most intimidating glare, which only serves to make her laugh harder.

"Let me know you got home safe," she calls as I make my way out the door to my car.

The temperature has dropped significantly since the sun went down while we were inside. Though the days are sunny, there's a chill in the air that serves as a stark reminder that winter has barely melted away in Massachusetts.

The road back to my place is empty, which isn't unusual for this time of night. My grandmother lives on the outskirts of Shine in one of the wealthy neighborhoods on a fair bit of land, which is great for me. It makes it feel less like I'm living at home and more like I have my own place, even though it's not. Not really, anyways. She's made it clear that the cottage is mine to do with what I like, but it still feels like hers, even though I doubt she's stepped foot in the place for years.

I'm singing along to the radio when my car starts vibrating, and it feels like I'm being pulled to the side of the road. I slow down and instantly recognize the thumping noise of a flat tire.

"Goddammit," I grit out, pulling over to the side of the road. "Of fucking course."

I press the button to pop the trunk of my practical sedan. People would think I'd have some fancy top-of-the-line car, but they'd be wrong. My parents probably would've given me the money to pay for one if I'd asked, but like most things, I never bothered. It's not like I can't afford a car on my own. Besides, it's my brother who they have to worry about driving a safe car or having enough for groceries, rent, and bills. The man is over thirty years old and still gets a fucking allowance from my parents—even though he hasn't visited in years. I take a bit of pride in not having turned out like my brother, though it was entirely possible had I not been the one who my family depended on from such an early age. No skin off my nose. The last time I spoke to him wasn't exactly a pleasant conversation, and that was five years ago.

My body is bent over, my top half in the trunk as I try to get a solid grip on the jack and spare tire when a gust of wind sends my skirt flying over my ass. I'm too damn annoyed that I'm in this ridiculous predicament to begin with to give my exposed rear anything more than an eye-roll. At least it's late and no other cars are driving home from work.

That relief is short-lived when I hear the loud rumble of a motorcycle engine on the otherwise empty road.

It couldn't be. There's no way the universe would be *that* cruel.

I stand up straight and slowly turn to see a black Harley pull off to the side of the road. Knox parks his bike before he swings his long leg over the seat and stands. It may be dark without any streetlights, but I swear to God, the man is wearing an annoyingly hot smirk across his full lips.

"Need some help?"

Yeah, into my trunk so I can shut it and die of embarrassment.

CHAPTER THREE
KNOX

I wasn't in the mood to spend the night drinking at Thorn and Thistle, but I let Cash talk me into stopping in with everyone for a beer. With the roads clear, we've all been taking our bikes out as much as we have time for. Spring is like fucking Christmas for bikers who live on the East Coast.

Linc said the girls were there having drinks with Mia. I didn't want her to feel uncomfortable with me being there—because she usually seems on edge any time I'm around, but it's not exactly like I could tell my brothers that. They'd probably look at me like I'd grown two heads or something. I'm not generally the type to give a shit if I make people feel uncomfortable, but Mia is different. And that's a can of worms I'm not ready to open.

When I walked in, I was on the phone with Ozzy. He wanted to make sure I was going to be around tomorrow so we could talk about some new business with an outfit in Michigan. The Monaghans have been busy brokering new gun deals, and they're still throwing plenty of business our way, so we need to iron out some details.

I hung up with Ozzy and walked to the little table that Cash was sitting at behind the girls and my brothers when I overheard Lucy say something about someone giving Mia a hard time. Instead of sitting, I walked over and stood behind her, wanting to know if she was in some kind of trouble. I'm not sure what made me do it, but hearing that someone is giving her grief doesn't sit right with me. Of course, she said she could handle it. That seems to be her MO from what I've witnessed from her since she came sweeping back into town. Mia's here to take care of her grandmother—although from what I know of the woman, she doesn't need it. She works full-time, is involved in community events almost as much as my mom, pitches in when Maizie needs a sitter for her son—hell, I don't know when the woman sleeps.

Not that I've been paying attention or anything.

We didn't exactly run in the same circles in high school, but I was well acquainted with her brother Nolan. He played on the football team with us and was friends with Ozzy's sworn high school nemesis. He never started any shit with us like that prick did, but he didn't exactly try to stop it either. When he graduated, Nolan came to some parties at the clubhouse, but we threw his ass out when he was caught dealing at a party. That shit didn't fly then, and it wouldn't fly now. That's one of the things we don't allow in Shine. We keep the streets of our town safe from the bullshit that a lot of other MCs would gladly welcome, which is why we've been able to mostly fly under the radar and the citizens of our town aren't raising pitchforks or some other stupid shit to try to run us out. That, and my mom throws herself into every charity event she can and ropes us all in right along with her.

It was always Mia picking her brother up from parties when he was too drunk to drive, and she was the one who would be cleaning up at their house when their parents were out of town and Nolan would throw a high school kegger. Not that we attended many, but there were a few team parties that Linc would convince us to go to back then. Mia reminded me of a silent little housekeeper, making sure spills were cleaned and any broken bottles were quickly disposed of so no one would cut themselves on the glass. But she never partook in the festivities. I didn't think much about it when I was a dumb eighteen-year-old guy in high school. I was just there to make sure no one fucked with my brother or my best friend. But thinking back to that time, that's what stands out to me.

As usual, my presence seemed to make her even more uncomfortable, and she left soon after I arrived, offering her seat at the bar to me along with a double thumbs-up. I had to hide my chuckle at the awkward gesture because I didn't want her to think I was laughing at her. I took the seat when she walked out the door but wasn't really in the mood to be sitting at a bar. My brothers like to give me shit about being a hermit or a loner, but the fact of the matter is, when I don't feel like being around a group of people, I don't. It's not uncommon for me to leave a bar or party to go home to my quiet house on the other side of town. I love my brothers. Love my club. But I love my solitude just as much, and I'm not one to be pressured to hang out when I'm not feeling it. And tonight, the last thing I feel like doing is sitting in a bar.

"I'm heading out," I say a couple minutes after Mia leaves.

"Shocking," Linc replies with a grin.

I shrug because it's not as though I can argue, but I really don't care. Standing from my seat, I throw a couple twenties on the bar.

"You taking care of the round?" Maizie asks.

"No, Cash is," I reply. "That's for you."

She doesn't argue but gives me a grateful smile when she puts the money in her tip jar.

Cash gets up from the table behind him and stands next to me. "Since I'm apparently paying, how 'bout another round, darlin'?" He shoots Maizie one of his oh-so-charming Southern boy grins, and Wyatt shoots lasers at him with his eyes. Good. Maybe if he thinks Cash is flirting with her, he'll get over whatever's holding him back and finally make a move. The knowing smile Cash gives Wyatt tells me that was the point.

"See you fuckers in the morning," I say and head out the door to my bike.

The night has become chilly, but that's never stopped me from taking the long way to my house. Cold air I can deal with, ice and snow? Not so much.

I'm a couple miles out of town when my headlight illuminates a familiar car on the side of the road. And a familiar ass—I would know since I've stared at it more times than I'm willing to admit—is sticking straight up in the air as Mia rummages around her trunk for something.

I pull over and park my bike. Mia straightens, her skirt unfortunately covering what has to be the most bitable backside I've seen in a long while before she turns toward me.

"Need some help?"

Mia closes her eyes and dips her head, mumbling something to herself before looking back at me.

"It's just a flat. I've got it covered, but thank you."

Walking over to her car, my arm brushes against hers that are crossed over her chest as I reach into her trunk to pull out the spare. "Mia, there is no way in hell I'm leaving you on the side of the road to change a flat, so deal with someone helping you."

She inhales a sharp breath at the light contact but takes a step back to allow me to lift the tire.

"This is awfully light," I say with the spare in my hand. "I think it's flat."

"You've got to be kidding me," she mutters, scrubbing her hands over her adorably freckled face.

"Afraid not, sweetheart."

Mia's body sags for a moment before she lets out a long exhale, then she stands tall—well, as tall as she can at barely over five feet—and pulls her phone from her pocket.

"Who are you calling?"

"Um, a tow truck?" She says the words as though the answer is obvious.

"In Shine? At ten o'clock at night? I can guarantee Rusty is about five beers deep by now if he's not already asleep."

That's one of the things about a small town like Shine. One tow truck driver who promptly clocks out at six p.m.

"Dammit." Her already tense jaw clenches tighter before she shakes her head. "Okay, I'll call a cab or an Uber then. It's fine. You can go."

"Did I not make myself clear earlier? I'm not leaving you alone."

Damn, this woman really isn't used to anyone doing something simple to help her out, is she?

It's obvious she wants to argue, but she stays quiet and gives me a quick nod before pulling up a rideshare app on her phone.

"Shit, they want an address," she says and lets out an adorable groan of frustration.

I look around the deserted road and the empty field on either side. "Yeah, that's not happening."

"It's fine. I can call Lucy or Charlie."

"They're each about four sheets to the wind, never mind the usual three. Come on." My head tilts toward my bike. "I'll give you a ride."

Mia releases a heavy sigh as her hand grasps the red stone pendant she always wears around her neck. She slides it back and forth on the dainty chain like I've seen her do so many times when she's uncomfortable.

"On that?" she asks, pointing to my Harley.

"I don't see any other mode of transportation around," I reply, taking a dramatic look up and down the otherwise empty street.

Her light-brown eyes close on a pained exhale, and the pendant drops as she bites her bottom lip. The urge to release that lip from her teeth with my thumb is strong, but instead of reaching out to touch her, I ball my fists at my side.

"Hold on one sec," she says, then leans back into her trunk, pulling out something long and black. "Turn around."

I do as she asks, and a few seconds later, she tells me it's okay to face her again.

"Do you carry a wardrobe in there with you?" I ask, noticing the tight black leggings she pulled on under her skirt.

"I had some workout clothes in my trunk. Figured I'd rather not flash all of Shine my ass cheeks."

Mia rubs her arms, trying to warm them through her thin sweater. "We should go. It's not like it's going to warm up anytime soon."

"You don't have a jacket stuffed in there, do you?"

"Unfortunately, no. I was in a hurry to get to the bar and forgot it at work."

She closes her trunk, and I walk back over to my bike. When she turns back around, I'm pulling my cut off and hanging it on my handlebars so that I can remove the thick sweatshirt underneath.

"Um, what are you doing?" she asks when I pull the material over my head.

"What's it look like?" I ask, handing it over to her. "You can't ride with a sweater and nothing else. You'll be a popsicle by the time we get back to your place."

She takes my offered shirt, and I turn to grab my cut and put it on over the flannel I was wearing underneath. Facing her again, Mia is wearing my too-large sweatshirt, and I swear for a split second it looks like she's smelling the collar. She looks at me and releases the fabric before I can be sure that's what she's doing, then quickly turns back to her car.

"What about my stuff?" she asks, grabbing what looks like a computer case and a large purse.

"That's what saddlebags are for, sweetheart."

She walks over to where I'm standing next to my bike, and I get a good look at her practically swimming in my sweatshirt. Shit, I like the look of that a lot more than I have any right to.

After she hands me her things and I have them locked tight in the leather saddlebags hanging on my bike, I hand her my helmet.

"You ever ridden before?"

I don't know what Mia has done with the last ten years of her life. For all I know, she could have been riding around with God knows who when she was living God knows where for the last decade.

"Nope, I'm a virgin." Her eyes close, and her adorable nose scrunches at what she just said. "That's not...I didn't mean..." she stutters out.

"I know what you meant, sweetheart. Don't worry, I'll go slow." I toss her a wink and watch her already rosy cheeks turn a deep crimson.

When Mia has the helmet on and fastened, I step forward and graze her neck and under her chin to make sure she has the strap snug enough. Her breath hitches at the contact as heat races up my arm.

"Just making sure you're locked in. Since it's your first time and all."

Mia closes her eyes for a moment and lets out a sort of chuckle-groan combination. "Please don't ever tell anyone I said that."

"Wouldn't dream of it. I don't kiss and tell."

Her eyebrows shoot up her forehead as her widened gaze flicks to my mouth, then back to my eyes.

"You know what I mean," I say, but now all I can do is think about having her full pink lips pressed against mine.

Turning away from the woman who is tempting me in all kinds of ways—even though she's doing nothing but existing—I throw my leg over my bike.

"Put your hands on my shoulders for balance, and get on like I just did," I instruct.

When she steps up to me, we're nearly eye level considering I'm six-three and sitting, and she can't be more than five-four or so. Her small hands slide over my shoulders, and when I inhale, the light floral scent of Mia's perfume invades my senses. She smells like the spring that's blooming around us. It's distinctly feminine and sweet, just like the girl settling in behind me.

"You can put your feet here," I say, pointing at the pegs, "but steer clear of the pipes. They'll burn the shit out of you."

Mia nods and rests her feet on the pegs like I showed her, but her hands are resting on her thighs. That's not going to work.

I kick-start my bike then settle into my seat. "Your arms go around my waist, sweetheart. Don't need you falling off the back."

She places her hands at my waist, but she's holding herself stiff behind me. I slide my hands over hers and pull them to my front. "I won't bite, honey."

Her front presses lightly against my back as she clasps her small hands together, and my entire body warms with the gentle pressure.

"You lean when I lean, yeah?" I turn and look at her, and she nods. "Okay, hold on."

I put the bike in gear, and we glide onto the street before I open it up and begin flying down the dark road. Mia lets out a squeal and presses herself completely flush against my back, squeezing me around my waist tighter than she was before. *Much better.*

Though I try to contain it, I chuckle at her reaction and place one hand over hers, which are gripped together at my front. "Relax, sweetheart. This is supposed to be fun," I call back to her.

"Do you know where you're going?" she asks over the noise of the wind rushing past us.

"Yup."

When some shit went down with another club who tried to take Lucy back to the cult compound where she grew up, I followed Mia home to make sure she got there safely. That night is burned into my brain, and part of me regrets the way I spoke to her after it all went down. It was the beginning of her avoiding me like the fucking plague.

Riding with Mia isn't like anything I've ever experienced. I'm not one of those guys who will only allow an old lady to ride with him. That shit is stupid, if you ask me. But having this girl behind me who has barely spoken to me, the sweet girl who gets so fucking uptight around me, I wonder if she doesn't like me or if she's scared of me. And yeah, there's a twisted part of me that feels like maybe a little corruption is in order. I imagine her tied in my ropes that I've only used with women who understand things like safe words and...and why the hell am I letting my mind go there? This is a simple ride home for Chrissake. Mia is so far from the other women I've played with or simply had any sort of sexual relationship with. She's kind, innocent, and, let's be honest, out of my league.

But that thought doesn't make me remove my hand from hers or stop me from wishing I was taking her back to my place instead of dropping her off at hers. From the moment I saw Mia Dawson back in town—all grown up, carrying herself with a certain self-confidence I never remembered her having—I wanted to know what she looked like under that adorable-as-fuck skirt and sweater set that screams *school librarian*. The woman must have about thirty of them hanging in her closet. Then I went and screwed the entire thing up by scaring her last year when the club needed her to stay quiet about a couple things she saw. Since then, I've made sure to steer clear, but there was no way I was leaving her on the side of the road tonight.

We pull up to her grandmother's house and she directs me to the back, where a small cottage sits a good bit away from the main house.

The second I stop in front of her little walkway and turn my bike off, Mia hops off like her hair is on fire. She stumbles a bit, which is perfectly natural if you aren't used to riding a bike, but I whip my hand out and catch her by the arm before she face-plants onto the dirt road.

"Thanks. Shit, my legs feel like Jell-O," she says with a shaky laugh.

If she were any other girl, I'd show her how easy it would be for me to make her feel like that over and over.

There's nothing I love more than watching a woman come undone under my ministrations. Especially when they're tied up and can do nothing but succumb to every last drop of pleasure I wring from their bodies. But she's not...and I need to stop imagining what she would look like at my mercy, with nothing stopping me from making her fall apart over and over again.

I'm quickly realizing that having her this close to me for the ten minutes it took to get her home may have been a mistake on my part.

"Okay then...thanks for the ride," she says, more uncomfortable than she was when she got on my bike. She's taken my stony silence and me trying to talk myself out of doing something that would be monumentally stupid—like wrapping her small frame in my arms and slamming my mouth to hers—as me being an asshole. Again.

Mia begins undoing the buckles of my saddlebags to retrieve her belongings as I clear my throat, trying to will down my half-hard dick.

"I'll have Rusty tow your car to the shop in the morning."

"Oh, you don't have to—"

"Mia. It's as good as done. I'll have the tire fixed and the car dropped off here tomorrow."

She wants to argue. I see the urge clear as day on her face, but I hold her stare and she finally relents, giving me a soft smile, then shakes her head.

"Thanks, Knox."

When she turns, I realize she's still wearing my sweatshirt. I could ask for it back, but the thought of her wearing my shirt, even if it looks more like a dress on her, does something inside of me that excites me—and maybe even scares me a little. I never intended to allow myself to have any feelings for the little librarian, to bring her into a world she's too sweet for, but what's that they say about the road to hell?

When she gives me a shy wave before stepping through her doorway, I have to force myself to stay seated on my bike. I want to press my lips to hers in front of her door, to feel her hands on me again like they were when she was hanging on for dear life. When the door shuts behind her, I let out a sharp exhale.

"Get it together, fucker," I say out loud to myself as I start my bike and head down the dirt roadway that will take me back to the main street and away from temptation.

"You look worse for wear," Cash comments as I'm pouring myself a cup of coffee the next morning.

"And you're up early. Are we in the habit of talking to each other about our sleeping schedules now?"

Cash's head rears back at my irritation. "Sorry, Mr. Grumpypants."

It's not like he's wrong, though. I saw myself in the mirror before I rode over this morning, and it was not pretty. The little bit of sleep I did manage wasn't the most restful I've had in my life. Thoughts of a sweet librarian in my shirt and nothing else kept racing through my thoughts, then my dreams when I did manage to get a couple hours. Half the time was spent telling myself all the reasons why starting any sort of anything with Mia was a terrible idea, while the other half was spent shooting down every reason I have for not wanting to involve her in this life, in my life. Basically, I fought with myself for an entire night, and I'm paying the price this morning. And taking it out on everyone else.

"Fuck off," I say, rather than apologizing to our club treasurer without any heat behind the sentiment. "Why the hell are you up this early anyways?"

He scoffs. "Oh, now you want to know?"

"I'm beginning to regret asking," I reply.

Cash sends me a half smile before taking a long pull from his coffee mug. "I have to take Cece to the shelter. You and her seem to share the same sleeping habits, but when she can't sleep, she bakes. A lot, apparently."

"Why can't Jude or Lucy do it?"

Cash shrugs. "I don't know. She called and asked me."

"Are there still many women from the compound there?"

Last year, when the club saved Lucy from her insane father's cult compound, all the men were killed in the attack—and rightfully so. But that left families with no way to survive without some help. Good thing we had a place we could relocate them to. Some had distant relatives they were able to contact in the outside world, but not many.

"Not really, but there's other women there with kids who are partial to Cece's baked goods."

Several yips sound from the hallway, followed by a baritone, "Get back here, asshole."

I look at Cash, who rolls his eyes as a golden fluff ball runs past me, looks around, then squats in the middle of the clubhouse and pees on the concrete floor.

"Oh yeah, so that happened last night." Cash tilts his head as Wyatt walks toward the puppy.

"Bad dog," he says to the puppy, who is now sniffing his way around every available surface. He walks over to the dog and picks him up, carrying him through the slider to the back of the property.

"Ozzy know about this?" I ask.

"He does. And he isn't thrilled," the man himself says, walking out of the hallway, presumably from his office, and looking at the widening puddle in the middle of the floor. "Goddammit," he mutters, walking behind the bar, grabbing a roll of paper towels and cleaning the spot.

"Make the prospects do that shit," I say when he stands and throws the soiled towels in the trash.

"Wyatt's dog, Wyatt's responsibility," Ozzy grumbles.

"Looks like you're the one cleaning his messes," Cash adds, being an unhelpful asshole.

"I just don't want the clubhouse smelling like piss. But Wyatt knows he's on dog duty."

Ozzy is pouring himself a cup of coffee as Wyatt returns with the skinny puppy in his arms, scratching him between the ears. "I couldn't leave him there, Oz."

"At least take him to the vet and make sure he doesn't have rabies or some shit," Ozzy grouses.

I watch the puppy in question lick Wyatt's face enthusiastically. "I think you're good on that end. How did this come about?"

"Poor little guy was eating trash outside of the bar last night. Didn't see his mama or any other pups around, so I brought him back here. Gonna head to the vet in a bit, then to the pet store."

"He have a name?" I ask.

"Not yet. Nothing's seemed right," Wyatt answers.

Ozzy shakes his head as he sips from his cup, then leans against the bar. "This is an MC clubhouse, not a fucking animal rescue."

"He could be the club dog. Kind of like a mascot," Wyatt says, setting the dog on the floor. He immediately starts running his nose along the ground. I really hope he isn't looking for somewhere to relieve himself again. I don't think Ozzy would take too kindly to the dog using the concrete as his own personal pee pad.

"I think I'll refrain from having a puppy who pees everywhere as a fucking mascot, Wy," Ozzy says, then looks at me. "Let's talk." He nods toward his office, signaling for me to follow.

Ozzy settles behind his large oak desk that's been here since Trick was president—hell, probably since Gramps was—as I get situated on the black leather chair in front. This office hasn't changed since his old man used to run things. Same brick walls with the same pictures hanging from them. Only difference is a few more pictures have been added throughout the years Ozzy's taken over.

"The Monaghans have some new deals with an MC in Michigan, the Iron Disciples. Want us to be the middlemen. We'll be responsible for delivery."

"Monaghan is working his way across the country?"

"Michigan isn't that far. After the bullshit with the Bone Breakers, I think he's playing it a little safer. Wants to deal with clubs that we already have a good rapport with."

The Bone Breakers were the fucking assholes who tried to kidnap Lucy, and she and Jude ended up putting three of them to ground for their efforts.

"Figured you wouldn't mind heading up the run since I seem to recall you having a particular fondness for one of their bunnies," Ozzy says.

"Amber still around?" Not that I'm interested anymore. And not that I'm going to tell Ozzy that.

Ozzy shrugs. "One way to find out."

"When are we headed out?"

"End of next week," he says, then arches a brow. "After your birthday party."

I groan and swipe a hand over my face. "I hate celebrating my birthday."

"I know, but Tanya loves this kind of shit. And what makes her happy makes my old man happy. And what upsets her—like you possibly thinking you can blow the entire thing off—upsets my dad. The man may be too broken to ride, but he ain't too broken to kick both of our asses."

"Why would you get a beating?"

"Because I'm your prez, and he'd be just as pissed at me if I let you skip it."

Trick has never laid a hand on either of us, but there're some men you just know not to fuck with. Not that I'd ever defy him, even though I no longer answer to him. Trick and Gramps were the family I never had while growing up. The first to show me and my brother how real men treat the people they care about. I'm as likely to purposely disappoint either of them as I am my own mother, who is also Trick's old lady.

"Linc already made me promise to be there," I concede.

"Oh, you poor bastard, having everyone here to celebrate you and the day you were born. It must be so fucking hard for you."

I grin at my president and best friend. "Asshole. Just wait until you marry Freya and all eyes are on you."

"Fair. I'm still trying to convince her eloping is the way to go."

Last year, Ozzy and the club were charged with the task of protecting his high school sweetheart who he hadn't seen in fifteen years. Worked out pretty well for both of them, if you ask me.

"Oh, yeah? And how's that going?" I ask.

"It's not."

I laugh because if there's anyone who hates attention as much as I do, it's the man sitting across this very desk.

"Alright, I'll get with Monaghan about the particulars of the pickup from Boston," I say.

"Cillian's handling this one. Seems both of us are getting used to delegating a few things."

Cillian Doyle is Finn Monaghan's second-in-command and, as luck would have it, is now Nova Reed's fiancé, making us one big, happy family of criminals.

"Thought Cillian ran the casino and the brothel?"

"Looks like even Finn's lieutenant is working on the whole delegation thing, too. Plus, he and his woman have been helping Liam's brother with a few things."

That's one thing I'm happy to not be a part of anymore. Liam Ashcroft is Jude's brother and has been a major player in taking down all kinds of sex trafficking rings throughout the world. We've helped out a few times when shit was too close to home, but I don't have the patience to deal with all the undercover shit that comes along with it. If you deal in selling women, I'd rather show up and kill every last one of the assholes, which is basically how we would help. But having to shake hands with those pieces of shit to get intel? Yeah, I doubt I could stomach it and would probably put a knife in their gut instead of playing the games Liam and his team do.

"I'll give Cillian a call, then," I say, standing from my chair. "That all?"

"No, can you smack Wyatt upside the head on your way out?"

"What for?"

"Plenty of reasons, I'm sure, but this particular time is for bringing that fucking dog home."

"Nah, think I'll look into getting him a little sidecar, though. Then he can take his new buddy out with him."

"If you do that, I swear to God I'll strip your patch. And his."

I shrug but can't help the chuckle that escapes. "We'll see."

"Party in three days, fucker."

"Yeah, yeah."

CHAPTER FOUR
MIA

Have I been sleeping in the sweatshirt Knox let me borrow since the night he took me home? Yes. Am I embarrassed that my schoolgirl crush may be turning into something weird and creepy every time I inhale his scent on the collar? Also yes. But it's not every day the man I fantasized about from the first time I saw him at fourteen loans me an article of clothing. Granted, at fourteen, my imagination was much tamer than it is now, but can anyone really blame me? The man smells like sex incarnate, laced with a hint of motor oil.

True to his word, Rusty came to tow my car first thing the next morning. Thankfully, my grandmother has a couple spares, so instead of driving the little red sedan that I usually do, I took one of her luxury cars to the school. I won't lie and say I didn't enjoy the hell out of the plush leather interior, but I was nervous as hell the entire way to and from work. God only knows what it would have cost to get fixed if someone had accidentally rear-ended me, or if a stray rock had hit the windshield, or any other thousand things that could have happened. If this is the stress that comes along with driving a high-priced vehicle, I'll stay happy with the perfectly sensible and economical car that I've had since I graduated college.

When my car was returned to me, Rusty asked if I'd driven through any construction sites, which I thought was strange considering there isn't construction work being done around town at the moment. When I told him I hadn't, he thought it was odd, seeing as I had a couple nails in my tires. Apparently, the reason my tire had gone flat was from puncture holes. Then, when I asked him for the invoice, he looked at me like I had some unexplained growth protruding from my forehead.

"It's been taken care of," he told me.

"That's not possible. I didn't get anything from your garage or the tire shop," I replied as he got back in his truck.

"Talk to Knox. He covered it all."

Rusty slammed the door and was obviously uncomfortable while I was standing there with my mouth hanging open, confusion and surprise running through my mind. Why would Knox take care of everything for me? He barely tolerates me. Not leaving me to freeze on the side of the road last night is one thing, but paying for a tow and a new tire is too much.

I should have called Lucy or Charlie to get his number so I could thank him, but I didn't. Leave it to them to read too much into it or something. Or leave it to me to somehow give myself away as a creepy weirdo who's been sleeping in the sweatshirt he lent me. Or changing into it when I get home from work.

Honestly, at this point, I'm a little worried about myself.

Good thing I'm going to see him tonight to give it back—and bake him a pie or maybe some cookies as a thank-you. I hate showing up to birthday parties without something in hand. This way, I don't have to agonize over what to buy the biker, who I know next to nothing about other than the fact he likes to ride, makes growly noises on occasion, and cranks up my heart rate every time I'm within a twenty-foot radius of him. Also, nothing says thank you for handling something for me that I could've absolutely handled myself—but it was nice not having to for once—like baked goods.

I rummage through my cabinets to see what I have on hand and realize there's only about half of anything needed for cookies or a pie. Looking at the clock hanging on my wall, I curse the time, realizing there isn't enough of it to run to the store to grab more ingredients.

Walking across the expansive yard to the main house, I open the French doors of my grandmother's white colonial home that leads to the kitchen.

"Grandma?" I call into the house. "Are you home?"

"In the sunroom," she calls back, and I make my way through the hallway and past the dining room, living room and library and find her sitting in her white wicker rocking chair with a book in her hand, surrounded by her plants and flowers that she keeps healthy and blooming all year round. This is one of my favorite rooms in the house, and hers, too, if the amount of time she spends in here is any indication. The room is still encased in glass that she uses to weatherize it every winter so her plants don't freeze. Once the chilly temperatures let up a bit more, she'll take the glass panels down to allow the warm air inside.

"What are you reading?" I ask, taking a look at the paperback in her hand.

Years ago, I bought her an e-reader, but I'm not sure she even took it out of the box. When I asked her about it, she said she loved the convenience but preferred the feel of a book in her hand and the smell every time she opened a new one. Can't argue with that.

"Some historical book about Scottish royalty," she says with a completely straight face.

I read the cover of the book that has a dashing, shirtless man with long, wavy hair holding a woman in a flowing gown as though he's about to kiss her.

"*The Highlander's Embrace.* Sounds educational, Grandma."

"It's very educational, my dear. The things I'm learning about kilts..." She leans back in her chair and fans herself with the book before shooting me a wink.

I huff out a laugh and shake my head. God, I love this woman.

"I need to borrow some stuff to make cookies if that's okay."

"Of course, Mia. You don't have to ask. As long as you leave me a few," she says, setting her book on the small glass table beside her and standing from her chair.

"You don't have to get up. Stay and enjoy the sun."

She waves me off as she passes by. "I'd rather spend time with my favorite granddaughter."

"I'm your only granddaughter," I reply, following her down the hallway back toward the kitchen.

"Good thing, too. It would be awful of me to have favorites if I had more than one."

When we get to the kitchen, my grandmother begins pulling various items from the pantry and refrigerator.

"It's fine. I can do it, Grandma."

I notice everything she's pulling out are ingredients for my lemon raspberry tart with cream cheese glaze, which also happens to be her favorite.

"Oh, I'm just helping you get started."

I chuckle and begin organizing the items on her white marble countertops.

"Who is this for anyway?" she asks as she pulls two mugs from her cabinet and puts water in the kettle for tea.

"I'm going to a party at the Black Roses clubhouse tonight for Knox's birthday. Tanya is making a big deal out of it, and I don't want to show up empty-handed."

"Knox? Is he the gentleman who gave you a ride home on his motorcycle the other night?"

"He is," I say with a laugh. I don't think I've ever heard of him referred to as a gentleman by anyone.

"Nice boy and his mother is an absolute gem. Great football player, too."

One thing many find shocking about my grandmother is her love of football. When my brother played, she made it to every game. Even after he graduated, you could still find her in the stands on Friday nights, cheering for our local high school.

"What time is the party?" she asks.

"In a couple hours. I'll have enough time to bake this, then finish getting ready."

"It's been a while since I've seen Tanya and her boys," she says as she fixes us two cups of Earl Grey. "I should invite her over sometime. It would be nice to have company. Being an old lady trapped in this big house can get lonely."

It takes everything I have in me to stifle my laugh. There are many things that I could say to describe my grandmother, but *old lady* and *trapped* would never come to mind. But I know a setup when I see one.

"Grandma, would you like to come with me? I'm sure Tanya would love to see you."

"Oh, well, if you insist," she says, giving me a half smile as she takes her tea to the little café table in front of the large window in the kitchen that overlooks her expansive backyard.

"I do."

"Well, you'd better make more than one tart then."

We pull up to the clubhouse with not one, not two, but three tarts for the party. Once my grandmother told me that not everyone is a fan of lemon, I set about making a strawberry and vanilla tart. In reality, I think she wanted both, but it still got in my head. All I could think about was Knox making that face that people make when they try something you baked. They want to be nice, so they smile, but then you see that grimace before they try to discreetly throw whatever they ate in the trash.

I may be overthinking this a tad.

When we walk into the clubhouse, me carrying two dishes and my grandmother carrying the third, I'm struck with how normal and festive this is. There are streamers and one of those colorful metallic *Happy Birthday* banners hanging behind the bar. A few kids are running around, and I see the families of some of the men who work at the shop. Nothing like the biker party I was afraid I'd be walking my grandmother into, even though Charlie said the party wouldn't become more adult-focused, shall we say, until later.

Tanya is setting food on the large table that runs along one of the walls when she sees me and my grandmother. Her face lights up and she walks over to us, wrapping me in a warm, if not awkward, hug, considering I'm holding two dishes.

"Hi, sweet girl. I'm so happy you could make it." She turns to my grandmother. "It's so good to see you, Mrs. Dawson."

"Tanya, I've told you a million times to call me Elaine," she chastises with a smile.

"Yes, ma'am."

My grandmother laughs and shakes her head.

"Don't be too hard on the girl, Elaine. It's not often you find kids with manners these days." This comes from a man I recognize as Ozzy's grandfather, Arthur Lewis, or Gramps, as he's most often referred to. If memory serves, he founded the Black Roses when he came over from England with his wife who has since passed. I recognize him as the man in the stands at all of his grandson's football games, cheering louder than anyone else in attendance. Back then, I wondered what it would be like to have a family so outwardly and unabashedly supportive that they didn't care about the looks other parents would shoot them.

"I'm hardly a kid," Tanya says, feigning insult.

"Talk to me when you reach my age, sweetheart," Arthur shoots back. "Not that Elaine looks like she could possibly have a granddaughter who's already graduated college."

"I'm well past graduation," I say.

"Blasphemy," Arthur declares. "Let me take that from you, Elaine. You come sit with me, and we can catch up."

My grandmother actually giggles when he takes the dish from her hands, then holds his arm out as if he's properly escorting her to one of the tables set up in the clubhouse.

"Thank you, Arthur," she says as I watch them walk away.

"Don't mind him. He's a harmless flirt," Tanya says, chuckling beside me.

"It's not him I'm worried about," I reply, and Tanya laughs even harder.

"Come on. I'll put this on the table." We head over to the spread that's already set out, and she removes the lids from the pans. "What are these?"

"Raspberry lemon tarts with a cream cheese glaze."

"That sounds delicious," a deep voice says behind me.

Tingles shoot up, or maybe it's down my spine. I don't know which direction they're flying, to be honest, but I feel like I'm lit up like a damn Christmas tree.

"I made a strawberry one, too, just in case you aren't a lemon fan," I blurt out. "Not everyone is, and I wanted to make you something as a thank-you. And a birthday gift. Happy birthday, by the way." *Shut up, Mia.*

"Oh my God, Knox loves lemons. He used to eat them like oranges when he was a baby. I thought it was the weirdest thing," Tanya says, looking at her son with love shining in her gaze. "Sorry." She waves a hand in front of her face, and I notice a slight sheen in her blue eyes that match her son's. "I always get emotional around my boys' birthdays."

"Well, here," I say, practically shoving one of the tarts into Knox's chest. "This one's yours."

Knox looks surprised by my sudden assault on him with a tart pan. I nervously laugh before looking down to find a fork on the table, then hand it over to him.

"Enjoy," I say as he takes the fork from my hand, probably afraid I'll shove that at him and accidentally stab him or something.

I turn on my heels and walk away, silently berating myself for that incredibly uncomfortable show of...shit, I don't know what the hell that was.

"Hey, girl," Lucy says as I practically plow right into her. "I think you need this." She shoves a cup in my hand.

"What is it?" I ask, lifting the cup to my lips.

"Sprite and—"

I take a giant gulp before she can finish.

"Irish whiskey. Heavy on the whiskey."

It burns going down but helps me refocus all the same. Being around Knox for thirty seconds scrambled my brain, but I'm a grown-ass woman. I'm not some weak-kneed fourteen-year-old girl who gets twitter-pated being so close to her high school crush, for God's sake. Okay, fine, apparently that's exactly what I am, but it doesn't mean I can't pull my shit together and act like the adult I've grown into.

"Why is Knox looking at you like he's utterly con-fused?" Charlie asks, walking up to us, her gaze ping-ponging between me and the biker.

"It might have something to do with me shoving a pan in his chest." I take another swig of the drink Lucy so mercifully handed me a moment ago. "Or it could be that he's afraid I'm going to have an menty-b at his birthday party because, for the life of me, I can't open my mouth around the man without being completely awkward." Taking another gulp of whiskey, I realize the cup is nearly empty, and my lips tip down in a little pout.

"Could be," Charlie replies, giving me a pitying look.

"I don't know why you two dance around this. Just bang it out already," Lucy says.

"Thank you for your completely unhelpful advice," I say, shaking the cubes in the now-empty cup. "But the only thing I need is another one of these." I let out a breath and look at my two friends, who have seen the way I turn into a bumbling idiot around the man. "Knox doesn't have those kinds of feelings for me. He thinks I'm the same gawky teenager I was when I first met him. He doesn't even like me."

Lucy and Charlie give each other a look that says I'm full of shit.

"I don't think that's the look he generally shoots you, my sweet, naive friend. Do you ever wonder why not a single one of these guys has made a pass at you? Or why when you show up to the clubhouse looking like an absolute smokeshow out of your normal school librarian clothes, they keep their eyes purposely averted from that delectable ass?" Lucy asks.

I look down at myself, wondering what the hell she's going on about. I'm in a light-pink sweater that hangs off one shoulder paired with dark jeans and heeled boots to give my shorter stature some height. It's nothing compared to what I've seen women wear around this clubhouse. Though, these are my favorite jeans that even I have to admit makes my ass look fantastic. But still. I'm not, nor have I ever been, someone people consider *sexy*. I'm cute, which is fine with me.

"I'm not always dressed like a librarian. It's not like this is my first party here, either. They've seen me plenty of times wearing something similar."

"And yet they all keep a respectable distance," Charlie says, nodding as though she agrees with our delusional friend.

"I figured it was because we're friends. Like it's some show of respect or something."

"Oh, it is," Lucy says with laughter lacing her words. "But not because we're friends. Because Knox said you're off limits. None of these guys are going to go against their VP."

"That's crazy, though. He's never hinted that he sees me as anything more than a nuisance when I'm around."

I think back to all the times he's been stoic and silent in my presence, never giving me a smile or any sort of acknowledgment. Then I think back to the way it felt to be behind him on his bike. About how he squeezed my hands that were clasped at his waist. How he waited until I was inside my house before he drove away.

"I can only tell you what Jude told me," Lucy replies

"What are you telling people about me, Lucifer," Jude says, coming up behind Lucy and grabbing her around the waist before he pulls her back into his chest.

"Girl talk," she tells him before she turns her head, placing a kiss on his lips.

Loud sounds of laughter and a dog barking are enough to break them apart, and we all turn to watch Colby, Maizie's son, running through the clubhouse with a small ball of yellow fur chasing after him.

"Hopefully they tire each other out," Maizie says, walking up to the group of us as we watch the scene unfold. Colby drops to the floor on all fours and starts barking at the puppy like he's a dog himself. He laughs hysterically when the dog starts jumping all over him, licking at his face. All the while, the five of us look on with smiles on our faces.

"Who's dog?" Charlie asks.

"Wyatt's. And believe me when I tell you Ozzy is none too happy about it," Jude answers.

"Well, if he ever needs someone to take the puppy to the park, I'm sure Colby would be ecstatic," Maizie says.

"They say every boy needs a dog," Lucy says to Mazie.

"But not every mother needs another living, breathing responsibility in her life. Doggy dates are one thing. Keeping another living creature alive and well is something else entirely."

"Fair," Lucy says before turning to me. "You want another?" she asks, pointing at my drink.

"God, yes," I reply, and she grabs my hand, leading me to the bar.

A few hours later, after the food has been devoured and the clubhouse erupted in a melodious rendition of

"Happy Birthday to You," I find my grandmother sitting at one of the tables with Arthur, Maizie, and a very tired-looking Colby.

"You about ready to get going, Grandma?"

She looks at me with a smile in her eyes. "I don't want you to have to leave, dear. Maizie was just saying that she needs to get this young man home. I'm sure she can give me a ride."

Maizie looks surprised that she was volunteered, maybe even a little uncomfortable with the suggestion. "Of course, Mrs. Dawson."

"Please, call me Elaine. You'll make me feel old."

"Nonsense, Elaine. You haven't aged a minute since the days we spent freezing our asses off at the football games," Arthur interjects.

"You're good for my ego, Arthur Lewis," she says, standing from her seat and grabbing her pocketbook. "I'm serious about having you over for coffee. I expect a phone call from you next week."

"It's a date," he says, sharing a smile with my grandmother that goes on a little too long.

"Come on, son. Time to go," Maizie says, rubbing Colby's back.

"Can Pepper stay the night at our house?" he asks before crouching down next to the dog sleeping at his feet.

Maizie smiles at her son, then turns to me. "Wyatt let Colby name the dog. His name is now Pepperoni—Pepper for short." She turns back to Colby's pleading eyes.

"Not tonight, but I'll make sure to let Wyatt know you want a sleepover soon, okay?"

It takes everything in me not to laugh. I'm sure Wyatt, not Pepper, would love to be invited for a sleepover at Maizie's. The fact that those two haven't seen what's right in front of them is crazy to me.

My grandmother stands and gives me a kiss on the cheek before walking to Tanya, who's talking with Knox and Trick and thanking her for inviting her. At that, I do laugh, considering the woman invited herself through me.

"I think I want to be Elaine Dawson when I grow up," Maizie says, watching the regal way my grandmother commands the attention of everyone around her, including the former Black Roses president—both of them—and the tall vice president standing next to her.

"You and me both, sister."

I give her a hug goodbye and turn to Arthur who is watching my grandmother being led out of the clubhouse with her arm looped through Colby's. My heart twists for a moment, thinking that my grandmother deserves great-grandchildren of her own. Not that she'll be getting them anytime soon. Between me and my brother, who should probably stay far away from even the thought of having kids, the poor woman will have to settle for being the honorary great-grandmother to my friend's kids.

"Tanya and I are headed out, too, Dad," Trick says as he walks up to the table. "Time to let the kids have their fun."

"You know, there was a time when we stuck around for the fun," Arthur says.

"And our time has come and gone," Tanya replies as she walks up and lays her head on Trick's arm. "Plus, I'd rather not see what my sons get up to when I'm not around, thank you very much." Tanya turns to me. "I'm so happy Elaine came today, Mia. She is an absolute riot."

I smile at Tanya. "I didn't have much of a choice, but I'm glad she came too."

"Well, she's welcome anytime." She turns back to Arthur. "You ready, Gramps?"

"Oh, fine. Take my old bones home," he says, standing from his chair.

When they leave, I look around and find Lucy and Charlie at the pool tables with Linc, Jude, and Wyatt. Jude is sitting at one of the bar tables, sipping on a beer, when I walk over and have a seat on the other side of the round table.

Lucy is, of course, wiping the floor with Wyatt as she attacks every shot with practiced efficiency.

"You gonna play next?" I ask the Englishman.

"He's still sore about the last time he lost to me," Lucy supplies after sinking the eight ball and holding out her hand to Wyatt. He rolls his eyes and hands over a twenty, slapping it into her palm.

Lucy shoots him a gleeful smile. "Pleasure doing business," she says while folding the twenty before shoving it in her bra.

"I thought I was getting better," Wyatt says sullenly.

"You are, sweet cheeks. Just not good enough to beat me." Never let it be said that Lucy isn't a boastful winner. She looks at Wyatt's pouting face and scrunches her nose. "Okay, now I feel bad about taking everyone's money."

"Why?" Jude interjects. "They're the stupid arseholes who lose it."

Lucy pretends to think about that for a moment. "True." She shrugs, then looks at me. "Let's go, sister, you're up."

I groan and shake my head. "Come on, Lucy. You and I both know I don't have a shot in hell at even getting any balls in the holes."

Jude snickers and I send him a withering look. "You're a child."

"I'm aware," he answers.

"We can play teams. I'll give you Jude, and I'll take Wyatt. That keeps us pretty evenly matched," Lucy offers.

"Hey," Wyatt protests, but none of us pay his offense any mind.

"Lucifer, I'm perfectly happy sitting here with my beer, watching you wipe the floor with everyone," Jude says, then takes a long pull from his bottle.

Lucy sticks her tongue out at her man. "You're no fun anymore."

"Careful, love. I have no problem hauling you over my shoulder and showing you how *not fun* I am for the rest of the night."

"That's not the threat you think it is," she responds.

Before either of them can say anything else, another voice is heard over the noise of the clubhouse.

"If I have to stay, you have to stay," Knox tells Jude as he comes to stand next to my chair. "Mia and I will play you and Wyatt," he tells Lucy.

Oh shit.

"It's okay, really," I tell him. "I suck at pool, and Lucy has a mean streak when she wins."

"She doesn't scare me," Knox says with a cocky tilt to his lips.

"No, I don't suppose she would," I mumble to myself before exhaling a deep breath. "Okay, fine."

Knox holds out his hand to help me from my seat, and I slip my slightly damp one into his palm. There's no reason I should be having this reaction to him. I'm either a blubbering idiot around this guy or a sweaty mess. There is no in-between.

Lucy grins and begins racking the balls in the little triangle as Knox and I head over to where the cues are hanging on the wall.

"When I tell you I'm not good, it's not because I'm some secret pool shark. I really do play like shit," I warn Knox.

"Honey, I've seen you play. I know how terrible you are."

The frown on my face makes him laugh. God, that's a good sound and not one I hear much from him.

Now that I think of it, all the times I've been here, I've yet to see Knox with a cue in his hand. "I don't think I've ever seen you play, though."

"I grew up in this clubhouse. When Ozzy and I were kids, there wasn't a lot for us to do, so he and I would fuck around with trick shots. I'm a little rusty, but I think we can give Lucy and Wyatt a run for their money."

I love my friend and would destroy anyone who would hurt her or cause her harm, but even I have to admit it would be kind of fun to see the smug smile wiped off her face if Knox and I actually won.

His optimism perks me up, and I smile up at the tall man. "Let's do this."

Wyatt breaks and no balls go in, but there're a couple set up that don't look like too difficult of a shot.

"Ladies first," Knox says, tilting his head toward the table.

I find what looks to be the easiest shot and bend over the table, steadying the cue in my grip. Pulling the stick back, I aim it at the cue ball to thrust it forward. It hits one of the solid balls and...misses. To her credit, Lucy doesn't display the arrogant smile she usually has on her face any time anyone else misses a shot when playing against her. Wyatt goes next, hitting one of the striped balls in a pocket, then misses on the next.

Knox takes his shots, and before I know it, he's sunk three balls before he misses again. This time, Lucy does, in fact, shoot him a smirk.

"Well, well, well, what do we have here?" Lucy says as she eyes Knox.

"Oh yeah, love, I may have never mentioned that Knox was the only brother to offer any sort of challenge when we used to play," Jude says from his seat at the cocktail table.

"Slipped your mind?" Lucy asks, giving Jude a mean side-eye.

"Yup," he responds before taking another swig of his beer.

She lines up her cue and takes two shots before missing the third.

"You're up," she says with a smile toward me.

I bend over, and just before I take my shot, I feel a warm and rather large presence behind me.

"Here, let me show you," Knox says before he leans over me. He adjusts my hold on the cue stick, and I'm immediately tense.

"Breathe," he says in my ear, and I do, taking a long, steadying breath, then releasing it on a slow exhale.

"Good girl."

And with that, I fucking melt into him. All the tension I was holding leaves my body, and when he backs up, I take the shot and the ball goes in.

Chapter Five
Knox

Mia squeals in delight when she makes the shot, and I have to contain the wide smile that threatens to burst from me. She turns to me with a grin bigger than I've ever seen on her face. Her eyes hold a slightly dazed look. I'm not sure if it's because she can't believe she made a shot or if she can't believe the way she reacted to being so close and me calling her a *good girl.*

The way she melted into me had my dick half-hard in an instant. I had to back away; otherwise, she would have felt it. And honestly, I'm not sure how she would have reacted.

The way she shoved that fucking tart in my chest when she showed up with her grandmother was surprising and pretty funny, but I didn't dare laugh at her. It's obvious she's nervous around me, has been since I saw her a year ago at Thorn and Thistle, but that's not the reaction I want from her. I much prefer the response she gave moments ago. The way she relaxed instantly when I told her to breathe. Then, when she followed directions so perfectly and I told her she was a good girl...hell, I was not expecting that. I'd considered it a possibility, so I may have been testing the waters a bit to see how she responded. It was everything I hoped for.

One thing I've always prided myself on is my ability to judge any situation or person for their subtle—or not-so-subtle—cues. It's a skill that went hand in hand with spending a handful of years in a house that could be wildly unpredictable. Being in the MC has made it necessary to hone that particular ability. Mia has spent her life taking care of everything and everyone around her, maybe even people who don't deserve that kind of care. I see it in her eyes. She's of the mind that if she wants something done right, she's going to have to do it herself.

Never in a million years would I want to take that fierce independence from her, but some of that control? Yeah, that's something I think she needs to let go of sometimes. I've been around her plenty of times in the last year since she's been back. Watched her far more than someone like me should. She's wound so damn tight. There've been times when it looks like the weight of the world rests on her shoulders, and she's doing everything to stay afloat. Lucky for her, I like taking that control. When she allows it. *If* she'll allow it. But I think I'm on the right track with her.

"You did good, honey," I tell her, and she beams as I hold her excited gaze.

"If you two are done eye-fucking each other, Mia, you get to take another shot."

Fucking Lucy.

I shoot Jude a look and he holds his hands up in surrender, indicating that he has as much control over his woman as any of us—none. It's not that Lucy means harm. But she tends to say whatever she thinks the second it comes to her mind—which is all well and good, except right now because she just embarrassed Mia and broke our connection. To Mia's credit, she simply rolls her eyes at her friend's antics and plays the comment off before she takes another shot.

I allow myself a brief glimpse at her delectable ass and appreciate the way those tight jeans make her legs look a thousand miles long. The thought of what it would feel like to freely run my hand up the back of her thighs, over her curves, and wrap my large hands around her slim waist makes my mouth fucking water. I have to tear my gaze away. Otherwise, everyone in this clubhouse is going to see what nothing more than the mere thought of touching this woman does to me.

Mia misses the next shot, then it's Wyatt's turn. He takes a shot, sinks it, then misses the next. Honestly, Lucy is a damn good pool player. She learned when she was on the run and used her natural talents to con people out of cash at the tables. But having Wyatt on her team is a disadvantage, and when I'm up next, I make every shot he leaves wide open, eventually sinking the eight ball.

Mia fucking giggles and holds her hand up for a high five. I huff out a chuckle and slap my palm to hers. But instead of letting go, I link our fingers together. I want to bring my mouth to her knuckles and swipe my lips across them, but before I can consider that thought further, Lucy butts in. Again.

"I want a rematch," she says.

Mia drops my hand, clearing her throat before looking at Lucy. "You're on," she says with a saucy smirk.

Girl's got a little fire under there. I like it. A lot.

Jude laughs as Ozzy and Freya walk over to where he's sitting. "I think I need a refill," he says and vacates his seat, gesturing for Freya to take it.

Truth be told, Mia is pretty terrible at pool. It's obvious it frustrates her to no end, and that's where a big part of her problem lies. She's too caught up in her head. It all leads back to her wanting control and doing everything "right." God, what I wouldn't give to seize that control and show her what it's like to be taken care of. At least a little, by someone who deserves that kind of trust. But the little voice in the back of my head is again telling me that she's too good, too sweet for someone like me.

"Wow, Knox, I didn't realize you were so good. I never see you play," Freya says.

"We were two brats who grew up in a clubhouse. Me and Knox used to play all the time," Ozzy says, standing behind her.

"Ah, the good old days," Linc says.

"They aren't that old, asshole," I mumble as I rack the balls on the table.

"Someone gets a little touchy around his birthday," Linc says with a smile.

I'm not necessarily irritable around my birthday. I'm just not a fan of celebrating them. Linc is too young to remember, but the last birthday I had before coming to Shine was in a roadside motel with a gash across my forehead and a terrified mother who was running from her abusive ex. I think my mom has spent the last twenty-five years of birthdays making up for that one where all we had was a vending machine cupcake and bruises. That's why I let her make a big deal out of it—and why I don't walk out and go on a ride like I'd rather be doing. Well, maybe not this birthday. I'm pretty happy where I am right now.

"You two must have been heartbreakers in high school," Charlie says with a laugh. "I can only imagine all the girls fawning over the football players."

Mia swivels her gaze toward Charlie with wide eyes and a look I can't quite decipher.

"I only had eyes for one girl in high school," Ozzy says, kissing the crown of Freya's head. "Linc, on the other hand..."

Charlie turns and looks at my brother with a raised brow. "Oh, a bit of a ladies' man, were you?"

"I don't know." He shrugs. "I don't remember any woman before you." He gives her a cheesy smile, and she laughs before kissing him on the mouth.

"Good answer," she tells him.

"Trust me, all the girls wished Knox and Ozzy would give them a second look. But they just left broken dreams in their wake when they walked the halls," Freya says with an exaggerated despondent tone to her voice.

Ozzy shakes his head and laughs. "You have a very active imagination, pretty girl. There were no breaking hearts anywhere."

The girls at Shine High, especially the cheerleaders, barring Freya of course, liked to have plenty of fun in the dark, but as soon as the lights were on, I was persona non grata. Not that it bothered me much. I was a dumb high school kid who couldn't care either way as long as I had a girl to make out with at a party or in the back of my truck.

"You went to school with them, Mia. Was it as tragic as Freya is making it sound?" Lucy asks as she shoots the break for the game of pool we're supposed to be playing.

A blush covers Mia's sweet cheeks as she studies the balls. "I don't really remember. I was only in school with them for a year before they graduated."

"But you were at most of their games, right? I'm sure there were plenty of girls with their jersey numbers painted on their faces," Charlie says.

"Not that I remember," Mia says, still looking at the balls on the table.

"Trust me, no one was cheering for two biker brats in front of their parents and the rest of the town." Ozzy isn't the least bit perturbed by his statement. It's simply a fact, but Freya's mouth tips down in a small frown.

"I hated the way so many people in school used to treat you guys," she says, and Ozzy squeezes her shoulder.

"I know, pretty girl. It was a different time back then. Plenty of people hated having the club call Shine home. Thought we were going to corrupt their kids or some shit."

"Unfortunately, there're still some assholes like that around," Mia says.

"Doesn't matter. Fuck those people," Lucy chimes in.

Jude lifts his beer bottle. "Hear, hear, Lucifer."

An hour passes of playing pool, talking shit, and filling Charlie and Lucy in on a few high school stories.

"You should have seen Freya," Ozzy says. "Seeing her ready to knock Trevor Adam's head from his shoulders was a thing of beauty."

"I got a good shove in until you stepped between us," Freya says with a laugh. "Then you had to go and steal the glory for yourself," she teases.

"Freya's a scrapper. Good to know," Lucy says with a smile toward the woman.

"Half those guys are reliving their glory days with their buddies at a Wednesday night bowling league—divorced and paying child support and alimony out the ass now," Linc says. "Especially if their wives meet with Freya."

My prez's old lady has made quite a name for herself as a family law attorney in Shine. She usually takes on as many pro bono cases as she can manage, especially for the wives of men like Trevor Adams.

"Didn't your brother play football with the guys, Mia? Was he team Ozzy or team dickhead?" Charlie asks.

Ozzy, Linc and I share an uncomfortable look. Nolan hung out with Trevor, but he was always on the outskirts. After graduation, he would come around the clubhouse on his piece-of-shit bike every once in a while, but none of us really liked him. We discovered at one of the parties that he was dealing coke. Me, Linc, and Ozzy stepped in and made it abundantly clear that shit wasn't tolerated at our clubhouse or in our town. Last I heard, he left Shine not long after Mia went to college.

"He did, but we don't really talk anymore. My parents hear from him every once in a while, but after I left Arizona, I haven't tried to contact him."

Interesting that she says she hasn't tried. Does that mean he has? Mia doesn't seem like the type to cut someone out of her life, especially if that someone is family.

"What happened? You never talk about him." Lucy asks, nosy as fucking ever.

"Maybe she doesn't want to, love. Leave it be," Jude says.

Mia sets the end of the pool stick she's holding on the floor, leaning into it a bit as though she's using it as support.

"It's okay." Her other hand grabs the drink she has sitting at the edge of the table, and she takes a healthy swallow. "My parents sent him out to Arizona to live with me. They paid our rent, and I worked and went to school to pay for bills and food. Nolan did...nothing, which was pretty typical. He'd go out at night and usually wouldn't come home until I was getting ready to leave for class or to go to my shift at a coffee shop on campus. One day, I got home early and he was passed out on the couch with a bunch of baggies of white powder in front of him on the coffee table. I woke him up, and he said he was holding it for a friend. Of course, I was furious and threatened to kick him out, but he swore up and down it would never happen again. Then I started getting bills from credit card companies with my name on them. The only thing was, I'd never signed up for them."

"Jesus," Charlie breathes out, and Mia nods with a pinched look on her face.

"Yup. I threw him out and told my parents what happened. They didn't try to defend his actions or anything, but I know they started sending him money. They'd ask me to go to whatever friend's house he was staying at to try to talk to him but never flew out to do it themselves. It was a mess, to be honest. And, as usual, I was tasked with cleaning it up." She shrugs and looks at Lucy. "Are we still playing, or what?"

Lucy perks herself up and nods. "Yeah, it's your shot."

Mia sends her a tight smile and takes the shot, no one bringing up her asshole brother again.

Mia and I win another game, then Lucy and Wyatt win the other. Our two teams are tied neck and neck when the clubhouse door opens and a few girls from the strip club show up.

"Heard there's a birthday boy here tonight," one of the girls says, walking up to me at the pool tables. "It's been a minute, Knox."

The woman smiles and tosses her red locks over her shoulder as she comes to stand next to me.

"Hey, Heather," I say, giving her a pleasant smile.

Heather and I used to have fun together. She's been working at the club for a couple years and likes to consider herself as more than a stripper who takes her clothes off for men who shove money into some barely there G-strings. Heather likes to give a performance, an experience, and occasionally that includes using ropes. When I saw her perform for the first time, I was impressed, and she made it known to me that she likes to play off the stage as well.

"I've missed seeing you around. You know, I came up with a new routine. I'd love to get your thoughts on it." Her hand brushes my forearm, and I subtly move my arm just out of reach.

Heather and I have never had a relationship or rather, any sort of commitment. Neither of us is in a place where that's what we want. She does her thing, and I do mine. And sometimes, we meet up to scratch an itch. But I'm also not an asshole who's going to make her feel uncomfortable and give her a rude brush-off.

"Been busy," is all I say, but I try to keep my tone as neutral as possible. Mia is on the other side of the table, pretending she isn't paying attention, but I am. The way she stiffened and her hand went to her necklace as soon as Heather touched me did not go unnoticed.

"Well, let me know if you have a free night," she says and smiles before going to the bar where the rest of the girls are getting drinks from a very captivated prospect.

"It's getting late," Mia says before she hangs her stick back on the wall. "I'm going to head out."

"Oh, come on, it's barely eleven," Lucy says. "We need our final match so I can claim victory."

"I'm getting pretty tired too, actually," Charlie says, giving Mia a small smile before turning to Linc. "Take me home?"

"That's the best offer I've had all night."

"It had better be your only offer," Charlie says, swatting him in the chest.

"Lead the way, Charlie Pie."

Charlie groans with the use of my brother's nickname for her, but we all know she loves it. "Come on, Mia. We'll walk you out."

Mia gives Charlie an appreciative smile while Lucy pouts next to her.

"Lame," Lucy gripes.

"I'll play you, Lucifer."

"As long as you promise to keep the crying to a minimum," Ozzy interjects.

"I *do not* cry," Jude retorts with an air of offense.

Mia gives Lucy a hug, promising that they're still on for working out in a couple days. When she passes me on her way to the door, her smile is once again tight. "Happy birthday," she says, then brushes past me, following Linc and Charlie.

Jude reracks the balls, and I head to the bar to get myself another beer.

Fuck, I did not like the look of disappointment on Mia's face. And I hate that I care about what she could be thinking about what is or isn't going on with Heather. Just when I thought she was relaxing around me, it all got shot to hell, and now she's back to being stiff and uncomfortable around me.

"Another beer, Knox?" the prospect asks.

"Yeah. And a shot."

He sets the beer and a small glass in front of me, filling it with my favorite Irish whiskey.

When he moves to put the bottle back, I grab the base. "Leave the bottle."

Fuck it. It was nice while it lasted, but if tonight proved anything to me, Mia's too sweet for this life. And for me.

Happy *fucking* birthday to me.

The next morning comes way too damn early. When I peel my eyes open, I let out a groan of discomfort. Looking over to the other side of the bed, I'm relieved no one is sleeping next to me. The events of the rest of the evening after Mia left with Charlie and Linc are a bit hazy, which means the whiskey did exactly what it was supposed to. I sit up in bed and rub the ache in my temples. Shit, maybe a little too well.

My shirt is off, but I slept in my jeans, which always leaves me feeling like I haven't gotten a good night's sleep. Although I suppose that could be due to the copious amounts of whiskey I poured down my throat. The last thing I remember is Lucy throwing money at the girls who were giving the prospect the time of his life while he sat tied to a chair. I may have had something to do with that little idea.

Climbing out of bed, I make it into the bathroom and turn on the shower as hot as I can stand it. After brushing my teeth, I step under the scalding spray to wash this hangover from my body. There's shit to do today, and I don't need to be riding around smelling like a distillery. Braxton and I are going to head into Boston and take inventory of the guns we're set to run to Michigan next week.

Several of the guys are sitting on the large black leather sectional, eating giant breakfast sandwiches when I emerge from my room.

"Your mom dropped these off this morning," Jude says through a mouthful of food.

I grunt my response and head behind the bar to grab a cup of coffee.

"Place doesn't look half-bad," I say to the room, noticing that all the trash, glasses, and beer bottles from last night aren't anywhere to be seen.

"Ozzy woke up the prospect a few hours ago to clean up," Wyatt says.

Everyone has a little chuckle. Listen, if someone wants to patch in, we aren't going to let them nurse a hangover like a little bitch. They knew exactly what they signed up for.

"From what I remember, he had a good time last night," I say.

"Not so much this morning," Ozzy says, coming from the hallway with a grin on his face.

We had to do the same shit when we wanted to patch into the club out of high school. And I seem to recall Trick and Gramps being just as pleased about watching us do the grunt work when we were hungover as much as Ozzy and I enjoy it.

My attention turns to the large TV hanging on the wall. There's a reporter talking about the authorities finding the body of a dead girl just outside of Boston.

"The victim has not been identified by police, who, at this time, are still investigating the cause of death. Sources say the woman was found in a shallow grave with carvings over her stomach. We are also told that they are looking into the possibility that the woman could have been reported missing last year after authorities uncovered the bodies of three missing women in New York. We will report more as information becomes available. Back to you in the studio."

I turn to Ozzy and raise a brow. "New York?"

Several months ago, Jude and his brother were involved in dismantling a sex trafficking ring with the Monaghans. The asshole in charge was the head of the Bratva in New York. He went after Eoghan Monaghan's woman, who was also the dickhead's daughter. They caught up to him and wiped him from the planet with the help of his son, Nikolai, who now runs shit in New York. It could be nothing, or it could be something. But if someone is selling women this close to us, there's no way in hell we're going to let it stand.

"I'll give Finn a call and ask him to check in with Nikolai. If this shit didn't die in our state with Farina, I want to know," Ozzy says.

Braxton comes out of the kitchen and sees me, shoving the last bit of his sandwich in his mouth. "Goddamn, if your mom wasn't living with Trick, I'd ask her to marry me today," he says, rubbing his stomach.

"And I'd be committing patricide tomorrow," I say. "Ready?"

"Yup, let's go."

Nothing like a long ride to rid me of the remnants of this hangover.

Chapter Six
Mia

"Grandma, where are you?" I call as I walk through the back door of her house.

There's a truck in the driveway that I don't recognize, which could mean a myriad of things. Could be a landscaper—my grandmother wants a few things done now that the weather is warming up. Or she could be deciding to redo one of her rooms as an indoor sauna or something. The choices are honestly endless when it comes to her.

What I did not expect to find was my grandmother sitting in her formal living room while serving Arthur Lewis a cup of tea from the set she uses for *special* company.

I stop in the doorway, and my grandmother catches my eye. "Hello, Mia. Would you like to join us, dear?" She tops off Arthur's cup and offers him a small plate with a napkin and what looks to be a slice of one of the tarts I made for Knox's party.

That sneaky woman.

Arthur turns and gives me a charming smile. "Good to see you again, Mia. Please, sit with us."

Offering Arthur a smile, I walk into the room since I don't want to be rude and have a seat on the other side of the couch my grandmother is occupying.

"Would you like a slice of raspberry lemon tart?"

I shoot my grandmother a rueful grin and chuckle softly. "No thanks. I'm meeting Charlie and Lucy in a bit. Just wanted to check on you before I left to see if you needed anything while I was out."

And to see if there were going to be construction workers traipsing around the property in the coming weeks.

"Oh, I'm fine." She sends a smile to Arthur. "We were discussing the finer points of the importance of a defensive line over an offensive line for draft picks that we see for next season."

Anything having to do with the rules of football is completely lost on me. For all the time I spent at football games for my brother, I never actually learned anything about the sport. My parents didn't care that I hated watching football—well, except for one player—and would make me sit with them to watch the game. Appearances mattered, after all. Their daughter's free time? Not so much. But I'm incredibly happy that my grandmother has someone to talk sports with because it certainly isn't me.

"Elaine, I forgot what a fan you were. Patrick and Ozzy share a love for football, but they put too much importance on offense over defense, and honestly, they aren't nearly as charming or well-versed in the sport as you." Arthur takes a small bite of the tart on his plate. "Delicious. Did you make this?" he asks my grandmother.

"Oh, no. Mia is the baker in the family."

"Yes. And I could have sworn this is one of the desserts I brought to Knox's party," I say.

"There were so many dishes out. Who's to say why this one didn't get eaten?" She shrugs innocently, but her smile gives her away.

My grandmother is many things, but sly is not one of them. I have no doubt this woman somehow hid the tart so she could bring it home.

"Well, thank goodness you didn't let it go to waste," I say before turning my smile to Arthur. "Do you have any favorites, Arthur? Maybe I can have something ready for you the next time you pay my grandmother a visit."

It's been a long while since my grandmother had a man over. I honestly don't remember the last time she entertained anyone who wasn't part of her knitting club or our local Rotary club. Plus, I like the way Arthur smiles at her—and vice versa. There's something to be said for that Lewis charm.

"My mum used to make the most delicious sticky toffee pudding. It's been years since I've had it. Not since my wife passed. She was the baker in our family."

"I do remember Janine's pies. I swear they were the envy at every bake sale. Those old biddies would get so mad when everyone would buy a raffle ticket for her pie," my grandmother says with a warm smile.

"Do you remember when Brenda Linders had a near meltdown insisting it was rigged in Janine's favor?" Arthur asks, his body shaking with laughter.

"I do. I also remember Brenda's apple crumble tasting like wet cardboard." She rolls her eyes as she sips her tea.

"Damn, Grandma. Vicious."

"I couldn't help that all my guys were particular about their pie," Arthur says, shooting my grandmother a wink. They share a laugh, which tells me they knew damn well the Black Roses did, in fact, rig the raffle.

I check my phone and see a text from Charlie telling me that she, Lucy, and Maizie are waiting for me at the coffee shop.

Standing from my seat on the couch, I face my grandmother. "Alright, you two have fun." I turn to Arthur, who stands from his seat and holds out his hand.

When I slide mine over his, he covers it with his other hand. "It was wonderful seeing you again, Mia. I hope to see you around the clubhouse more, too."

"Now that it's warming up, Lucy wants Charlie and I at target practice, so I'm sure you will."

Arthur gives me a smile with an amused glint in his eyes, although I'm not sure why my answer has him entertained. Maybe it's the thought of Lucy schooling all the guys in the club a time or two at their outdoor range. From what Charlie has said, when she showed Jude up the first time she shot a gun, the look of shock on his face was pure gold and the talk of the clubhouse for weeks afterward. My friend is a certified badass, so I suppose if anyone can teach me to shoot straight, it's her.

"Wait, wait, wait. You're telling me that Arthur Lewis is at your grandmother's house having tea right now?" Lucy asks as the four of us are sitting at our favorite little coffee shop—Cool Beans—before we head to the farmers' market.

"They've known each other forever. Since way before I was born. I don't know"—I shrug as I sip my latte—"I think it's nice that she has a gentleman caller."

Lucy throws her head back with a laugh. "Have you gotten into your grandma's stash of historical romance? *Gentleman caller.*"

"I like a good romance every now and again." Or every night when I read myself to sleep.

"Well, I, for one, love that Arthur is spending time with Elaine," Maizie chimes in. "She has always been so kind to me and Colby. She used to be friends with my grandmother, too. When my grandma passed, she helped organize everything for me, considering I didn't have a clue about funeral arrangements, and my grandma and mom weren't exactly on speaking terms."

Life hasn't been fair to Maizie, and her parents have only made it harder. Though her mom seems to be coming around, she's not always in the best frame of mind after her mom visits her and her son.

"Jesus, does everyone know everyone in this town? I swear, you could throw a rock and hit someone's nanna who knows your nanna and remembers every little detail about your life," Lucy says.

Maizie and I look at each other, then turn to Lucy.

"Yup," I say.

"Pretty much," Maizie says at the same time. "Welcome to life in a small town."

"I like this small town a hell of a lot better than the one I grew up in. At least everyone here supports each other for the most part. Trust me, it could be worse," Charlie says.

Charlie has shared that where she came from, though small as it was, no one wanted to get involved with anyone's business. Even if they knew what went on behind closed doors was often violent—at least in Charlie's case.

"It wasn't always like that, either," I say. "It took a long while before the good people of Shine realized the club wasn't running around trying to corrupt its innocent boys and girls. They caught a lot of flak, especially after the shooting at the clubhouse."

Years ago, when Trick was president, the Italian Mafia had a problem with the Black Roses and shot up the clubhouse right before Thanksgiving when everyone, kids included, was there celebrating. I wasn't around, but I remember hearing about it and all the rumors about Freya leaving school after she was caught in the cross fire.

Though I don't think anyone necessarily forgot about it, they realize there hasn't been an incident since. For as seedy, or I don't know...unlawful as they think the club is, they can also recognize that Shine has remained largely untouched by a lot of the other problems that small working-class towns have. There aren't drugs on the streets, people aren't afraid to be out after dark, and I'm sure there are plenty of people who don't even think to lock their doors at night. Shine is a safe haven, and I believe that's largely thanks to the Black Roses making sure no one messes around in their town.

"I know one girl in particular who could use some corrupting," Lucy says, eyeing me over the rim of her cappuccino.

She laughs when I roll my eyes and wave my hand in front of me, indicating for her to just come out with it. "And there it is. Wow, it took you a whole"—I check the time on my phone—"fifteen minutes to make a reference to me and Knox."

"Woah, sister. I didn't say anything about Knox. That was all you," she says.

Charlie groans next to me. "Lucy, you are many things...and completely obvious *is* one of them."

Maizie and I bark out a laugh as Charlie holds Lucy's glacial stare. It takes about three seconds for the two best friends to break into a fit of laughter before Charlie turns to me.

"In all fairness, though, I'm pretty sure I didn't imagine the steam rising from you and Knox the other night," Charlie says while dramatically fanning herself.

"Ohhh, what did I miss?" Maizie asks.

"Nothing," I say, turning toward her, then back to Charlie and Lucy. "There's nothing going on between us. Jesus, until the other night, I wasn't even sure he liked me. He's always so stiff and gruff around me." I sit straight in my chair and do a piss-poor impersonation of the biker. I furrow my eyebrows and pull the corners of my mouth down in a deep frown, much like the expression Knox usually wears around me.

"Add in a growl. It would make it more realistic," Charlie says.

"I don't think he usually growls, at least not around me. But holy shit, when he was helping you with that shot, I swear to God, even I was getting a little hot under the collar," Lucy says.

Maizie's eyes dart between Lucy and Charlie before landing on me. "You and Knox, huh? Can't say I didn't see that coming."

"I already told you. Nothing is going on. He gave me a ride home the other night and then we played pool at the clubhouse."

"Wait a minute, sister," Lucy says, leaning over the table between us. "You didn't say anything about a ride home. When was this? Was he on his bike? Why didn't you call me? Was riding with him everything you ever dreamed of?" She fires off her questions in rapid succession, the last being the most ridiculous.

"I got a flat tire on the way home the other night when we went for drinks. I was about to change it when I heard him pull up behind me. Thank God, too, because my spare was flat, and I wasn't going to get a tow that late." I remember trying to think of every plausible excuse I could think of to not hitch a ride with Knox. Not that I was opposed to getting on his bike. The exact opposite, actually. I just wasn't sure if it would be possible for me to suppress all the teenage fantasies of him whisking me away on his motorcycle enough to not embarrass myself.

"So you rode on the back of his bike? Did you invite him in and give him a proper thank-you?" Lucy asks with her lip tipped up in a wicked smile.

"What would that be? A roll in the hay, or would a blow job have sufficed?" I ask with an arched brow. "I said thank you and walked inside. I have a little more self-respect than to fall all over him because he's a decent man who wasn't going to leave me stranded."

"Girl, it's not about self-respect. But I'm glad you have it. I wish more women did. *And* I wish more women didn't tie their self-respect to some antiquated idea of being sexually repressed," Lucy says with her brow arched as she gives me a scolding look.

"Jesus, I am not sexually repressed. And I don't tie the two together. Everyone is free to be who they are, and they'll get zero judgment from me. But making sure a woman isn't left stranded on the side of the road is bare minimum in my book and doesn't warrant an invite into my bed." A deep breath rushes out of me. "It's just...it's Knox." I close my eyes and massage my temples with my fingertips, trying to stave off the tension headache building there. "I'm well aware of the fact that I have him on some sort of pedestal as the ultimate bad boy crush." I tilt my head down and cover my face with my hands. "God, that sounds so stupid."

When I look back up, the girls all have varying degrees of pitying smiles on their faces. I don't know which is worse, what I just said about Knox or the looks they're giving me now.

"Listen, I know I'm not his usual type. No reason to look at me like that."

"Oh no, honey," Lucy states in an unusually sympathetic tone. "We know you've had a crush on the guy forever. It's the fact that, for some reason, you don't think you're good enough for him or something. None of us like seeing you feel so uncomfortable around him. That's the look."

"I'm just not...Heather."

"Who?" Maizie asks.

"You'd already left when the girls from Midnight Rose came to the party for Knox's birthday," Charlie says. "Heather is one of the dancers. She seemed to know Knox on a more *intimate* level than the other girls, and she stopped by the pool table when they were playing to say hello."

"And she's a gorgeous, leggy redhead," I add.

Charlie tilts her head in my direction. "And that."

"Mia, look at me," Lucy says, and I turn my head toward her. "I'm not Heather, either. Neither is Charlie, and neither is Maizie. We're us, and you're you. If Knox wanted a *Heather*, he could have easily had her that night, but he didn't touch any of the girls. In fact, after you left, he got good and drunk, then went to bed."

"It's fine, really," I say, trying to give the girls a reassuring smile. "I'm sure everyone has that one crush they always felt was totally out of their league." I look around the table, and the girls all have blank expressions on their faces.

"I grew up in a crazy cult that wanted to marry me off at sixteen," Lucy says.

"My one and only crush I had when I was younger turned out to be an awful human being who tried to sell me and is now..." Charlie slashes her finger across her throat.

"I'm a single mom who doesn't have the time, energy, or interest in anything having to do with anyone who has a penis," Maizie offers.

"You guys could at least pretend to relate to me," I grouse and raise my eyes to the ceiling. "Man, I need new friends."

"No, you have perfect friends who love you. However, what we won't do is let you talk bad about yourself. Mia, you're gorgeous, loving, and have one of the kindest souls I've ever known. Remember, Knox is just a man. He isn't some guy who has a magic dick that will completely transform your entire life," Maizie says.

"Well, you don't actually know that for a fact, do you, Maiz?" Lucy asks with a grin. "It could have superpowers."

Maizie scoffs. "Please. The last guy who tried to convince me of that wasn't close to having anything magical about his dick or his personality once the tequila wore off," she mumbles.

"Okay, as fun as it is talking about magical dicks and my embarrassing high school crush, we should probably hit the market. I still need to finish up a few details on my proposal and go over it one more time."

"How many times have you already proofed it?" Lucy asks.

I shoot Lucy a look that says I'd rather not say. "Once more can't hurt."

The farmers' market is crowded. It's the first of the season, and the residents of Shine are more than happy to be emerging from their homes now that the weather has thawed a bit, although there's still a slight chill in the air.

"Let's stop by Cece's table," Lucy says.

When the Black Roses rescued Lucy, they took the women from the compound and many of them went to the women's shelter in town. Cece went to live with Lucy and Jude and has made so many strides since leaving the hell both sisters were raised in. But I know Lucy worries about her. Though she came to Shine quiet as a church mouse, she's been finding her voice, according to Lucy. And apparently, that voice has gotten louder and angrier as time has gone on. If there's one person to soften Lucy's rough edges, it's her sister, but I know she worries that she isn't handling things correctly. There was so much that happened to the girl in the years Lucy spent on the run, and most of it we still don't know because Cece won't discuss it.

"How's she been?" Charlie asks as we weave through the crowd.

Lucy lets out a breath and shrugs. "Okay, I guess. She doesn't really talk to me about anything. I was so happy to have her home in the beginning, and we were focused on making sure she understood that she was safe around Jude and all the guys. These last few months though, there's this other side of her that I didn't see, or maybe didn't want to see...I don't know. But she's angry. She won't open up about it, and the only way I really have to judge what she's feeling is by the music she blares when she's baking. Sometimes, it's somber, and sometimes it's the loudest scream metal you could imagine. Jude stays away when that shit is blasting. He tried to turn it down once, and he told me she looked like she was ready to grab a knife from the butcher block and stab him with it."

"Have you convinced her to talk to someone yet?" Charlie asks.

"Nope. She said it doesn't matter. That they can't magically take away what she went through, so what good will it do to relive it now?"

"Shit," Charlie breathes out.

"Yup. The only thing I can do at this point is keep showing up for her and make sure she knows that no matter how hard she rebels, gets angry, or yells, she's still loved and still safe."

"She's been great with Colby," Maizie says. "He lights up every time she comes over to hang out with him."

Cece has been babysitting for Maizie. Lucy's mentioned that the only time she sees glimpses of the sweet and playful girl she remembers from their childhood has been when she's around Colby.

"I'm glad she's spending time with him," Lucy says. "It gets her out of the house and makes her happy."

Maizie shoots Lucy a smile as we approach the booth surrounded by shelves of bread, with Cece sitting behind a table draped in a light-blue tablecloth.

Lucy's gaze travels over the half-empty shelves, and she shoots her sister a smile. "Hey, looks like you've been selling a lot."

"It helps to stock up when you hardly sleep," Cece replies, looking around at the loaves of bread and small homemade pastries.

"You should talk to Betsy at Cool Beans. I'm sure she'd love to carry some of your pastries," I say in a bright voice usually reserved for the kids at school. It's hard seeing her like this. When we first met, she was so quiet but seemed hopeful. Now, it's as though a sullen teenager has taken her place. Not that anyone can blame her.

"Maybe," is the only response she gives.

"Well, I, for one, am always up for more treats," Charlie says as she grabs a napkin and picks up some sort of berry Danish before reaching into her purse to fish out cash, then hands a couple bills to Cece.

"It doesn't seem right to charge you. You're like family," Cece says.

"Good thing I like supporting my family's new business ventures," Charlie says, and Cece reluctantly takes the cash from her hand.

Charlie bites into the Danish, and a satisfied moan escapes her throat. "So worth it," she says around her mouthful.

I grab one for myself and hand Cece the money before taking a bite. "Oh my God, Cece, I think these are better than Betsy's." I feign a look of guilt as I glance at the people walking past, then back to Cece. "Don't tell her I said that." I give her a conspiratorial wink, and she tilts the corner of her mouth in an almost smile.

"Here's the girl I was looking for," a feminine voice calls from behind me. I turn and there stands a stunning redhead, her face free of makeup, with two other girls standing beside her, just as tall and just as exotically beautiful without any effort. "This is the amazing baker of those scones and pastries Knox dropped off a couple weeks ago. I remember him saying you planned to have a booth here."

"Hey, Heather, how are you?" Lucy asks.

Heather leans in and gives Lucy an affectionate hug while my friend shoots me an apologetic look over the redhead's shoulder.

"It's so good to see you," Heather says. "Knox told us this was your sister, so of course we had to come down here and load up. Not to mention, I haven't been able to get those apple turnovers out of my head since I tried one," she says, looking at Cece with a wide grin.

Of course she has to be gorgeous *and* nice.

"I've been working on some different recipes. I have peaches and cream and vanilla blackberry now, too," Cece says.

"Girl, I'll take everything you have. I work tonight, and there's no doubt in my mind the other girls will be ecstatic if I walk in with these." Heather smiles while Cece starts wrapping up the dozen or so different pastries she has left, then looks at me. "Hey, I met you the other night at the clubhouse at Knox's birthday party."

"Not officially," I say.

"I'm Heather." The woman holds out the hand that isn't clutching the pastry, and I shake it.

"Mia."

"Mia and Knox have known each other since they were in high school," Lucy says.

"Seems everyone in this town knows either knows each other from high school or church or something," Heather says.

Lucy laughs. "I was just saying that earlier."

"Good thing I'm a transplant, I guess. No one remembers my awkward phase," Heather says on an embarrassed laugh.

Yeah, I'm so sure she went through the same tragic phase of braces and frizzy hair as the rest of us mere mortals.

"Where are you from?" Charlie asks.

"Boston, actually, so not too far."

"What on earth brought you to Shine?" Lucy asks.

"I met Sylvie, Midnight Roses' manager, at a club there. She liked my work, and I wanted out of the city." Heather shrugs. "I like a quieter life, and working for the club is honestly the best decision I've made. The stories I could tell you about some of the places I've danced at would make your hair stand on end."

I have a feeling Heather doesn't know the particulars about Charlie and Lucy's former lives. It's doubtful she could say anything about what she went through that would compare. *God, stop being a judgy bitch, Mia.*

"Well, I'm glad you're happy working there. Ozzy certainly wants all the girls to feel comfortable," Charlie says.

"All the guys are great." Heather points her smile at me, and I feel how brittle the one I return is. Jesus, I'm jealous of a woman over a man who, until last week, I hardly had any interaction with in my entire life. This is not me, and to be honest, I'm not enjoying this side of myself at all.

"It was nice meeting you," I say, trying to sound like I mean it. There's no reason for me to be an asshole to the girls standing in front of me. I've never been the one to behave or even think like this, and I'm not about to start now.

"You, too. I'm sure I'll see you around sometime."

Great. I'm so looking forward to that—especially if Knox is around, and I feel two feet tall again, like I did the other night.

Okay, so obviously I have work to do. Baby steps.

"I need to get going," I tell the girls. "Thank you for the pastry, Cece. Actually, let me get a couple loaves of bread, too."

I plan on eating my feelings tonight, and what better way to do it than with Cece's homemade rosemary sourdough?

After paying for the bread, I give the girls a hug goodbye and tell them that we'll meet up later in the week for drinks or something. Charlie was talking about Linc going on a run with Knox and Cash later this week, so that would be the perfect opportunity to make sure Knox isn't around. I feel like an idiot for my reaction at the clubhouse...and an even bigger idiot for feeling like I was run off by the leggy redhead—who is apparently extremely nice and supports the small business of one of the club's family members.

Before leaving the market, I stop and grab some homemade fig and jalapeño jam to go with the bread. When I get to my car, there's something on my windshield. A beautiful bouquet of white tulips.

Huh.

I throw the bread and jam in my back seat and grab the flowers. No note, but they are gorgeous, wrapped in butcher paper, and tied with string. I'm not sure they were meant for me because who the hell would be leaving me flowers? But I set them on my passenger seat and head home to put them in water. Hopefully the person they were meant for isn't upset that they didn't get them.

But hey, they sure brighten up my otherwise dreary day, so I'll call that a win for me.

Chapter Seven
Knox

"Well, well, well. I expected to have one of your grunts driving everything out to us, not the lieutenant of the Monaghan family," I say, standing outside of the clubhouse as Cillian Doyle steps out of a Sprinter van and opens the door of the luxury sports car his fiancée came in.

"Nova wanted to visit with the girls and say hello to Ozzy," Cillian replies as another car and two motorcycles pull in behind him.

Nova hops out of the car and waves in my direction before walking over to Charlie's car, giving her—then Lucy—a long hug when they step out.

Cillian strides over to me, and we shake hands, but his attention is focused on the woman who stole his wallet, then his heart, in New Orleans several months back.

"I hear congratulations are in order," I say.

We watch as Lucy grabs Nova's left hand and whistles loudly as she takes in the huge diamond on her finger that I can see shining from here. "Good job, Cillian," she yells to him.

He smiles and laughs. "Have her tell you about how she found it," Cillian calls back and laughs.

"Now don't go telling all my secrets," Nova says in a sweet Southern accent I've never heard her use before.

The usually stalwart lieutenant shakes his head with a chuckle before turning back to me. "Figured you'd want to use a new van rather than that beater you've been driving since we've been doing business."

I nod, examining the vehicle as Cillian leads me to the back and opens the doors. He lifts the floorboard, revealing the hidden compartments underneath with the guns nestled in safely. Then he opens the false side panels, another hiding spot for the merchandise we're taking to Michigan.

"Liam had this lying around. Said if we wanted to use it for our business, we were more than welcome. It's hooked up to GPS that only we have access to, just in case."

No one is expecting any trouble on our little business trip, but we've all learned to play it safe the last couple years, especially between the Italians and the New York Russians. Not to mention the Bone Breakers—who are still without answers as to where three of their guys vanished to. They already tried to fuck with us once when we weren't prepared, and there won't be a second time.

"Hey, Cillian, good to see you," Ozzy says, walking to meet us at the back of the van with Cash behind him.

Cillian shakes Ozzy's hand, then Cash's.

"Thanks for the phone call," Cash says before looking over toward Nova. "She's happier than I've ever seen her."

Before Cillian proposed to Nova, he called Cash to tell him. He grew up with Nova and her older brother, Cooper. After Cooper's death, Cash hadn't spoken to Nova for over a year. She held a grudge the size of Texas against the club. But when she needed protection a few months back, Ozzy took her and her best friend in. Then we assisted the Monaghans in making sure there were no loose ends that could come back and bite her. The two started talking again, and he was the closest thing she had to family. Well, we all are now. Nova may not have anticipated being taken into the fold, but if there's one thing about the Black Roses, it's that we take care of our own. Cooper was ours. Therefore, by extension, so is his sister.

"You're the only family she has left. I'm not big on the tradition of asking permission, but I thought I should at least let you know," Cillian says.

Cash's lips tip up in a small grin. "What if I would have said *over my dead body?*"

"Like I said, I wasn't going to ask permission. Do you honestly think she would have let you tell me no?"

"I don't think Nova has ever let anyone tell her what to do a day in her life." Cash laughs and slaps Cillian on the back. "Good luck if you ever try."

"Trust me, I'm well aware of my woman's stubborn streak."

"You haven't even begun to understand a stubborn streak until you've lived with a young woman in the midst of her teenage rebellion years," Jude says as he and Linc walk over.

"I'm assuming you aren't talking about Lucy?" I ask.

"Jesus, I wish. At least I know how to handle her. Her sister, on the other hand? Haven't the faintest, except to stay as far away from it as I can."

"Sounds like a good plan to me," Ozzy says.

"I'm one door slam from taking the damn thing off the hinges," Jude grumbles.

"She's gone through a lot in her short life. I think she deserves a little patience, dickhead," Cash says.

"Fuck off, arsehole. Me and Lucy have been nothing but. Something's gotta give, and I'm afraid it may be my sanity before long."

"I'll see if my mom can rope her into some volunteer work. She has a way of getting people to open up and talk about their shit," Linc offers.

"I'm more than happy to give it a try. Little Bit needs something to occupy her time," Jude says, using the nickname that Liam, Jude's brother, coined for her the first time they met.

My eyes stay on Cash, and I think about his reaction to what he perceives as Jude saying anything remotely critical of Cece. Lately, it seems he's been at her beck and call. Jude doesn't seem particularly concerned with the idea that our treasurer may be taking a more than brotherly interest in her, but it has alarm bells ringing in my head.

Before I have a chance to think any more on the subject, Ozzy says, "Alright. Let's get the bikes loaded in the back so you guys can hit the road."

Cash and I cover the hidden panels and walk over to our bikes parked in the gravel lot. We'll be putting them in the back and driving. None of us have ever been stopped by law enforcement on one of these runs. When traveling, we keep it at the speed limit and tend to take as many back roads as possible so as not to attract attention on the open highway where we can. But we always make sure to have some sort of cover story in case local cops see a bunch of bikes with a van and get a hair up their ass. Plus, it never hurts to have the van when we make trips, just in case something happens with one of the bikes.

Once we have everything loaded, we head back into the clubhouse, and I head to my room to pack a bag so we can get the hell out of here. I throw a couple changes of jeans that I keep here in a bag and start digging around in my closet for a few warmer shirts. I think back to the night I gave Mia a ride home on my bike, seeing her in my sweatshirt. Fuck, she looked good. And now that I think about it, she still has that sweatshirt. For all I know, it's balled up in the back of her closet—and now I'm thinking about her bedroom and how honored I'd be if she let me see it firsthand.

A knock sounds at my door, and Braxton peaks his head in. "Ready?"

I zip up my bag and haul it over my shoulder. "Let's go."

It takes twelve hours to get to the Iron Disciples clubhouse outside of Detroit. And I was stuck in this fucking van the entire time with Cash skipping through every damn radio station on the drive. When he was bored with that, he connected his phone and started skipping through those songs. Drove me up the fucking wall. He's lucky he's one of my brothers. Had it been anyone else, I would have tossed the phone out the window, then threatened the asshole with a myriad of creative ways I would torture him if he touched the damn radio again.

I may be slightly irritated, but fuck, riding in a cage for twelve hours will do that to a man. I don't care what I have to promise; someone else is riding back to Shine in the van with Cash. Ozzy will have my head if we're short a treasurer when we get home.

Jude, Braxton, and Linc climb off their bikes slowly, bodies aching from so many hours riding. Strange as it may seem to any rational person, I envy every stiff muscle they're stretching out. Long rides have a way of centering me, and I could use that right about now. When Linc was locked up, I would make the ride to the prison he was in states away every couple of months. It was a two-day ride there and back for a few hours with my brother, but there was no way in hell I was going to leave him to rot for six years. The Iron Disciples were always happy to have me spend the night when I made the trip.

"Knox," a voice calls from the door of the clubhouse. I turn to see Silas, the Iron Disciples president, walking toward us, holding out his hand.

"Silas, good to see you."

We met the president before he held the title years ago at a meet in Kentucky. Someone had pissed off Ozzy for who knows what. He had a bit of a temper for a few years after we joined the club. The guy swung, Ozzy ducked, and the asshole hit Silas. Without missing a beat, Silas punched the other guy in the face, and it was utter mayhem in that little bar until the bartender pulled out a sawed-off shotgun and blew a hole in the roof. Probably less damage than what was being torn apart in the bar. The local assholes who didn't appreciate having bikers in their town ran off, and we went to another bar down the road and nursed our split lips and bruised ribs over beers and shots of whiskey. Been friends ever since, but this is the first time we've facilitated any sort of business between their club and the Irish. Truth be told, if it wasn't for Finn expanding his gun business, we wouldn't have brought this to them. At least Finn was smarter this time around and chose to do business with a club we already have a relationship with.

"Got rooms set up for you guys," Silas says after saying hello to the others with me. "And Amber's been looking forward to your visit." Silas directs the last bit of information toward me.

"I'm pretty fucking wiped after the drive, but I could go for a beer," I say.

Amber is a nice girl, and we've had our fun together the times I've been here for a night or two when I would come visit Linc, but I'm not interested in having a roll in the sheets with my old hookup. Not when the only woman who's been running through my mind these last few weeks has been a cute-as-hell librarian who makes a mean tart.

"We have plenty of that, brother." Silas waves his hand, and we follow him inside.

His clubhouse is similar to ours. Concrete floor, pool table, but no dart boards, which Jude has harassed him about nearly every time we've been here. A bar that's well stocked, though it doesn't have quite as much Irish whiskey as ours, but if all goes well, that will change sooner rather than later.

A few of the guys who have been members since we met all those years ago come over to say hello.

"Jude, it's been a fucking minute. Heard you got yourself shacked up these days with a hot little thing with a penchant for firearms," Vaughn says, giving the Englishman a back-slapping hug.

"And couldn't be happier about it," Jude replies. He used to make the trips out here with me when I'd ride through on my way to visit Linc.

"Why don't you bring her around? Afraid she'll take one look at me and leave your sorry ass?" Vaughn asks.

Jude shakes his head and grins. "I'm afraid you'll say something stupid, and she'll shoot you. But if you want to take the risk, I'll be more than happy to bring her next time we're in town."

Vaughn lets out a boisterous laugh and grabs Jude around the shoulders. "I've missed you, asshole. Let's get a drink."

Vaughn, Jude, and Linc head over to the bar, followed by me and Silas. Before we have our beers in hand, an arm wraps around my middle. I look down to see fingernails painted bright red. A woman with bleached-blonde hair—that was a different color last time I was here—looks up at me with what I'm sure is supposed to be a sultry smile on her bright-pink lips.

"Hey, Knox. Good to see you," Amber says, her finger traveling dangerously close to my belt buckle.

Carefully untangling myself from her touch while trying to make it look as natural as possible is no small feat. Amber's a nice girl, and if the guys see that I'm not interested, it will raise the kinds of questions I don't have the answers to right now. But having Amber's hands on me is uncomfortable and feels wrong.

"Hey, Amber. How've you been?"

She looks slightly confused at my action, but like a good club bunny, she doesn't question or get upset by my clear disinterest.

"Good. I was happy to hear you were going to be in town. Was hoping we could catch up."

She looks at me with a coy smile that tells me her version of catching up is naked in a bed. Can't blame the girl for giving it one last shot.

"It's been a long drive. I'm pretty tired. Think I'll be heading to bed here in a minute. Alone." I don't want to be a dick, but I want it perfectly clear that I'm not interested in having her there with me.

She smiles, but it doesn't quite reach her eyes. "Got it. Have a good night, then." She turns and heads toward a group of a couple other bunnies and a few brothers hanging out around the old pool table.

When I sit down at the bar, Cash casts his scrutinizing gaze in my direction.

"What?" I ask, nodding in thanks toward the prospect when he hands me my beer.

"What was that?" Cash asks, tilting his head toward Amber and the other group.

"Not sure what you mean." I know exactly what he means, but like hell I'm going to talk about what—or rather who—has been playing through my head.

Cash nods a few times before turning and resting his forearm on the bar, then he picks up his bottle and brings it to his smirking lips. "Whatever you say, brother."

Jude and Linc walk over with Vaughn behind them.

"Fancy a game of pool?" Jude asks me. Since the night of my party, he has been relentless in trying to get me to play again. Hell, before that night at my party, it had been a long-ass time since I'd picked up a pool stick. Which brings my thoughts back to the woman I was playing with.

Through the years of Jude being a brother, we've played a few times, but life got busy, and I moved into my own place, so the nights of staying up until sunrise, drinking, and shooting the shit with my brothers are few and far between. When Linc was in prison, I spent a lot of time at my mom and Trick's place, helping with various projects or just enjoying a home-cooked meal. She told me it helped having me around, seeing that one of her boys was safe and sound. My mom knew the dangers of this life, and she accepted them long before Linc and I were in the club, but that didn't mean she didn't worry. If I could ease that by spending more time with her while Linc was locked up, I was happy to do it.

"Nah, I'm going to hit the sack. Being stuck in a van with this fucker"—I point my thumb at Cash—"was exhausting."

"Fuck you, dick." Cash rolls his eyes.

"No thanks." I give him a wide smile which he returns by raising his middle finger in my direction.

When I stand from the bar, my hand clamps down on Linc's shoulder. Being here with him when I spent so much time at this clubhouse without him is bringing up emotions that I spent years keeping under lock and key.

"We're leaving early. Make sure you get your beauty sleep. Oh, and you're riding with Cash on the way back," I inform my brother.

Linc laughs and nods, not particularly upset that he won't be riding back to Shine. He knows me well enough to know I hate being stuck in a cage and was probably expecting the driving arrangements to change. "Ok, brother."

"Silas," I call, turning toward the president, who's sitting a couple seats down with a bunny attached to his side. "Same room?"

The man jerks his head toward the hallway. "You know the way. See you in the morning."

I walk into one of the rooms the club leaves empty for guests who travel through and need a place to crash. I toe off my boots, strip out of my jeans, and rip my shirt over my head before falling into the queen bed. Grabbing my phone, I set my alarm, then open the photos. My mom sent a few pictures from my birthday party the other day. I pull up the one with Mia's face, mid-laugh as she sits with Maizie and Colby. Fuck, she looks good with that smile. It's rare that I see it from her in person, but my mom caught the perfect shot—and I've spent more time staring at it than any reasonably sane man should.

Originally, we were going to take two days getting back to give our bodies a break from the long ride, but

I changed the plan at the last minute, which was fine with Jude and Linc. They have women to get back to. I, on the other hand, don't, but I'm also done lying to myself and pretending I don't wish I did. Being here is making me remember all the reasons this life can be painful for the people we love. Our freedom—shit, our lives—could be taken at any moment. I *could* run from this feeling I have every time I look at this picture or imagine Mia on the back of my bike like I've been doing since the night I gave her a ride home. I *could* ignore the tightness in my chest when I think about her finding a nice, respectable man to settle down with, watching her give him the smiles that should be mine. And maybe I should. No, I *definitely* should, but doing what I think is right and what I want are two completely different things.

I close the photo and set the phone back on the nightstand before turning off the light and rolling to my back with my hands behind my head.

I'm done. Done denying myself what I really want and think I can't have. Done letting my past of never thinking I was good enough for someone like Mia dictate my life from here on out. I want to get back to Shine and prove I'm the exact kind of man who is worthy of the little librarian, and I'm done letting the bullshit in my head stop me from going after what I want.

My alarm goes off at seven in the morning. I have no idea what time everyone else went to bed, but I'm ready to hit the road. When I walk out into the main area of the clubhouse, it's quiet. Heading into the kitchen, I go about making myself a pot of coffee when Cash strolls in, showered and looking ready to get on the road.

"Morning," I say, leaning against the counter as he opens the fridge, probably hoping for at least a loaf of bread or something to put in his stomach.

"Gotta say I appreciate the hospitality here, but the lack of food is mildly concerning. What the fuck do these guys eat?" he asks, closing the refrigerator door.

"Yeah, they don't have anyone who makes sure to keep the refrigerator stocked and shit like we do. Not every club has a Tanya who likes to make sure her boys are fed." I nod over to the pizza box, and Cash lifts the lid, revealing a couple slices of what I'm pretty sure are at least a day old.

He curls his lip and looks at me. "Let's go get some breakfast. By the time we're back, the other three should be up. I'll even be nice and bring something back for them."

My eyes shift to the coffeepot—which is almost done brewing—and my stomach rumbles. "Yeah, that sounds good."

We head into town and park the van on the side of the street. There's a little coffee shop next to a small mom-and-pop jewelry store. I smile at the older woman turning her *closed* sign to *open*, and my gaze falls to a pair of earrings in the window. They have a red center stone nestled in a silver design that's similar to the necklace that Mia is always wearing.

"Hold up," I say and turn to go into the store.

"What are you doing?" Cash asks as we step through the door.

"What does it look like?"

The woman has moved behind the counter and smiles when we approach.

"Can I help you find something today?"

"Yeah. I saw a pair of earrings in the window that I'd like to get."

The woman and I walk over to the display in the window, and I point to the ones I saw. When we walk back to the counter, she hands me the earrings so I can take a closer look, I guess. I've never bought jewelry for a woman, so I'm not exactly sure what the protocol here is. I saw them, I liked them, and I'm going to buy them.

I nod and hand them back to the woman. As she's ringing me up, Cash seems to be chomping at the bit to ask me a million questions. Questions that I haven't had answers to. Hell, I may not have them all now, but I'm not afraid of him or anyone else asking anymore.

When I finish paying, we walk next door to the coffee shop and order a couple cups of coffee and a couple breakfast sandwiches for us to eat here, then a few more to bring back to the clubhouse with us.

Cash has been silent about the seemingly odd excursion we went on, but that changes as soon as we sit at the table with our coffee.

"What are you doing?" he asks.

"Drinking coffee," I say, taking a sip from my cup and wincing a bit when the hot liquid burns my tongue.

"You know what the fuck I'm talking about. You've been a moody fuck and more in your head than usual. Last night, you brushed that bunny off, then went to bed, and this morning you're buying jewelry. Last I checked, you don't have your ears pierced and these aren't exactly your style," he says, pointing to the small bag sitting on the table.

"Wow, I didn't realize you paid such close attention. I don't know whether I should be touched or scared that you're falling in love with me."

"Fuck off. And don't try to change the subject. Who are the earrings for, Knox?"

"Mia," I answer simply.

Cash sits back and blows out a breath. "You sure that's wise? She's not exactly old lady material."

My spine stiffens with his remark. "And Cece is?"

Cash's eyes go wide, surprised that he's being called out, before he quickly tempers his features. "What does she have to do with anything? We're talking about you."

"Yeah, and I don't like where the conversation is going. Freya isn't someone who you would call 'old lady material,' but she and Ozzy make it work just fine. Are you saying Mia's too good for me? Because you'd be right, but that doesn't change the fact that I'm interested."

"The girl barely talks to you. How could you possibly be interested?"

"The girl's name is *Mia*," I say, giving Cash a stern look. "And I've known her for a long time. I don't know, there's something about her. Like when I see her laughing or smiling, I want to know what it would feel like to be the one she turns to with that smile. She's good and sweet. I could use a little sweetness in my life."

"She's also friends with Lucy and Charlie. Are you sure you want to risk pissing that one off?" he asks, and we both know he isn't referring to Charlie.

"I could ask you the same thing. You're the one who's at her sister's beck and call."

His gaze travels to a spot on the wall over my head as he considers his answer. "Cece needs someone on her side who she doesn't have to hide her feelings from."

"Is she hiding them from Lucy?"

Cash works his jaw back and forth before he responds. "Look, I'm not going to talk about what she confides in me."

"I didn't realize you were her big brother or something."

"I'm just a person she feels comfortable around who isn't always trying to get her to talk about her past. That's all," he says.

Now it's my turn to shoot him a skeptical look. "That's all?"

"Yup," he replies. "Unlike you with your fucking interrogation."

"That's rich, considering how this conversation started." I take a sip of the coffee that's cooled down from the molten lava level of heat it was a few minutes ago. "Be careful there, brother. I don't want to see either of you get into something you don't know how to get out of. And I sure don't want to have to clean the brain matter if you hurt Lucy's sister. I don't think even Jude would have your back with that one."

"I can say the same to you."

We're silent for a few minutes, each of us in our own heads, considering what the other said.

"Enough of this feelings bullshit. Let's get back to the clubhouse and get on the road. If we're driving all fucking day, I'd like to get to it," Cash says.

Grabbing the extra sandwiches and the coffee, we step out into the bright Michigan morning. Cash is right to an extent; Mia isn't a typical old lady. And that's one of the reasons I want her and think she's too good for me at the same time.

It's about time to find out if she feels the same.

CHAPTER EIGHT
MIA

"You want another?" Lucy asks, pointing to the glass in front of me. Charlie and I decided to have a little date over at Thorn and Thistle since Linc and Jude are on a run. I have to admit, I like the idea of being able to hang out with two of my friends without the chance of Knox showing up with their men. But on the other hand, there's a part of me that's a little sad that there's no chance of seeing Knox tonight. It's seriously a total mindfuck.

"Sure, why not? I'm celebrating."

I finally finished the proposal to the school board for the improvements that the library needs, and it's absolute perfection if I do say so myself.

Which I do.

It's been years since anything has been updated in the library. The former librarian was not in favor of changing anything, happy with the status quo. When I came in, I would inquire about things here and there but was constantly told it wasn't in the budget. But this year, with the donation we're expecting to come in from the spring festival, there's no way they're going to say no to me. Plus, Charlie already told me she'll drive me home so I can get up to any trouble I care to. Not that there's much trouble to get into in Shine on a Friday night, but I appreciate the sentiment all the same.

The bar is on the busy side considering no one has to work tomorrow. There's a lull in the music, so I grab my purse and rummage through it, finding a few dollar bills.

"I'm going to put some music on. Anyone have any requests?"

"None of that girly pop you ladies seem so fond of these days," one of the regulars says from the other side of me.

"Shut up, Will. Don't act like I don't hear you humming along to those songs," Lucy replies, then looks at me. "Play the poppiest of pop songs your little heart desires. Will loves that shit."

The man groans, and Lucy sticks her tongue out at him.

"Be careful with that tongue, Lucifer. I have plans for it later."

A wide smile stretches across her face, and Lucy walks around the bar to Jude. She jumps in his arms and wraps her legs around his waist, kissing him as though there's no one else in the room.

Inappropriate? Yes.

But damn, I wish there was someone I could climb like a tree anytime the mood struck.

These vodka sodas may be getting to my head.

"I thought you weren't coming back until tomorrow," she says as he walks her back toward the bar and sets her down.

"Knox wanted to get back, and I wasn't going to argue."

I look over and see Charlie giving Linc a welcome as though he just got back from war.

Laughing, I shake my head and head over to the jukebox. As I'm putting in my song selections, I feel a presence behind me and a hand reaches for the number pad on the old machine.

"Do you mind?" a deep voice asks from behind me.

"Um...no, go ahead," I say to Knox, whose soft breath tickles the side of my face as he presses a few numbers, making a selection of his own.

The air has stalled in my lungs at his nearness, and I'm struck motionless with his heat at my back and that scent of cedar with a hint of motor oil surrounding me.

"Breathe, sweetheart," he whispers, and I swear to God my knees feel like jelly, but I do as he says.

He stands straight, adding only a couple inches between our bodies. When I turn, there's a certain heat in his eyes that I'm not used to seeing, though I suppose that could be wishful thinking.

This is all so confusing. It wasn't that long ago he barely talked to me and kept his distance. Now, whenever we're in a room together, he's near enough to hear when my breath stutters. It's as though all my girlhood fantasies are coming to life, and honestly, it's kind of scaring the crap out of me. I know how to appreciate him from afar, but I'm wholly unprepared to have him so close and in my space.

"Hi," I say dumbly as I stare into his blue eyes. "You guys decided to come back early, I see."

Smooth, Mia. Real fucking smooth.

His lip tips up at the corner, and goddamn if that half smile doesn't send tingles racing down my spine.

"We did. Didn't feel like being on the road longer than I had to." A look of uncertainty crosses his face, but it's gone only a moment later. "The guys didn't at least. I figured they wanted to get home to their women."

"Glad you made it back safely," I say, then slide out from where I'm standing between Knox and the jukebox. Being this close to him is doing things to my body that I wasn't prepared for. I wasn't expecting to see him, and I have no defense against letting him see how his mere presence affects me. Usually, if I know he's going to be around, I can mentally prepare, so I don't make an ass out of myself. Well, not every time, seeing as I practically attacked him with a dessert a few nights ago. It's a work in progress.

I walk back over to the bar and grab my drink, taking several long pulls from the straw, nearly finishing it in one go. Lucy looks at me with concern in her gaze, but I give her a wide smile. She knows what Knox does to me and how out of sorts I am when he's around. Of course, she also thinks it's ridiculous and I should just pull up my big girl panties and flirt with him to see where that takes me.

God, I want to. I wish I had her confidence. I want to be the one who gets the hello kisses Charlie and Lucy get from their men. I want to be the one who has a man who looks at me the way theirs do with them. But that's never been my story. I've always been the one with sensible sweater sets. The nice girl, the reliable friend. Sometimes I wish I had it in me to be bad.

Jesus, the vodka is definitely going to my brain.

Nothing to do but order another.

It's a nice dream, but this is Knox I'm talking about. If he were interested, I'm sure he'd have made it known. Not that I would have the faintest idea what to do or what it would look like if he did.

"How about a round of shots?" Jude suggests.

"Yes," I reply, probably a little louder than necessary.

Lucy smiles and goes about pouring the guys their customary whiskey. Though that's my usual drink of choice, I opt for something a little smoother.

"Can I buy you another drink since apparently I insulted your music tastes earlier?" Will asks next to me.

"No," Knox responds, shoving his way between Will and me.

Well, okay then.

I lean around the behemoth of a man and smile sweetly at the perfectly nice one sitting on the other side. "You didn't insult me, Will. I played something special just for you." When the latest Top 40 hit comes on, I smile even wider, and Will laughs before turning to his friends.

"That was a little rude," I whisper to Knox.

The man shrugs as though he couldn't care less and says nothing else. Okay, guess we're back to silence with the occasional grunt to break up the quiet.

Lucy hands us our shots, and I immediately take mine.

"Uh, I think you're supposed to wait," Charlie says with a giggle.

Lucy chuckles along with her and pours me another. "Am I going to be cutting you off tonight, my friend?"

"I have a driver, and I'm celebrating. I think I'm allowed a night to get a little wild."

Lucy raises her brows and looks at Knox, then back to me. "Sister, you can be as crazy as you want. In fact, I fully support this side of you." She gives me a pointed look with a not-so-subtle nod toward the man next to me before handing me the glass.

"How about a toast, Lucifer?" Jude says as Lucy raises her glass.

She thinks on it for a minute, then a broad smile stretches across her face. "Here's to the top and here's to the middle. Hopefully tonight, we all get a little."

Jude barks out a loud laugh before we all take the shot and slams his glass on the bar. He grabs Lucy by the back of her neck and smashes his mouth to hers. "You'll be getting more than a little, love."

"Promises, promises," she teases as she collects the glasses and checks on her other customers.

Two hours pass and several shots are poured and toasted. I'm feeling light and happy even with the man sitting next to me. Maybe that's what it takes to feel less awkward. I just need to drink copious amounts of vodka around Knox, and all my worries simply disappear. I laugh at my silly thought and Charlie gives me a dopey smile while tangled with Linc on the other side of me.

"What are you giggling at?" she asks with a slight slur to her words.

"I like vodka. I should drink it *all* the time," I reply, throwing my arms out wide, nearly knocking over the beer bottle sitting in front of Knox. He grabs it in the nick of time.

"You have really good reflexes," I tell him. "Like a cat. Are you part cat?"

I look around his head as though little ears are going to suddenly sprout out of his hair.

"No, sweetheart. Just a man," he says, his lips tilting in an almost smile.

"That's a good look on you. When you smile." I point my finger at his mouth. "Not that you smile much. You're very serious all the time."

I make a stern face and growl at him. When his eyebrows raise, I laugh again.

"Yeah, that's the face all the girls made when I did my impression of you. I think it's pretty good though." I turn toward where Linc and Jude are sitting and make the same face. "See, it's good, right?"

"She looks just like you, brother," Jude says, not trying to contain his laughter in the slightest.

"Stop egging her on," Lucy says, looking at Jude.

I'm giggling as I turn back to Knox who is wearing a glare pointed directly at Jude.

"There it is." I lean forward and bop Knox on the nose, and the look of surprise on his face has me throwing my head back in hysterical laughter.

"Oh, I love this song. Come on, Charlie, let's dance." I hop off my seat, a little wobbly on my feet, but who cares? This song is everything, and I can't fight the need to shake my ass to it.

Charlie laughs as I spin her, then I start shaking my hips from side to side with my hands in the air, belting out my very own perfect rendition of the song. I start jumping up and down, tossing my head back and forth before I grab an empty beer bottle from one of the tables to use as a microphone.

"You guys should really have karaoke in this place. It would be so fun," I call out before I start singing again, twirling around and around before I feel myself going down. Before my face meets the ground, a pair of strong arms grab me and pull me back upright.

"You okay?" Knox asks with a look of amusement on his face.

"Uh-huh," I reply, breathless from my dancing and stellar vocal performance.

He begins to walk me back over to the table, and I stumble over my feet, nearly falling flat on my ass.

"I think it's time to go, sweetheart," he says, steadying me once again.

My lips purse, and I blow out a raspberry and scrunch my nose, thinking about his suggestion. Considering I'm seeing two of him at the moment, he may have a point. "Okay," I concede.

I hold his very strong, very tight arm as we continue the laborious journey of seven steps back to my seat at the bar and grab my purse, digging for my keys.

"Why do I have so much crap in here?" I ask out loud, sifting through my bag. Receipts and loose cash from when I got change for the jukebox tumble around the cavernous bag, along with a few pens and an inordinate amount of lip balm.

"Ah-ha." I hold my keys above my head in a triumphant flourish, waving them around until someone grabs them from my hand.

"You aren't driving," Knox says, giving me a stern look.

"Of course not. I was going to give them to Charlie."

I look over at my friend, who is sloppily making out with her boyfriend.

She lifts her head and looks at me. "I'm not driving, either. Linc can give us a ride home."

"I've got it," Knox says.

He slides the strap of my purse over my shoulder and grabs my hand. "Come on, trouble. Time to go home and sleep it off," he says and starts heading for the door.

"Wait, I have to pay," I argue before we get to the door.

"I already did," Knox tells me without slowing down as he walks outside with my hand still clasped in his.

He unlocks my door and helps me in the car.

"Thank you, Jeeves," I say, then burst into a fit of giggles.

Knox arches his eyebrow in question.

Fuck, that's sexy.

"What is?" Now the eyebrow is coupled with a smirk.

"Huh?" I ask.

"Something about something being sexy…"

Double fuck, I said that out loud.

"I don't know what you're talking about. Do you hear voices? You may want to talk to someone about that."

Knox laughs and shuts the door. I'm pretty sure I got out of that one.

As he drives my car back to my grandmother's property, I flip through the stations on the radio until I land on a song that was popular in high school.

"I used to love this song," I say, swaying in my seat.

"You gonna sing this one, too?" he asks with a little snicker.

"Hey buddy, my singing is spot on. I have the voice of an angel." I hold my nose in the air with a huff of offense. It doesn't last long before he's chuckling next to me, and I smile, unable to hold my anger.

"God, I had such a crush on you in high school." My heavy head rests against the back of the seat as I allow myself the rare indulgence of unabashedly staring at him.

Knox's head tilts to the side slightly, but he keeps his eyes on the road.

"If I were sober, I probably wouldn't be saying this, but I don't care. I thought you were the most handsome boy I'd ever seen. Shit, you looked more like a man than any other boys I had in my class," I tell him.

"You never talked to me. Pretty sure I was at your house a few times, too."

I laugh as though he said the most ridiculous thing. "Please, you had so many girls hanging all over you. I was just Nolan's little sister who was around to make sure no one broke my mom's vases or set the house on fire or something. I was never really *at* those parties, just kind of there, taking care of things, as usual."

"I don't remember who you hung out with. Actually, I don't remember seeing you much in high school other than when you played in band at the football games."

I groan, wishing I had another shot in front of me. "Be honest—you probably couldn't pick me out of a lineup. You were too busy making eyes at the cheerleaders."

Knox lets out a light chuckle and looks at me, then back to the road. "First of all, I never looked at the cheerleaders when I was in the middle of a game. Second, you're wrong. If I had a photo of you with the rest of the band, I would definitely be able to pick you out."

"Oh, please. There were plenty of times I saw you leave my brother's party with one of those cheerleaders."

"Yeah, I'd leave with them, then they'd act like they had no idea who I was at school."

My brows draw down, not quite comprehending what he's saying. "This could be the vodka, but I'm confused. Any of those girls would've been lucky to have a star player as a boyfriend. What do you mean they would act like they didn't know you?"

"I guess it sounds worse than it was. I was the kid from the other side of the tracks, and those cheerleaders were from opposite worlds. I may have been a star player, but it didn't change where I came from. I didn't have money, and their parents considered us biker trash. It was different back then than it is now."

"Ugh, that makes me so mad for you." I huff out my annoyance and cross my arms over my chest while Knox chuckles at my irritation.

"It was what it was." He shrugs as he turns into my grandmother's estate and down the dirt drive that leads to my little house.

When he parks, he turns the engine off and I open the car door, stumbling up the small walk to my front door. Knox is next to me in an instant.

"Want to come in? I never got to thank you for taking care of everything with my car. I think I have beer in the fridge." Did I just ask Knox Turner to come into my house for a drink?

"Sure."

Oh my God. Knox Turner is going to come in.

He unlocks my front door since he still has my keys, and I flip on the lights once we're inside.

"Living room is through there," I say, pointing to the right. "I'll grab you that beer."

He nods, making his way into the living room, and I watch him for a brief moment. It's so fucking crazy to see him in my space. He walks over to the small bookcase I have and peruses the titles, smirking at my romance selection.

"The remote is on the coffee table if you want to put something on."

Jesus, am I going to actually watch TV with the man?

"I'm not much for TV," he answers and takes a seat on my beige couch.

I head into the kitchen and open the fridge, pushing everything aside until I find the two bottles of beer shoved in the back. Then I open my freezer and pull out a bottle of vodka. Taking a healthy swig, I set the bottle on the counter. What is actually happening right now? What possessed me to invite this man in here? I don't have men over to my place. I grab the bottle and take another long swig.

Fuck it.

I want to be that girl. *Tonight, I am that girl.* I put the vodka away and take the two beers back into the living room, handing him one. He nods in thanks, and I have a seat next to him.

"How about some music?" I ask, not knowing what the hell to do with myself.

"Sure."

I stand and head over to the dock and set my phone in the holder, connecting it to the speakers before I put the music app on shuffle.

"I really like this band," Knox says.

I turn around to walk back over to the couch, trying to put a little sway in my step because that just kind of feels like something someone would do when they're trying to seduce the hot biker on their couch. But my shin knocks into the corner of the damn coffee table.

"Ow, shit!" When I bend down to rub my sore bone, I lose my footing and fall over.

"Fuck," Knox says and rushes over to me.

He kneels beside me before running his hand over my leg, and I burst out laughing.

"It would hurt a lot more if I didn't have so much alcohol running through me."

Knox shakes his head, but he's wearing a smile. "It probably wouldn't have happened if you weren't drinking in the first place. May I?" he asks when his hand finds the hem of my pants.

I nod dumbly, feeling a rush of heat where his hand is touching my ankle. "S-sure," I stutter out.

He lifts my pant leg, and though there's a red line where my shin made contact with the wood, there's no blood.

"I think you'll survive," he says, standing, then holds out his hand.

Grabbing the hand that was just *touching my leg*, I let him haul me off the floor. We're so close, standing in the middle of my living room. This isn't the first time I've been this close to him, but it is the first time we've been alone like this.

Now or never, Mia.

I anchor myself by grabbing his waist and lift on my tiptoes so I can reach his mouth.

And to my absolute horror, the man puts his hands on my shoulders and gently pushes himself away.

"Oh my God," I say, jumping away from him. "I can't believe I just did that." Warmth creeps up my neck and into my face, which I'm sure looks like a fucking tomato from embarrassment right about now. "I'm so sorry. You came in for a thank-you beer, and I practically tried to eat your face."

"That's a little exaggerated. Look, Mia—"

Before he can get a word out, my hand clamps over my mouth. The warm feeling that I thought was from humiliation has turned into what feels like a tsunami in my stomach.

"Oh shit," I say before running to the bathroom in my room, flipping the toilet seat up and emptying the contents of my stomach—a.k.a. all the vodka I've consumed—into the toilet.

Moments later, the light in the bathroom switches on. If my eyes weren't already closed, I would be squeezing them shut, wishing like hell the man who turned on the lights was not, in fact, standing in my bathroom watching me heave. Well, he came after I was finished—oh wait, thought that too soon.

I begin retching again, but this time, a soothing hand caresses my back. Another hand gathers the hair I was desperately trying to keep out of my face into a ponytail as all the liquor I've ever consumed in my entire life is trying to reappear and be purged from my body.

When the rolling of my stomach ceases, I nearly collapse onto the floor, exhausted from the exorcism of alcohol.

"Do you think you're done?" Knox asks in a gentle voice.

"Yeah," I croak out, too mortified to meet his eyes.

His boots move from where he's perched himself on the edge of my bathtub while helping me. He walks to the sink, and I hear water running before he comes back with a cool washcloth.

"Tilt your head up, sweetheart."

I do as he asks, and he wipes the damp cloth over my face.

"Not exactly how I pictured the first time you coming over would turn out," I say sullenly as he walks back over to my vanity. He grabs my pink toothbrush from the holder and squeezes toothpaste over the bristles before handing it to me.

"Help me up? I'd rather not brush my teeth over my toilet."

He reaches down and pulls me so I can stand in front of my sink. When I rinse my mouth, he hands me some mouthwash, too.

"You give really good puking-after-consuming-too-much-alcohol care."

Knox chuckles and leans against the wall. "I used to live in a clubhouse full of bikers. I had to help all my brothers to bed at least once. And usually, they didn't make it to the toilet."

I scrunch my nose in disgust. "Let's not talk about that." Then something he said strikes me. "What do you mean *used* to?"

"I got my own place a while ago. I still spend some nights at the clubhouse, like if there's a party and I don't want to ride home. But once my brother moved in with Charlie, I got my own place, too."

"I had no idea," I say as I walk over to my bed.

Knox disappears again and comes back with a glass of water and sets it on my nightstand. Then he goes back to my bathroom, and I hear him rummaging around in my medicine cabinet. He returns with two pills, placing them next to the water.

"Think you can get yourself changed?" he asks, handing me the pair of pajamas I have sitting on the chair in the corner of my room.

I grab them from him and begin pulling my pants down my legs. Knox clears his throat and turns as I make quick work of my pants and top.

"I'm decent," I say, and he walks over to my bed and pulls the covers back.

"Okay, trouble. Time for you to pass out."

Climbing into bed, Knox turns off the light, but his outline is still illuminated with the moonlight from my window in the otherwise dark room.

"Sorry I'm such a disaster. Thank you for taking care of me," I say as my eyes close.

I swear I feel his finger brush across my cheek as he whispers, "There's nowhere else I'd rather be."

Then sleep overtakes me.

Chapter Nine
Knox

I could have left Mia alone in her house and called one of my brothers to come get me. But I didn't. Instead, I made myself comfortable on her couch for the night. I'm not sure why. Maybe I wanted to make sure she didn't wake in the middle of the night and get sick again, but that's not entirely true. With the amount the poor girl threw up last night, I don't think there was a chance there was anything left in her system to get rid of. No, the reason I stayed was because I wanted to be here in the morning when she woke up.

When we were in Michigan, I decided that the time for talking myself out of what I really wanted was over. I don't know where this is going, but I have every intention of figuring that out. At least now, I know she has similar feelings toward me if her drunken attempt at a kiss is any indication. I know she's attracted to me, but that could mean anything. If I wanted just a night with her, I may have taken her up on her offer when she tried something. But having a drunken one-off with her isn't my end goal, and I'm afraid that's what she would've considered it. I need her completely sober and able to understand that I want more than that.

I head up the walkway to Mia's house, juggling the cups of coffee and the breakfast I picked up from Cool Beans. I figured she wouldn't mind if I stole her car for a few minutes as long as I came back bearing gifts.

When I checked on her this morning, she was still out cold. It took a hell of a lot of willpower to not crawl in bed next to her. She looked so damn comfortable lying tangled up in her blankets, snoring softly. To be honest, I doubt she thought I would stay the night, so waking up with me next to her would have probably been the shock of a lifetime.

I unlock the door and walk inside her little cottage. The folded blanket and pillow I slept with are still on the couch. I veer right toward the kitchen, and there stands Mia, hunched over her sink, the smell of brewing coffee in the air.

"You gonna puke again?" I ask.

She jumps about three feet in the air, obviously not hearing me walk in.

"Jesus Christ, are you trying to give me a fucking heart attack?" Her hand is on her chest as she breathes heavily, her chest rising and falling rapidly against her thin nightshirt.

I smirk and set the coffee on her small dining room table, placing the keys next to it.

"I didn't realize you were still here," she says, tucking her unruly hair behind her ear.

She's obviously embarrassed, and I'm obviously an asshole because I think it's the cutest damn thing I've ever seen.

"I wasn't. Took your car to grab coffee and breakfast."

"You spent the night?"

I nod. "I did. Went out this morning and just got back. I'm surprised you didn't realize I slept on the couch or stole your car."

"The only thing on my mind when I woke up this morning was coffee."

"Well, I have something I think you'll like better than whatever you're brewing."

I pull the coffee cup from the travel container and hand it to her. "Caramel latte with a dash of cinnamon."

Mia looks at me, stunned for a moment, before she accepts the cup I'm holding out for her.

"I didn't realize you knew my coffee order." When she takes a sip, her eyes roll back in her head, and she lets out a little sigh of contentment.

"There's not much I miss. Not like you haven't been around the clubhouse sipping on that."

"You should try it." She holds the cup out to me and I grab it, taking a tentative sip. Do I enjoy a frou-frou flavored coffee? No. But it does make me wonder what would happen if I kissed her now so I could taste it from her lips instead of this paper cup.

"I'll stick to black," I say, handing the cup back to her. "I also picked these up." I pull the breakfast sandwiches from the bag. "Wasn't sure if you liked bacon or sausage, so I grabbed both."

She turns toward her cabinets and grabs a couple plates. As she's reaching for them, her shorts ride up the back of her thighs, exposing the smallest inch of the curve of her ass. Thankfully, I'm able to stifle the moan that's ready to spill from my throat.

Jesus Christ, why was I such a gentleman last night?

When she turns, she takes the paper towels from the counter and walks over to the kitchen table in front of the little window that overlooks her front yard.

"Sit, sit," she says, waving at one of the three chairs she has around the table before having a seat herself.

Mia grasps the bacon sandwich, takes a giant bite out of it and releases another moan. Fuck, at this rate, I'm going to be taking a cold shower the second I walk through my front door.

"Thank you so much for this." She takes another bite and sets the sandwich on the plate, looking at her lap, then back to me. "Listen, about last night—"

"Mia, seriously, don't worry about it. You got a little too drunk. I was more than happy to help you out."

"I appreciate it. Honestly, I don't remember anyone ever taking care of me. It's usually the other way around."

"To be fair, I don't think I've ever seen you that drunk."

The embarrassed chuckle that escapes her makes me smile. "Yeah, can't say I've ever invited a guy in and then had to run to the bathroom before I puked on his boots.

Or tried to make out with a guy after eating shit on my own damn floor."

"I didn't mind that part. Any of it really. I mean, I could do without the puking again, but everything else was cute."

She sends me one of those looks that says she thinks I'm full of shit. "Are you so used to drunk women throwing themselves at you that it's second nature to turn them down?"

I set my sausage breakfast sandwich on my plate and cross my arms over the table, looking her dead in the eye. "There's a reason why I didn't take you back to your room and make you scream my name until the sun came up. Let me make sure you understand because I think you may have one idea that's pretty far from the damn truth."

Her eyes widen but she stays silent and allows me to speak.

"We've never kissed. Until last night, I wasn't even sure you thought of me in that way. Or if you saw me as just another brother in a club you occasionally hang out with because two of your best friends have men in the club. True, last night confirmed it for me—"

"And I'm the cute little friend that has no business thinking she has a shot in hell with you. It's okay; you don't have to sugarcoat it." She clears her throat, but her gaze has dropped to some spot on the floor she feels the need to stare a hole in.

"Mia, look at me." Her eyes meet mine, and she's wearing a smile I'm not fond of. It's one that says she's used to hearing the bullshit that she just spewed and she'll put on a brave face in front of me.

Fuck that.

"I didn't let anything happen because you were too drunk. Not because I didn't or don't want to. When we take that step, it sure as hell isn't going to be some drunken night that you might not even remember."

"Trust me, I'd remember," she mumbles, more to herself than to me, so I continue.

"I stopped it before it started, so you didn't wake up thinking I'd regret it, or worse, I was afraid you'd have regrets."

She nods slowly and grabs her sandwich, taking another bite. "That...makes sense."

"I'm not some dumb biker out for a good time. I respect you too much to take advantage." No matter how much I wanted to.

"I would never call you dumb, Knox. And I certainly would never accuse you of taking advantage."

She looks like she wants to ask another question, but before she does, she thinks twice and stays silent.

"What?"

Mia shakes her head and takes a sip of her coffee. "Nothing. I'm sure you have a million things to do today. I don't want to keep you."

She's putting that wall up again. The one I hate because it means she's overthinking everything and selling herself short like she seems to do too much. Since I'm more of an actions-speak-louder-than-words kind of guy, I finish my sandwich in one last big bite and wipe my hands on a paper towel.

"You know what always seems to help me when I'm hungover?"

Mia turns her head slowly from side to side with a confused look on her face. "No..."

"A long ride on my bike." I stand from my chair and hold out my hand. "Come on. Let's see if it works for you, too."

It doesn't take Mia long to get ready before we drive to where my bike is at the bar. There aren't a lot of places I'd feel comfortable leaving my motorcycle overnight, but everyone knows Thorn and Thistle is owned by the club, and no one would dare fuck with it, not if they wanted to avoid a trip to the hospital with shattered hands.

Mia follows me out to my place in her car so I can grab her a helmet and jacket. I bought a little piece of land, and on it sits my small three-bedroom house. The outside isn't much to look at right now, but I've been fixing it up. As soon as it gets a touch warmer, my mom swears she's going to come over and finally get the yard in order. Lord knows what the woman has in mind, but she fucking loves that kind of shit, and honestly, I can't be bothered with picking out flowers and bushes or whatever shit she has planned. All the work I've put in has been on the inside.

"I didn't realize you lived so close to my grandmother," Mia says when she parks her car behind my bike.

"It's a left instead of a right and you're at my place in a few miles."

I've always thought it was strange that the "other" side of town is so close, but my entire life, I was made to feel like it was worlds apart. At least when I was younger. These days, those lines blur more and more.

We walk up the steps to the front porch that I spent a shit ton of time sanding and staining over the summer. When I open the door, Mia steps through, and I take no small amount of pride at the impressed look on her face. The small entryway opens up to the living room with the kitchen to the right, nothing separating the two rooms except a black marble breakfast bar. I refurbished the wood ceiling and beams before painting the walls a deep hunter green. My mom thought it was going to be way too dark, but I fucking love how it turned out. And I love seeing the look on people's faces when they walk in and see all the work I've put into the place.

"Wow, Knox. This place is beautiful." Mia walks across the plush throw rug covering part of the original wood flooring and looks out the French doors I put in that lead to a deck my brother and I built last year. "I bet you can't wait for it to warm up so you can spend more time out here."

"That's what firepits are for," I say, pointing to the one that's surrounded by overstuffed outdoor furniture.

"You don't strike me as the kind of guy who does a lot of entertaining."

I bark out a laugh. "I'm not. But my mom and brother like to show up here and force me to be social."

"You like the solitude life," she says, looking around the expansive property without another house in sight.

"Depends on who wants to come over, I guess."

I'd be lying if I said seeing Mia in my space didn't feel right. It's almost as though something has settled in me even though we haven't really talked about this change in our dynamic. Seeing as I have no real experience with any kind of relationship beyond the typical friends-with-benefits situation, I'm going out on a limb here suggesting we should at least have a few words about where I'd like us to go. It doesn't take a genius to realize Mia is the type to need things spelled out. Her mind is amazing, but it tends to run in the opposite direction of what I'm trying to convey if I don't use my words with her carefully. Novel concept for me, but here we are.

"Let me grab you a helmet and a jacket."

Leaving Mia in the living room, I head to my garage and find a helmet and a jacket that my mom left over here. When I return, Mia eyes the contents of my hands with suspicion.

"Just had that lying around, huh?" she asks.

"If you think this belonged to some woman I used to have over, you're wrong. My mom likes to ride, and sometimes she goes out with me, so she keeps a jacket and helmet here. Plus, I don't have random women in my space."

"So what am I?"

"Not random."

The shy smile that covers her face lights me up inside.

"Put this on, and we'll get on the road," I say, handing her the jacket before she slides it on over her light-gray sweater.

When we walk back outside, Mia puts the helmet on, and I help her with the chin strap. When I'm sure the helmet is secure, I put mine on and sit on my bike.

"Remember what I told you about getting on?"

She nods and I start the bike before she slides her leg over the seat behind me and settles in. Mia is more comfortable than she was a couple weeks ago when I gave her a ride home. Instead of tentatively placing her hands on my side, she wraps her arms around my middle, and I feel her relax into me almost immediately. Nothing like her rigid posture from before.

I ease out of my driveway and hit the main road. Mia laughs when I open up the throttle and go a little faster. I'm not breaking any speed limits, far from it, but I feel the excitement radiating from her. My property sits on the outskirts of Shine, and instead of going down the main street, I take us in the opposite direction to a little town about an hour from us. It's a relaxing ride, and we're treated to the beauty of spring blooming everywhere. Trees have fresh green leaves, and wildflowers are blossoming in the fields we pass.

I rest one hand on Mia's thigh as we travel the country roads, soaking in the pleasure of being able to touch her without her becoming wooden and nervous. I was a little apprehensive this morning about whether or not she was going to overthink last night, but the way she's relaxed behind me tells me the only thing she's thinking about is experiencing the openness and freedom of being on a bike. Just like I do every time I take a long ride, and just like I was hoping she would.

I pull into the parking lot of a small park with a lake. Ducks float peacefully in the water, and a couple families are here with their kids, seeing as the weather is starting to warm up.

When I park the bike and turn it off, Mia uses my shoulders to steady herself as she slides from her seat to solid ground. The smile tilting her lips reaches her eyes when she removes the helmet from her head.

"Feeling better?" I ask after dismounting and removing my own helmet, setting it on my seat.

Mia releases a deep breath and lets her head fall to her chest. "So much. I think the fresh air really does help."

I smile and grab the loaf of bread I brought with us before taking her hand in mine. It hits me that I've never held a woman's hand, at least not like this.

"Let's go feed the ducks."

A burst of laughter escapes me at the look on Mia's face.

"What?" I ask.

"You never struck me as the type to go around with duck food in your saddlebag."

"I think there's a lot you don't know about me," I say as we walk to the edge of the lake.

"I think I've been too scared to ask," she says.

I tilt my head, confusion in my gaze. "Why?"

Mia laughs again, but this one is in stark contrast to the light one a moment ago. "Do you remember being at Charlie's house when someone broke into Lucy's? You weren't exactly giving off the warm and fuzzies." She removes her hand from mine, and I hate the cold feeling it leaves me with.

"I know," I say on an exhale. "But you have to understand there were things happening that could have landed us in a shit ton of trouble if anyone found out what was going on."

"Why? Not saying I would have, but what would have happened if I told anyone what I saw that night?"

"Mia, there are certain things that happen in this life. If the wrong people find out about those things, there could be deadly consequences. Not just for us, but for anyone involved with us."

"I'm not an idiot, Knox. I know not everything you do is on the up and up in the eyes of the law."

"I would never call you that, but you have to understand—it's my job to make sure my brothers and their women are protected."

"I'm familiar with the responsibility," she mumbles as she looks at the water.

"Most of the time, I don't have the luxury of making sure everyone understands what's at stake in the nicest way possible."

She scoffs. "Gee, you think?"

"I don't think it works to ask nicely. Not in this life, anyways."

"You could have tried. With me, you could have asked, and I would've done that. For you, for Lucy, for the club," she says with irritation mixed with something that sounds like hurt.

"You're too good for this. Too good for me, but that's not going to stop me from taking it."

Mia releases a frustrated growl, and I have to smother my laugh. She's upset, but damn, she's also adorable as hell.

"You confuse the hell out of me, Knox. You barely talk to me when I get to town, then when you do, it's to threaten me to stay quiet—"

"I didn't exactly threaten you," I say, interrupting her, which seems to be the wrong move when she shoots daggers at me.

"You'll remember it how I say you remember it," she says, lowering her voice into a gruff impersonation of what I'm assuming is supposed to be me. "Then you barely talk to me for the last year, barely look at me."

"I did look, Mia. A lot. Just not when you were paying attention."

"See?" She waves her hand in front of me. "Then you go and say stuff like that. Last night, you pushed me away, then you stayed the night. Brought me coffee this morning and talked to me about *when* things are going to happen, not *if*."

"It sounds like you're upset because I'm not clear enough. Am I getting that right?"

"Uh, yeah, Knox. You haven't exactly been an open book."

Fuck it.

I drop the bag of bread to the ground and take a quick step toward Mia. My hands go to the side of her face before I crash my mouth to hers. She's still for a moment, and I worry I've made a mistake. Until her hands clutch my waist and she pulls me harder against her warm body. Kissing Mia is everything I dreamed. When I part my lips, my tongue darts out, tasting her lips for the first time, and she opens for me. No hesitation. Her taste is sweet, like the coffee she was drinking earlier, and I wonder why the hell I waited so long to do this. We lose ourselves in each other the way both of us have been wanting to.

I break the kiss and press my forehead to hers. "Is that clear enough for you?"

"Mm-hmm," she hums in response.

"I'm sorry I wasn't clear. I had to work out a few things in my head."

"Better late than never, I guess," she says with a light chuckle.

"To be fair, until last night, I wasn't sure I didn't scare you."

"Oh, you scare me. Just not for the reasons you probably thought."

My brow furrows before I press a gentle kiss to her pink lips. "I've never really done this before."

"Ah, a virgin. It's okay, I promise to be gentle." The corner of her mouth tilts in a smile as I remember her comment when she first rode on the back of my bike.

"I've never dated anyone."

Mia pulls back and looks me in the eyes. "Wait, what about Heather?"

"Heather?"

"Yeah, the girl who came to your party. She felt pretty comfortable touching you. I thought maybe something was going on between you two."

A smile ticks up the corner of my mouth. "Were you jealous, sweetheart?"

"Ah, yeah. Obviously. She's gorgeous and tall and—"

I cut her off with another kiss before she can keep talking. When her body relaxes into mine again, I pull my lips from hers.

"And you're beautiful and kind. The woman I want to take out on my bike, spend the day with, and take to dinner tomorrow night."

"Like a date?" she asks, the smile returning to her face.

"Not *like*. We're going to feed the ducks, then I'm going to take you home. Tomorrow night, I'm picking you up to take you out to dinner."

"I realize you're new to this, but most men ask, not *demand*, to take a girl out."

I bend and kiss her again, loving the little moan that escapes her throat.

"Good thing I'm not most men."

Chapter Ten
Mia

"So basically, you're telling me all your teenage fantasies have come to life, and I'm going home to make Colby mac and cheese with a side of carrots because his favorite color is orange, so naturally, he only wants to eat orange things," Maizie says as we're having a cup of late afternoon coffee.

"Tell him he'll turn orange if he doesn't eat anything else," I suggest.

"If that were a deterrent, believe me, I'd do it."

I met Maizie at Cool Beans after her day shift at the bar. She had a couple minutes, and I needed a friendly face. I got squeezed in for a last-minute wax and had a little extra time for a manicure and pedicure. And I've been freaking the hell out all day.

"It's ridiculous for me to be nervous, right? It's not like this is some blind date. I know Knox. I've *kissed* Knox." And I'm getting warm in certain places just thinking about it. For how rough his hands were against my skin, his lips were incredibly soft and tasted better than anything I could have imagined.

"I get it, hon. It's not every day you get asked out by your high school crush who has aged like a fine whiskey."

"True. I'm probably making too big of a deal out of this, though. It's only our first date. We may have nothing to talk about and realize the only thing we have in common is this insane attraction."

Maizie arches her brow. "Do you honestly believe that?"

"No. I think I'm trying to talk it down a little so I don't get my hopes up to be let down."

"And I think you must have had some really shitty luck with men if that's how you psych yourself up for a date."

"You wouldn't be wrong."

"Listen up, my gorgeous friend who wears a red polish like no one's business. Knox is beyond lucky that you agreed to go out with him. You're putting up walls before anything even happens. Believe me, I get the disappointment that can come from falling for your high school crush's charm, but that doesn't mean you should be talking yourself out of something great before you give it a chance."

"I guess I'm scared to go all in if this turns out to be nothing more than a nice dinner."

"Somehow, I very much doubt that's all it will be."

When I get home, there's something sitting on my front porch. I get out of my car and walk up the little walkway, bending down to pick up the gorgeous flower arrangement of white tulips. There's no card, but I can only imagine one person who would be sending me flowers today. A broad smile stretches across my face as I walk in my front door and set the flowers on my kitchen counter. Now I wonder if the flowers I found on my car were actually meant for me. Maybe Knox has been slowly dipping his toe into this whole dating thing, but he wasn't ready to come out and say anything. I kind of like the idea that he's been my secret admirer or something silly and cute like that.

Wow, cute and Knox aren't two words I'd ever thought would be used in the same sentence.

"You aren't half-bad with the whole *wooing* thing. I'll give you that," I say in an empty room. If Knox wants to spoil me with flowers and dinners, who am I to say no?

Looking at the time, I realize there're only about thirty minutes left before Knox is supposed to be here. As I rush around doing a little picking up, touching up my makeup, and getting dressed, I blast one of my favorite bands through the Bluetooth speaker I have set up in my living room. It's still chilly when the sun goes down, so I've paired my tight leather pants that I've always been hesitant to wear with a longer off-the-shoulder sweater.

It's not often I get dressed up to do much. If I'm having drinks with the girls, I'm usually coming from work. Every once in a while, I'll wear something cute to a party at the clubhouse, but I rarely go to those. Nope, my days are usually spent in what Lucy likes to call my librarian uniform, but I think it makes me look a little more, I don't know…grown-up? Being on the shorter side and still looking like I can pass as a college student would be great—if I weren't working around teenagers. I remember being terrified of the old librarian, but we all knew no shenanigans were going to happen with her around. I don't exactly have the same intimidating presence, so I have to use whatever I can to my advantage.

I walk out of my bedroom, belting out the lyrics to the song that's playing, and shriek when I see a tall man standing in my doorway.

"Sorry, I tried to knock," Knox hollers over the loud music.

I run over to the speaker and turn the music down so neither of us has to yell as heat envelops my entire body. I'm pretty sure that when I turn around, my face is the color of the bright-red nail polish I had done this morning.

"You look beautiful," Knox says, his eyes trailing over my body.

"So do you." He smirks, and now it's not only embarrassment running through my body. "I mean handsome. You look very handsome."

Knox is freshly shaved and wearing a midnight-blue plaid flannel, which makes his eyes even brighter than usual, and he's paired it with a heavy leather jacket and black jeans. God, the way his pants mold to his strong, long legs is the best jean porn out there—if that's actually a thing. And if it's not, it should be. Having him in my house and ready to take me on a date is so surreal and something I never thought would happen. A very girlish giggle threatens to erupt from my throat, but I keep myself contained. Barely.

"What's in the bag?" I ask, walking into the kitchen to grab my purse.

"Something you're going to be getting some use out of," Knox says, walking over to the small counter and placing the bag next to the flowers. "These are pretty."

I smile in his direction. "They are. I love fresh flowers."

When Knox bends to swipe an innocent kiss over my lips, it's all I can do not to throw myself at him. Screw the dinner. I want more of this.

He pulls away all too soon and nods toward the bag. "Open it."

A shy smile spreads across my face. I've never had someone bring me gifts, or even flowers, on a first date. For supposedly never having a serious relationship before, this man is knocking it out of the park.

"Lucy helped me pick it out," he says as I pull a black leather moto jacket from the bag. It's a simple design with a band collar and brass-colored snaps, but the leather feels buttery soft as I run my fingertips over it.

"Figured you'd prefer this over borrowing my mom's every time we go on a ride."

"I love it," I say, unzipping the jacket to try it on. When I slide the jacket on and zip it up, I place my hands on my hips and give Knox a bright smile. "How do I look?"

"Like I waited too damn long to take you out on my bike," he says, his appreciative gaze once again sliding over me. Considering two days ago I felt awkward over any sort of attention this man gave me, I've certainly become comfortable under his appraisal. I guess a drunken night of confessions is all I needed.

"Come on," he says. "Let's get going. I have another gift for you on my bike."

"I didn't take you for the whole *spoiling-your-date* type," I joke as I grab my purse and keys and lead us to the front door.

"Trust me, no one's more surprised than me," he says in that growly voice that makes my damn knees weak.

After locking my door, we head toward his bike that's parked next to my car. There's something about seeing his motorcycle there that warms me. For so long I've wanted to be the girl who he came to pick up. I used to fantasize about it when I was a teenager and would see him riding around town. I was desperate to know what it would be like to have my arms wrapped around his waist as we sped through the streets of Shine. Now I know, and I'd be lying if I didn't say it was just as good, if not better, than any fantasy I conjured.

He takes my purse from me and puts it in his saddle-bag, then hands me a different helmet than the one I was wearing yesterday.

"Figured if you were going to be on my bike, you should have a helmet of your own, too."

He's wearing a smile, but there's a touch of nerves in his blue eyes.

I put on the black helmet with a bit of sparkle that reflects off the light from my porch. "I love it. Seriously, if you keep spoiling me like this, you're going to make it impossible for anyone else to rise to the bar you've set so far tonight."

He chuckles and helps me with the strap. That's something I noticed yesterday, Knox's attention to detail and making sure I'm comfortable and safe.

"Well, that's kind of the point, sweetheart."

"Big words for a first date," I tease.

"I want to make sure we're on the same page here, Mia. This may be the first, but it's not the last. Not by a long shot."

He bends and kisses me again before lowering the visor on the helmet.

Damn him and his sweet words in that deep voice that has always made tingles shoot through me.

He gets on his bike, and I use his shoulders to keep me steady as I climb on behind him.

When he eases away from my car and gets to the road in front of the property, he opens up the throttle like he did yesterday. And just like yesterday, another excited giggle escapes. I feel his chest vibrate with laughter as his hand strokes over mine that are connected at his waist, squeezing for a moment before settling. Though I'm pressed against him from my chest to my thighs, that one caress of our hands feels more intimate than anything else. His touch is reassuring and thrilling at the same time. Like he plucked one of my girlish imaginings from my head and is making it a reality. And I really fucking like it.

We pull into the parking lot of a restaurant about twenty minutes from Shine. I love my little town, but the options for a romantic dinner date are limited to one restaurant. Thankfully, there are plenty of places around us in neighboring towns that aren't far. And if we can get there on his bike, I'm all for it.

Knox parks, and I slide off while he removes his helmet. When I lift mine from my head, my smile is beaming with excitement.

"I think I'm addicted to riding," I tell him as he stands from his bike and takes my helmet from me, setting both on the seat.

"Yeah?" His fingers swipe a few strands of hair from my forehead that came loose from the helmet. "So my master plan is working."

"Master plan?"

"Yes, it's very devious. Get you addicted to riding, then to me. And I'm already halfway there."

He tosses me a wink, then bends, giving me a quick kiss on the mouth before grabbing my hand and leading me inside the dimly lit restaurant. Knox gives the hostess his name, and she leads us to a table toward the back. The man made reservations. I repeat, *the man made reservations.* Knox thought ahead, didn't depend on me to take care of where we were going to eat dinner, basically took the control out of my hands so all I had to do was show up. Either the bar has been set ridiculously low in my head or he's just really good at this wooing thing, Probably a little bit of both.

"I've never been here before," I say, looking around the room. Each table is topped with low candles in thick white glass holders sitting on black tablecloths. The dark gray walls with wood beams running along the high ceilings and the large hanging industrial lights give the restaurant a cool but elevated feel.

"First for me, too," he says. "But I figured it was a step up from the diner."

"I happen to like that little diner."

Knox smiles. "That'll be our second date, then," he says as the waiter comes to get our drink order. Knox orders me a glass of red wine and himself a beer.

"How did you know that's what I wanted?"

"I've seen the bottles you and the girls toss back, so I figured it was a good guess. If you want something else, just say the word."

I shake my head and don't even try to hide my smile. "No. It's nice to have someone take care of things for me. That happens all of never in my life. And I really like the idea that you've been paying attention." My nose scrunches when I worry that I've said too much.

Knox has made it clear that he's all in on...whatever this is, but I'm not quite ready to trust it. It's almost too good to be true, and the last thing I want is to be let down. I have a feeling if that ever happened with the man sitting across from me, it would hurt more than all of my past relationships combined.

"Sweetheart, I've been paying attention since you came back to town. If we hadn't had the shit going on this last year that we did, I would have asked you out a lot sooner."

"I'm no expert on motorcycle clubs, but doesn't it stand to reason that whatever happened last year could happen again? What changed your mind?" *And are you going to change it back?* I think to myself, but don't have the courage to ask out loud.

The waiter comes back with our drinks and sets them in front of us. "Are you ready to order, or would you like a few minutes to look over the menus?"

Knox's gaze doesn't leave mine as he answers that we need a little more time.

"There was shit I had to work through in my head, Mia. It was a dangerous time, and I was scared because it seemed like the women were in the cross fire too much. But if you want full honesty, I was scared that you would look at me like all the other girls from high school. Or that I would be tarnishing you somehow. I'm not an accountant or a banker who comes home at six o'clock on the dot. That's not the life I lead, and it never will be. Sometimes I worry that you're too clean, too sweet for this life." Knox exhales a deep breath and the urge to somehow comfort him is strong. Instead, I sit quietly and let him continue because he needs to get this out. "I'm not clean, Mia. Being in the club, it means I'm a criminal, and I never want that to touch you. Honestly, I don't know how my brothers don't keep their women under lock and key."

Laughter bubbles from me. "Yeah, I don't really see that working with Lucy. Or Charlie or Freya, now that I think about it," I say, tilting my head to the side.

He laughs with me and leans back in his chair. "Yeah, you're probably right about that."

"Knox, if I wanted an accountant or lawyer or banker, I'm sure there are plenty of men my parents could set me up with. Hell, I've dated a couple, and I can tell you one thing"—I take a fortifying sip of my wine—"not a single one of them made me feel half the things I do when I'm around you. I never felt nervous around them because I wasn't excited to be around them. Imagine going your entire adult life without ever being as excited as you are with the man you've had a crush on since you were old enough to fantasize about kissing a boy. You barely knew who I was in high school, but I felt more for you than I ever did with any of those other guys." *Jesus Mia, for being cautious about going all in, you sure are giving him a lot of information he never asked for.*

Knox gets up from his seat, walks to my side of the table, and sits next to me. His hand gently cups the side of my neck before he leans in for a soft but firm kiss.

I'm breathless when he finally pulls away. "What was that for?"

Knox smiles and leans his forehead against mine. "Just something I needed to do."

He gets up and walks back over to his chair, and the waiter comes back again. God, this guy is probably getting so annoyed with us.

"Have you made your selections?" the waiter asks.

Knox chuckles, his mind probably going to the same place as mine. "I'll have a medium-rare steak." He looks at me, waiting for me to order.

"Sounds delicious."

He looks back at the waiter and tells him I'll have the same, letting the poor guy do his job.

"You want to know what I think?" I ask.

"All the time," he says without any hesitation.

I smile at his answer. "I think you're so focused on taking care of everyone else you haven't let yourself be taken care of. Or even allowed yourself to *want* to be taken care of."

"I don't need you to do that for me, sweetheart."

"No, you don't need it. But you spent so much time being the dirty secret of the girls in school, you never had someone on your arm who was proud to be there. I think you may have decided to hide behind that and decided it wasn't something you needed."

Knox arches his brow. "You seem to be speaking from experience a little there."

My head tilts back and forth as I consider what he said. "A little. Or a lot." I release a light laugh. "I've never had someone make reservations for dinner, buy me a jacket because they wanted me to ride with them, or order me my favorite red wine. No one has ever paid enough attention to those details except for me. It's nice being the one who doesn't have to plan and be in control at every turn. I think that's why I like riding with you so much. You have control, and I know I'm safe."

"You always will be with me."

"And I actually believe you when you say that. So, believe me when I say this, I'm so damn proud to be here with you. I'm fucking thrilled you asked me out even after the puke incident of the century, and there's nowhere else I'd rather be than on your arm."

A look crosses his face that I've never seen before, but if I had to guess, I'd say he looks impressed, maybe even a little awed.

"Goddamn, Mia." His eyes fall to the table for a moment before he meets my gaze again, holding it with intention, as though he needs me to *really* hear him. "You fucking amaze me."

"Right back at you." I smile and clink my wineglass against his beer bottle, throwing in a little wink for good measure. The laughter that erupts from him brings a wide smile to my face.

"What am I going to do with you?" he asks while shaking his head, his smile beaming toward me from across the table.

I can think of a few things.

CHAPTER ELEVEN
KNOX

After enjoying a meal of steak, potatoes, and salad, Mia and I get back on my bike. She gave me a lot to think about, and for once, I don't want to do that thinking alone. Having Mia wrapped around me as we take the long way back to her house is giving me a sort of anchored contentment I've never had with another woman. One I never looked for with anyone else. This sweet woman with a heart of gold that people have taken advantage of her entire life finds pride in being with me. This woman who has spent her life taking care of other people considers me to be worthy of that same attention, that same care. I've never had that. I know my club will back me no matter what; my brothers will always be there for me. But I've never asked because it's always been my job—my responsibility. Now, the woman behind me is telling me she wants it to be hers, and fuck if that doesn't make me want to let her. And it makes me want to be her safe place to land just as much as she wants to be mine. After all these years, all the shit we've been through, I think we both deserve that.

Pulling up to her house, I park my bike, and Mia slides off before I do. She removes her helmet and tries to hand it to me.

"Uh-uh. That's yours, sweetheart. Keep it here for the next time I pick you up."

She lets out a breathy laugh and shakes her head. "Sorry, I didn't know if you bought it as a spare to keep or if it was mine."

"It's yours. You aren't a spare anything," I say before I bend to kiss her. When our lips brush, I have to hold myself back from grabbing her and marching up the steps to take her inside and strip her out of these damn leather pants that had me salivating all night with how delectably they molded to her curves. This isn't a one and done, and I don't want her to think a single dinner means she needs to give her body to me. She's in charge, and if she doesn't give me the go-ahead for more than a goodnight kiss, then I'll get back on my bike and send her a sweet goodnight text when I get home.

Mia breaks the kiss and lets out a shaky exhale. "You want to come in for a beer?"

"Of course." Hell, I want to come in for more, but this is the part where she needs to lead, and I get to follow. She only had one glass of wine at dinner, so she isn't impaired, but that doesn't mean I would assume her invitation means anything more than a beer. I'm a firm believer in full and enthusiastic consent and need to get to know her better before I can start reading her mannerisms. Before I'll have a full understanding of what each breath and tremor of her body is telling me. That's crucial in the dynamics I like to play with. So, until I feel comfortable taking control, she's running the show.

Mia smiles and leads me to her door. Though I try to keep my eyes off her ass, I fail miserably. I've denied myself for so long. Being this close to her and being able to take in everything about her is intoxicating.

She grabs her keys to unlock the door, but I cover her hand with mine. "Let me."

"Um...okay."

It's one of those things I've done for so long it feels strange not to. If we're walking into an empty room or house, I like to be the first one in. Coming from the background I did, there's a certain heaviness you feel when something isn't right. It's one of those gut in-stincts I came to rely on when Linc and I were kids—and it served me well when I became a part of the MC. When I open the door and step inside without feeling that tingly sensation of something being off, I hold the door open for Mia to enter.

"Were you afraid that the bogeyman was going to jump out at me?"

"Well, he'd have to get through me first."

She laughs lightly and kisses me on the cheek as she passes. "I like this side of you, Knox."

Mia walks into the kitchen and pulls out a bottle of my favorite beer. When I quirk a brow, she smiles and opens it, handing it over to me.

"You aren't the only one who pays attention." She grabs a bottle of wine sitting on the counter and pours herself a glass, then giggles, shaking her head as though she's clearing her thoughts. "Sorry, I'm a little rusty, and having you here is like having my teenage fantasies come to life." She lets out an adorable groan. "What is it about you that has me admitting the most embarrassing things about myself?"

I laugh. She's so damn cute with her pink-tinged cheeks. I can't help myself. There's nothing about Mia that tries to put on pretenses, and I love her unfiltered confessions. I take her hand in mine, leading her into the living room.

"Tell me more about these teenage fantasies of yours," I say as I sit on the couch and pull her down next to me.

"That's like reading my diary out loud. I don't think either of us is ready for that," she says with a chuckle.

"Come on. Let's see if adult Knox can live up to whatever you conjured in that pretty little head of yours about teenage Knox." I give her a broad smile, and she stares at me for a moment.

"Picking me up on your bike and taking me on an amazing date was a great start," she says.

"So I nailed that one. What else?"

Mia releases a nervous giggle. "Are you keeping track? Like checking boxes off a list?"

"I mean, if you have a list you'd like to give me so I don't mess this up, I wouldn't say no."

Her eyes soften as she leans closer to me. "You don't need it. You're doing amazingly well all on your own."

She closes the small gap between us and brushes her wine-flavored lips against mine. It's the first time she's initiated anything physical between us. It makes me unbelievably happy that she's taken even the smallest initiative. The kiss is languid and slow, neither of us in a hurry to go further; we're simply enjoying the taste and feel of the other.

I pull away and brush my roughened fingertip down her smooth cheek, noticing the way her breath hitches. The way her eyes close for a brief moment. Each small response is filed away in the back of my mind, giving me a greater understanding of her physical reactions. Something that is vital to my type of play.

"What else, sweetheart?" My voice is soft as I try to encourage her to open up to me.

"Well, there was one in particular. It's kind of embarrassing, though."

My lips trail down the silky skin of her neck while notes of sweet jasmine fill my senses. I fucking love the delicate perfume she wears. It's the polar opposite of the cloying scent so many other women wear. Mia lets out a stuttering breath and squirms the tiniest bit next to me. Another reaction I file away.

"Um, I used to imagine being at a school dance and standing against a wall when one of my favorite songs would come on. You would appear from the crowd and walk up to me and hold out your hand. Then you'd take me into the middle of the gym and we'd sway to the music."

"And we'd just dance?"

She releases a light giggle. "Well, I was only like fourteen."

"Play the song," I whisper against her skin.

She laughs again and I'm not sure if I found a ticklish spot or if she's embarrassed. "What?"

I lift my head from her neck and look her in the eyes. "I want to hear the song that played in your head when I'd sweep you off your feet."

Her delicate nose scrunches, and I kiss the tip because, at this point, I can't *not* touch her.

After she presses a few buttons on her phone, a song I vaguely remember sounds through her speaker.

I stand from the couch and smile down at Mia. The sight of the rosy flush covering her cheeks makes my dick half-hard.

"Dance with me," I say, holding out my hand to her.

"Shit, you're really good at this," she mumbles and slides her hand into mine.

When she stands, I place her hand around my neck and she brings the other one up, clasping them together. My arms wrap around her, and we begin swaying to the slow beat of the music.

"You know, I've never done this before," I say as I draw her tighter against my front.

"What?"

"Danced with a woman." Sure, I've had plenty of dances, but not of this variety. "Am I doing it right?" I ask as we slowly turn in a circle.

"You're doing great," she says with a breath of laughter. "You want to hear another confession?"

"The answer to that question will always be yes."

"I've never done this either," she admits.

"What are you talking about? You didn't go to any high school dances or anything like that?"

"I was never asked."

I lift my hand from her waist and cup the side of her face, running my thumb along her bottom lip. "Their loss, I guess. Now we both have a first to share."

That brings a warm smile to her face, and my hand drops back to her waist as we continue to sway to the gentle beat.

"So, what else happened in this little fantasy of yours?" I ask.

"You would take me out of the dance, and we'd go for a ride on your bike. My dress would be blowing behind us in the wind. It was all *very* dramatic."

"It's a little late to go on a ride, but if you really want to, we can," I offer, even though that's the last thing I want to do right now.

Her light-brown eyes dart to mine. "Is that really what you want?"

I shake my head. "Not even a little."

"What do you have in mind, then?"

"This is your fantasy, sweetheart. I'm taking it wherever you want me to."

Mia's fingers slide up the back of my neck before she scrapes her nails down. It feels as though sparks are shooting down my spine when she raises herself on her toes and presses her lips to mine. Her kiss is tentative for a moment, but then her mouth opens, and I plunge my tongue inside, needing to taste her again. Fuck, I'll never get enough of her kisses or the soft moans that fall from her while we tease and taste each other.

Her touch travels over my shoulders and down the front of my shirt until she reaches the bottom. With a tentative touch, she moves her hands under my shirt, running her fingertips over the skin of my stomach. Her being this forward is exciting me in ways I never thought possible. Yeah, I've had women put their hands on me, but not like this. Not with gentle, exploring, if not slightly unsure, fingers. I fucking love that Mia is nervous, but she's following her instincts. It's about what she wants, and she's taking it.

"Is this okay?" she asks with a breathless whisper.

"More than okay. I fucking love your hands on me." I rock into her, showing her exactly *how* okay I am with everything she's doing. Her touch becomes bolder, and she runs her fingertips up the planes of my stomach and chest, then down, feeling every groove of muscle as she explores under my shirt.

When her arms circle around my waist, I bend and take her mouth in a forceful kiss as my hands run under the hem of her shirt. I'm holding on by a fucking thread at this point. Her soft skin under my palms erupts in goose bumps as my touch trails up and down her back. When her shirt lifts a bit, Mia raises her arms, giving me the signal to remove the fabric from her body.

Fuck yes.

I break the kiss, and the gray sweater she's wearing is off in mere seconds. I'm greeted with the exquisite view of her breasts covered by a black lace bra.

"You're stunning, Mia," I say in a low growl as I take her mouth again. The kiss is frenzied, our tongues stroking and teasing the other in an erotic dance.

Her fingers find the buttons of my shirt, and she begins undoing each one until it's open, then her small hands run up the center of my chest. When she reaches my shoulders, she slides the flannel off, leaving both of us naked—or mostly naked, in her case—from the chest up.

Her head dips forward, and she brushes her lips against my chest. A hiss escapes through my teeth, and my hands dig tighter into the smooth skin of her back, trying to keep myself from ripping the rest of our clothes off and sinking deep inside of her. That's not what I want our first time to be like. This night is about her pleasure and making sure she's one-hundred-percent comfortable with me. It's about showing her that if anyone is going to center her pleasure, it's going to be me. And I'm going to do it so thoroughly she'll know exactly who she belongs to.

"Are you alright?" she asks.

"I have your mouth on me. Trust me, I'm better than alright."

She smiles and holds my stare as she leans forward again, brushing her lips against my chest before her tongue darts out to taste my skin.

My hand tangles in her loose waves at the back of her head. "Fuck, Mia. You have no idea what I want to do to you right now."

"Do it. Don't hold back."

She has no clue what she's asking. Mia is innocent and sweet. All the things I'm not. But I have every intention of dirtying her up just a little tonight.

Releasing her hair, I clasp her hands and wrap them around my neck before grabbing the back of her thighs and lifting her in my arms. She lets out a squeak of surprise as her legs wrap around my waist. I walk us over to the couch and sit with my back against the cushions and Mia straddling my lap, her gorgeous tits nearly level with my mouth.

One of my hands tangles in her hair again, pulling her down to my lips for another explosive kiss while my other glides up her back until my fingers reach the clasp of her bra. With deft precision, the clasp is undone in a matter of seconds. Her breasts spill from the lace that was covering them as I guide the straps down her arms.

She cries out when my mouth attaches to one dusty-pink nipple, and a satisfied groan rumbles deep in my chest.

Her hands clutch the side of my head and her fingers tangle through the longer strands, pulling my hair while she writhes on top of me, rubbing on my hard length over and over.

"Fuck, I'm going to come if you keep that up, baby," I say through a hiss against her heated skin.

"Good."

I bite down on her nipple, not hard, just testing the waters.

Another cry escapes Mia, this one even louder than the first. "I'm going to come if you keep *that* up," she moans.

I file that away under things I need to know for later. Right now, I have other plans for my little librarian.

I roll over and position Mia against the couch, pulling her to the edge.

"You are definitely wearing these again, but right now, I need them off," I say as I undo the button of her pants and drag them down her legs. She's wearing black lace panties that match her bra, and saliva floods my mouth when I see the darkened lace at her center.

Instead of diving in and licking until she comes on my face, I lift her leg and place soft kisses along the inside of her calf, trailing my lips back and forth. Mia's breaths are shallow and fast while her gaze stays fixed on me, anticipating every move. My other hand traces soft circles on the inside of her other thigh, but I don't touch her where I know she desperately needs me. I like drawing this out, fucking love seeing the way her muscles ripple under my fingers. Hearing the breathy moans she lets out is like music to my fucking ears. Some may call it torture, but I like to think of it as getting to know her body and learning every little reaction she has to my touch. I'm not rushing a single goddamn thing.

"Please, Knox," she begs so prettily, and my lips move past her knee to the sensitive skin of the inside of her thigh.

"I'm getting there, baby. But first, I want to get to know every inch of you."

The hand that was on her leg skates up her stomach, her muscles quivering under my touch. When my fingers meet her breast, I plump the soft flesh, all the while kissing and tasting her skin. My hand moves over her breast, and I run her hard nipple through my fingers. Mia's back arches from the couch. So my girl likes nipple play. That's another thing I file away. My index of everything Mia reacts to is growing by the second, and I'm having the time of my fucking life filling it up.

My mouth reaches the crease between her pussy and thigh, and I take a long lick, wanting to taste every inch of her before I finally put my tongue where we both want it. Mia lets out an adorable growl and my lips quirk up in a smile, but I still refuse to stop my exploration of the softest skin I've ever tasted in my life. Her hand finds my head as she once again grabs two fistfuls of hair. I think my girl has had about as much teasing as she can take.

The lace of her panties is completely soaked, and the taste of her arousal explodes over my tongue when I finally take my first lick. Mia's hips jump from the edge of the couch, but I rest the hand that was playing with her full tits against her lower stomach to keep her still.

I lift my head from between her thighs and pin her with my stare. "You're going to have to stay still if you want me to lick this pretty pussy, baby."

She bites her bottom lip and holds my stare with burning desperation in her gaze as she nods quickly.

My hands move to the sides of her panties, and I drag them down her thighs, leaning back so that I can get them off her legs. Instead of tossing them on the floor, I shove them in my pocket and give Mia a wink.

"Do you have a panty fetish?"

"Just a Mia fetish."

I spread her legs wide and gently run my tongue over her slit. She exhales a shaky breath as she holds my stare, begging me with her eyes to hurry the fuck up. I smile and stare into her darkened gaze, her pupils nearly covering the rich brown of her irises from her heightened arousal.

My head lowers, but I never drop eye contact when I take a long lick, spreading her with my tongue. This is the first full taste I've gotten, and Jesus fucking Christ—I'll never be the same.

Mia's eyes roll back, and she lets out a string of expletives while I lick her over and over, dipping inside her, then twirling the point of my tongue over and around her plump clit. Her hips roll against my mouth, and I soak in every labored breath, every "*Oh God*," and her breathless "*Fuck, that feels so good.*"

Her moans become louder and louder as one hand pulls roughly at my hair and the other squeezes the cushion next to her ass so hard I hear threads ripping. Her hips elevate as she comes in my mouth on a long cry. I lick her through the orgasm, gathering every drop on my tongue as she writhes beneath me, lost in her pleasure.

When her movements slow, with the exception of the slight jerk of her hips as aftershocks tumble through her, I lift my head from her pussy and kiss my way up her stomach. Her arms wrap around my shoulders and a dopey smile is spread across her lips. I take her mouth in a deep kiss, sharing the delicious taste of her orgasm.

"That was…" Her head lolls to the side as though she's lost her ability to use her muscles.

"You're beautiful when you come in my mouth, Mia."

The image of her climaxing is burned into my brain, and the echoes of the noises that fell from her perfect pink lips will forever ring in my ears.

Leaning back, I wrap Mia's legs around me before I stand, taking several long strides to her bedroom. When I lay her on the bed, she reaches for my belt, but I take a step back. The confused look on her face is adorable.

"This night is about you, sweetheart. And I plan to make you come on my tongue at least twice more before I lie down next to you and spend the rest of the night with you wrapped in my arms."

"Wait, so we're not having sex? I mean, I'm not saying we have to or trying to pressure you—"

A laugh bursts from my chest. "Baby, I would never think you were trying to pressure me into something I didn't want to do."

"So you don't want to have sex with me. Okay, great." She grabs the blanket and pulls it over her naked body.

"That right there," I say as I sit next to her. "That's why I'm making tonight solely about you. I need you to know that this is about more than me getting off. You mean more to me than a quick lay. I need you to trust me with your body and your heart. This is how I'm going to show you. Don't get me wrong, I want to sink so deep inside of you that you feel me for the next week. But first I need you to trust me completely. Trust this"—I wave my fingers between us—"completely."

Mia blows out a breath and covers her pinkened cheeks with her small hands. "I never thought I'd be the one pouting over not having sex."

"Well, I am irresistible, so your frustration is understandable."

She giggles and removes her hands from her face. "Sorry, this has never happened to me before."

"Trust me, it's new for me, too." This is, in fact, the first time in history I've had a naked woman in front of me who I've been dying to feel wrapped around my cock and said no.

"No, I mean I've never been with a guy who made it about me. Who didn't go down on me for thirty seconds before deciding that was enough and skipping ahead to the main event."

My head rears back in shock. "Listen, I'm fucking phenomenal at oral, but it takes me longer than thirty seconds. Are you telling me no man has ever made you come like that?"

Mia laughs, but it doesn't hold any humor. "No man has ever tried. Except you."

"Jesus Christ," I mumble, shaking my head. "Watching you come on my tongue was the singular highlight of my fucking year, baby. Any man who would pass that up is a fucking idiot."

Leaning down, I press a kiss to her mouth and gently pull the blanket away. When she doesn't give me any resistance, I remove it from the bed completely and flip her over on her stomach.

"Hips up, sweetheart. I'm far from done worshipping this perfect pussy."

Mia laughs, but it's muffled by the pillow she has her face in.

"Uh-uh. When you scream for me, I'd better hear you. Those noises are mine, and the last thing you're going to do is muffle them. Understood?"

She lifts to her elbows and rocks her naked ass back toward me. "Understood."

I lick her from her clit to her opening, dipping my tongue inside to get another taste of her sweetness.

"Good girl."

CHAPTER TWELVE
KNOX

The first thing that registers when I wake in Mia's bed is that I'm alone. The next is the clamoring coming from the kitchen. I always had a feeling Mia was one of those early riser types, but I was hoping the three orgasms I gave her last night would've made her need a little more sleep. Guess I'm going to have to work harder on that; I sure as shit don't like waking up in her bed without her next to me.

I move to sit up, wincing at my poor cock. I was serious when I told her last night was all about her. My dick has never been so neglected since I was a kid in high school and the furthest a girl would let me go was a little tit grabbing. Fuck, I forgot what it was like to wake up like this.

Standing from her bed, I stretch my arms over my head and look down.

"Sorry, buddy," I say to the bulge in my black boxer briefs before grabbing my jeans that I left on her floor. Pulling them over my hips, I head to her bathroom. When I've relieved myself, I look around for my flannel, then remember it's still in the living room where Mia pulled it off me last night.

Fuck, thinking about the way she erupted under my touch is making me hard again.

Think of something else, Knox, anything else.

Not exactly an easy task when I'm surrounded by everything Mia.

Walking out of her room, I find her in the kitchen with her back turned toward me. It looks like she's making scrambled eggs as she hums the song we danced to in her living room last night. Apparently, I'm not the only one with memories of last night running through their mind.

I lean against the doorway of her kitchen and take a few uninterrupted moments to soak up the way her night shirt hits just below the curve of her ass that I spent time tasting and becoming well acquainted with last night. Lace peeks out from the bottom when she reaches for a plate, scooping the eggs onto it. When she turns, she jumps and lets out a little yelp.

"Good morning, sweetheart," I say, watching a rosy hue creep over her cheeks. I love that she does that, and I hope to God she never stops.

"You are determined to scare me whenever you can, aren't you?"

"Never, baby. But I can't say I hate the way your tits bounce in that shirt when you jump," I say, looking at her chest, then back to her face.

Her blush deepens as she sets the plate on her small kitchen table next to a plate of bacon and pancakes.

"Come here," I say and grab her around the waist before she can walk back over to her stove.

When my lips brush against hers, she relaxes into me and hums in contentment.

"That's better," I say, pulling away and running my thumb over her kiss-swollen bottom lip. "I'm not a fan of waking up without you."

Her eyes soften and her arms wrap around my waist. "But are you a fan of pancakes?"

A laugh escapes which brings a bright smile to her mouth. "Yeah, baby. I like pancakes."

"How about coffee?"

My head tilts to the side. "Is that a real question?"

Mia giggles and dislodges herself from my hold before walking over to the coffeepot and pouring me a mugful. She grabs two plates and a couple forks before heading back over to the table and waves at me to sit. We fill our plates, and when I bite into one of the pancakes, I moan with delight.

"Jesus, woman. They are delicious. I'm coming over every day for breakfast."

"It's the cinnamon and vanilla."

We eat nearly everything she made, and that's saying a lot.

"What do you have planned for today?" she asks.

I smile, loving the normalcy of talking about plans for the day with the woman across from me. This isn't something I ever enjoyed with any other women. Shit, I never *did* this with another woman.

"Gotta head over to Midnight Rose and go over a few things with the manager. Then I was going to help the prospect work on his bike for a bit. What about you?"

"Maizie, Lucy, and Charlie are taking Colby to the park, so I was planning on meeting up with them. Then I have dinner plans with my grandmother."

"When am I going to see you again?" I don't give a flying fuck if I sound like a needy bitch right now. Mia needs to know that I want to spend as much time with her as possible, and I want to make plans to actually do that.

"Maybe dinner on Tuesday?"

"It's a date. If your schedule opens before, let me know and we can grab a drink or something."

Mia smiles and looks from her lap to my face with happiness dancing in her eyes. "Yeah, I'd like that."

After helping her with the dishes, since she wouldn't let me do them on my own, I head home to shower and change clothes before taking my bike to the strip club. It's Sunday afternoon, and we don't open for another few hours, but I spot Sylvie's deep-red luxury sedan in the parking lot. The woman makes good fucking money working for the Black Roses and has been here since

Trick was president. She keeps drugs out of the club and makes sure none of the girls are ever trying to make some extra cash on the side by offering services that we don't allow on the premises. What the girls want to do on their own time is their business, but we run a legit establishment. Well, if you don't count the money laundering that runs through the place to clean the cash we get from other less-than-legal operations.

It's my job to take care of the books here—both sets—and to make sure Sylvie has everything she needs. That could run anywhere from stocking some particular alcohol that some of our customers prefer apart from our usual fare to making sure there's enough glitter for the girls. It's a lot of paperwork, mostly with the books, clean and not so clean.

Though Cash is the official treasurer, I have a good idea of what runs through the club. Anything having to do with money is a two-man operation. Not because we don't trust each other implicitly, but this way, that trust can never be called into question. It worked for Gramps and Trick, and it works for us.

Walking into the brightly lit space, thanks to the cleaners who are still here detailing everything before we open for business, I find Sylvie at the bar going through some paperwork.

"Hey, Sylvie," I say as I walk behind the bar and pour myself a cup of coffee. "How's it going?" I turn and offer her a smile.

She tilts her head to the side as she runs her gaze down to my boots, then back up to my face.

"There's something about you today. I can't quite put my finger on it. You seem more relaxed than usual," she says, still giving me a skeptical appraisal. "Oh wait, does this have something to do with the school librarian I heard about?"

My eyes squint while I sip my coffee. "How do you know about Mia?"

"That's right. Mia. Heard Heather say she was at your party and when she went to say hello, you brushed her off."

"I don't have anything going on with Heather." Especially not after last night.

"She didn't say you did. Just mentioned that she ran into the girls at the farmers' market and met your new woman. Said she was nice."

"I don't need Mia to be fodder for gossip around here."

Sylvie lets out a loud laugh, her head tipping back like I just said the funniest thing known to man. "Oh, Knox. You should know by now that when you get a bunch of girls working together or any time really, everything is up for grabs."

"Can you please make sure to shut it down if you hear it? Mia doesn't need people talking about her behind her back."

Her laughter stops, but her smile remains on her red lips. "You really like this girl. I've never seen you so protective."

"Yeah, I do." It's the truth, and I'm not afraid to admit it.

"Does she know about your other proclivities?"

Sylvie and I have always had an open and respectful friendship. Through getting to know her, I discovered she was a member of a sex club in Boston. Call it curiosity, but years ago, she took me as a guest. It was a night they had a shibari performance and I was instantly enthralled. The pleasure the woman on stage had by allowing her partner to tie her in intricate knots. The beauty and release she found in it captivated me. The marks left on her skin afterward when the ropes were taken off were wildly attractive to me. Sylvie, seeing my reaction, hooked me up with the performers, and they taught me everything I know about the art of shibari. Eventually, I became a member there as well. Finding women at the club to play with was easy. But aside from Heather, I've never had anyone in my real life who I thought would be into it. Or maybe I never found anyone I wanted to see with my ropes around them.

Until Mia.

"I haven't told her," I say.

"Camila and Andrés are having a show at the club in a couple weeks. Maybe you could take Mia so she can see what it's about. I'm sure they'd love to see you."

They were the couple who were willing to teach me years ago. I don't even remember the last time I saw either of them. They travel and give demonstrations and performances all over the world.

"I'll think about it."

Sylvie doesn't push, but she does give me something to think about. Seeing as Sylvie and I have been working together for several years, she knows me well enough to pick up on the fact that I'm done talking about this.

"Let's go to the office so we can go over a few things," she says as she gathers the papers she was reading when I walked in.

It doesn't take long for me to get everything I need. I sign off on the inventory restock. Not that I necessarily need to since Sylvie is good at her job. But Trick and Gramps drilled it into us that we need to make sure to dot every *i* and cross every *t* ourselves.

When I walk out into the parking lot of the club, I notice my bike sitting lower than it should be.

"Son of a bitch," I say, walking over. My blood pressure nearly shoots through the roof when I see the cause. There's a knife plunged into each of my tires.

I turn and stalk back into the club, storming into the office where our security camera screens are located.

"What's wrong?" Sylvie asks when I stomp behind the desk and grab the keyboard to look through the footage.

"Someone fucked with my bike."

"What?" she asks incredulously.

Everyone knows we own this club, and if they see a bike, it belongs to one of the Black Roses. No one has ever been stupid enough to do something like this before. But it looks like shit's changed.

It's been less than an hour since stepping through the door, so it doesn't take long to rewind the footage to when I first arrived. About ten minutes later, there's a figure on the screen dressed in baggy, dark clothes with a hoodie pulled over their head. The person isn't particularly tall, so it could be a shorter man or a taller woman. It's impossible to tell from the footage. I watch as they walk over to my bike, stick a knife in the back tire, then the front with quick precision. Then they keep walking like they're out for an afternoon stroll. I follow them on the monitor, changing frames until they're out of camera range. Never once did I see their face. Either they knew where the cameras were, or they were damn lucky they never turned toward one.

"Holy shit," Sylvie breathes out.

When I turn to her, shock is written across her face.

"I'm putting extra guys on tonight."

"Do you think we're in danger?" she asks, looking as though she's ready for a fight. Sylvie doesn't put up with any bullshit, especially when it comes to the club she runs—and her girls.

"No, but there's no way this is random. Everyone in town knows that bike belongs to me, and they also know this club belongs to the Black Roses. Since it was my bike they went after and not the building, I'm going to guess this has to do with us, not the strip club. But since it's my job to make sure everyone here is safe, I'm not taking any chances."

Sylvie nods and straightens her spine. She's been in this business a long time and has seen plenty of jealous partners walk through the doors at the various places she's worked, both wives of customers and boyfriends of dancers.

"You got your piece?" I ask.

Sylvie nods and points to the bottom drawer of the desk. "Always."

I nod and grab my phone from my pocket.

"Hey, Oz," I say when my prez picks up. "I'm going to need a flatbed and a few extra guys for security at Midnight Rose."

"What's going on?" he asks.

"Some asshole slashed my tires."

"What the fuck?" he grits out.

"Yeah. I don't think it has anything to do with the strip club, but I'm not risking it."

"Alright, I'll send Wyatt and Braxton, and I'll be right there. I want to look at the security footage."

"I did. Couldn't tell who it was, or if it was even a man or woman."

"Shit. Alright, I'm coming to check, just in case. Stay there," he commands.

"Where the fuck you think I'm gonna go?"

"Right. I'll be there in ten."

Ozzy disconnects the call, and I walk out of the office to the bar, pouring myself a healthy shot of whiskey. I shoot it down quickly, then slam the glass back on the bar before resting my fists on the wood in front of me.

I don't know who the hell that person thinks they were walking onto our property and fucking with our shit. But the one thing I do know is once I find out the who and the why, they're going to wish they'd never heard of the Black Roses MC.

Chapter Thirteen
Mia

I'm on a cloud this morning, riding high all through getting ready to meet the girls at the park. It's a little hard to get my eyeliner straight when I burst into a fit of very girlish giggles every time I think about Knox's goodbye kiss this morning. It's my favorite when he wraps his arms around my waist and pulls my body to his. Or maybe it's when he slides his palms up the side of my neck and drags my lips to his. Although, I really like the combination of the two. Who am I kidding? Any way that man kisses me is ridiculously hot. And now my neck and chest are red from imagining all the places he kissed me last night.

"Get it together, girl. You can't turn into a tomato whenever you think about the gorgeous biker you had in your bed last night." I laugh at myself, rolling my eyes while trying to talk myself off this high I'm on.

You know what? Screw it. Why am I trying to talk myself down? Am I a little scared I'm in over my head? Sure, but I think that's perfectly normal for anyone just starting something. I don't have anything to really compare this to. No other man gives me the butterflies I experience when Knox so much as looks at me, let alone anything else.

Looking at the time, I realize I was supposed to be at the park ten minutes ago. I quickly gather the rest of my things and throw on the jacket Knox gave me before grabbing my phone to text Lucy.

Me: *Leaving now.*

Lucy: *You better come bearing gifts since you're late.*

Me: *I'm not that late.*

Lucy: *I know, I just really want a coffee from Cool Beans so I'm guilting you into stopping.*

Me: *No guilt trip necessary. See you in a few.*

The entire way to the coffee shop, there's music blaring through my speakers as I happily sing along. It's a beautiful day, even if it's a little chilly, but the sun is out, and that makes me happy. Or it may have been the three life-altering orgasms I had last night. I laugh at myself again. God, if I show up to the park like this everyone is going to know what went on last night.

It scared me a little when Knox said he didn't want to have sex. I know it's so stupid, considering it was right after he went down on me, but insecurities have a weird way of rearing their ugly heads at the worst times. No, it's good he wants to take it slow and get to know my body before we take that step. Right?

Of course it is, Mia. Stop overthinking.

As I park in front of Cool Beans, I'm determined to keep my mood happy and light. No overanalyzing last night for this girl. I'm cool, calm, and collected.

I order four coffees and a hot chocolate for Colby, then have a seat while waiting for my drinks. When my phone rings, I fish it out of my pocket and look at the screen. *Unknown Caller.* Silencing the call, because the last thing I want to do is deal with some pushy salesperson, I put my phone back in my purse only to hear it ring again. Another *Unknown Caller.* Jesus, do these people have a way of knowing when you have your phone in your hand or something? I silence it once more, and thankfully it doesn't go off again.

"Mia, your order's up," Betsy says as she places the carrying tray on the counter. "I put a little cake pop on there for Colby," she says with a smile.

"Thanks, Betsy. Hey, has Lucy's sister reached out about you carrying some of her homemade pastries?"

"No, I haven't heard from her. God, that would be such a huge load off for me. I knew she was selling at the farmers' market, but I'd love for her to sell here too. It would be nice to sleep past three sometimes." Betsy laughs and turns to make the next order.

"I'll talk to her about getting in contact with you." Again. "See you later."

"Bye, sweets."

If Cece ever wants to get out on her own, she's going to have to do more than sell at the weekly farmers' market. I'll have to call her and set something up with Betsy. There's no way that's going to pay rent and utilities and...*Stop it, Mia.* You aren't responsible for Cece. All you can do is nudge her in the right direction, not make the decisions for her. Damn, that whole responsible fixer mentality is a bitch to get to shut the hell up.

When I pull up to the park, I grab the drinks and walk over to where Lucy, Charlie, and Maizie are sitting in the warm sun. Colby is running in the distance, his exuberant laughter meeting my ears as Wyatt's puppy excitedly chases him.

"I see you're puppysitting today," I say as I walk up to my friends and have a seat on one of the wooden park benches.

"Wyatt got called to Midnight Rose and didn't want to leave the dog alone," Maizie says.

"Oh, is everything okay?" I haven't heard from Knox today, but I know he was on his way there when he left my house.

"I didn't ask, and he didn't offer. He knows Colby loves that damn dog, so I think it was just a way for him to let them spend time together without me being able to argue."

"Would you have argued?" Charlie asks.

"No way," Maizie says. "I'm like a dog auntie. I get to have all the fun and none of the responsibility."

Lucy taps her cup against Maizie's. "Amen, sister." She takes a sip and eyes me over the lid. "Nice jacket."

I chuckle and roll my eyes. "You would know."

Lucy shrugs. "I have good taste."

"That you do," I say.

"I still can't believe Knox called you to help him get something for our little Mia," Charlie says. "I never thought the man had a romantic side."

"Ask Mia, I'm sure she's been seeing all kinds of different sides to Knox," Maizie comments with a smirk.

Instantly I feel the blush creeping up my neck. I know it's only a matter of seconds before my friends notice too. Love them as I do; they aren't ones to *not* dig into why I'm turning red.

"I'm definitely getting to know him and having a good time doing it," I say.

Lucy arches a brow with a slight upturned tilt to her lips. "How good of a time?"

"He took me to a cool little restaurant outside of town on his bike, and we got to know each other a bit more, then he took me home."

"That's it?" Lucy asks, obviously believing there's more to the story.

The heat in my cheeks has turned into an inferno, and as much as I try, there's no stopping the grin that spreads from ear to ear.

"No, I didn't think so," Lucy says, reading me like an open book. "Come on, tell Auntie Lucy everything."

"You're ridiculous," I say, throwing my paper napkin at her.

"That may be true, but that doesn't mean I don't want to know. Mia, this is the guy you've been fantasizing about since I've known you. Shit, probably since Maizie has known you."

Maizie nods. "True," she says, agreeing with Lucy.

"We're kind of invested at this point. Especially Lucy, it seems," Charlie says.

I exhale before taking a sip of coffee. "Okay, fine. We went back to my house, and I was a little awkward at first, but he was quick to put me at ease, then we danced and...other things." When I finish, I'm once again wearing a silly grin like I have for most of the day.

All three girls are staring at me with their mouths hanging open and eyes comically wide.

"You danced?" Lucy finally asks.

"Yeah, it was this whole *tell-me-what-you-used-to-fanta-size-about-in-high-school* moment. It was cute," I say.

"Jesus, I never thought I'd hear cute being used to describe anything about Knox," Lucy says.

"Well, I don't necessarily think that's something he's going to suddenly become known for around the clubhouse. He definitely showed me a side I'd never seen before last night," I tell her.

"Now that you mention it, I've noticed him smiling a lot more, especially when Mia's around," Charlie says.

"That's all well and good. But I want to know that he made you see stars after your little dance," Lucy says.

"Jesus," I breathe out.

"What? You deserve nothing less than to be railed all night by that giant of a man," Lucy counters.

"Yes, I saw stars. No, there was no railing. He said he wanted to get to know my body and wanted me to be comfortable before we took that step."

"I'm dead," Lucy says, dramatically falling against the back of the bench. "That is so unbelievably sweet."

"You don't think it's...I don't know...*odd* that he didn't want to go further? I mean, he got no 'relief' last night. I don't know any man who would—or I guess *wouldn't*—do that."

"That's because you're dating Knox. He obviously isn't like any other man you've dated," Charlie says before smacking Lucy's leg. "Sit up. You're being dramatic."

"What?" Lucy protests. "I can't help it if I'm completely blown away by this new development. Knox is a romantic and shit."

"I think it's safe to say we all see a different side of our men when we're alone," Charlie says.

Lucy tilts her head from side to side a couple times. "I think Jude is about the same."

Charlie rolls her eyes but continues talking as though Lucy didn't interrupt her. "And no, I don't think it's weird that he wanted to make it about you. There's a certain control I've always thought Knox had. He's not going to try to hump your leg the first time you two make out."

"Ugh, the leg humpers," Maizie says. "Sometimes I wonder what it would be like to have a night with a man who actually wanted to get to know my body and not stick it in, then turn over and fall asleep."

"Maybe when Wyatt comes over to pick up his dog, you can invite him in for a little scratch behind *your* ear," Lucy says.

Maizie shakes her head. "Nope. He's off limits. One, it would go against my no-biker rule, and two, I work for the club. I'm not about to put that in jeopardy. Not when I have that guy over there who depends on me," she says, pointing to her son. "I don't have the luxury of scratching anything with any member of the Black Roses."

"They would not fire you over something as dumb as having a one-off with one of their guys. Shit, half the girls at Midnight Rose have hooked up with at least one of the brothers," Lucy says.

Maizie shrugs and shakes her head. "Doesn't matter. Those girls don't have kids to look out for. If shit goes sideways for them, they can just pick up and leave. I can't."

Colby starts running toward us as if just remembering we're here, with the dog traipsing behind him.

"Can Pepper spend the night?" he asks his mom with pleading eyes.

"I don't know, bud. Depends on what time Wyatt gets home from work."

That reminds me that there seems to be something happening at the strip club that I know nothing about. Not that it matters. Knox and I aren't attached at the hip, and he certainly doesn't answer to me.

"Hey kiddo, I got you a hot chocolate, and Betsy put a little something in the bag for you," I tell Colby as I hand him the paper sack.

"Cake pop!" he yells, holding the sugary treat in the air.

"Great, just what I need," Maizie grumbles before taking another sip of her coffee.

We spent about another hour at the park so Colby could run off the sugar rush, then all of us headed home.

I still haven't heard from Knox, so I decide to shoot him a text.

Me: *Hey, everything Okay? Maizie said she was watching Wyatt's dog because he had to go to Midnight Rose.*

Is that too needy? Does it sound like I'm being clingy, calling him out for not having checked in with me? Jesus, I really need to stop second-guessing myself today.

Knox: *Hey, sweetheart. Just taking care of a few things. I'll call you later, yeah?*

Was that a brush-off?

For fuck's sake, Mia. Stop it.

Me: *Okay, talk later.*

I grab a bottle of my grandma's favorite wine and head over to her house. When I walk in through her kitchen, she's pulling a roast from the oven. She already has mashed potatoes and what looks like a green bean casserole in serving bowls on her counter.

"Wow, Grandma. It smells amazing in here."

She turns to me after setting the roast on the stovetop and smiles. "We'll be eating like kings tonight, my dear." She looks at the bottle in my hand. "And drinking like them, too."

I walk over to a drawer, pull out a wine opener, then grab a couple glasses from the cupboard. After pouring the wine, I hand my grandmother her glass, and she takes a long sip.

"Ahh, I needed that today," she says.

"What's going on?"

"I talked with your parents today."

"Yeah, that usually puts me in a drinking mood, too," I say and take another drink from my glass. It's not that I don't love my parents, but I can't say I necessarily like them very much. I can only imagine what little scheme they're trying to pull my grandmother into this time.

She laughs and sets her glass down before grabbing a knife and cutting the roast, then nods at the dishes sitting on the counter. "Why don't you take everything in, and I'll be right out with the roast."

I carry the mashed potatoes and casserole into the dining room, noticing she's already set the table. My grandmother loves to make a fuss over dinner. Though we don't do it every night, I always make sure to be here at least once a week for this particular meal. I see her nearly every day, usually for a morning coffee since she's an early riser like me, but I didn't stop by this morning since I was otherwise occupied.

My grandmother comes in carrying a huge serving tray, far too much for either of us to eat in one sitting.

"Why so much? There's no way we're going to eat all of that."

"Well, I wasn't sure if we were going to be dining alone. I thought maybe the man who left this morning on his motorcycle would be joining us," she says with a small smile playing on her lips.

I lower my head and groan. "Sorry, Grandma. I guess we've never discussed having overnight guests."

"Nonsense. That's your house now. And frankly, it's about time that you had a man spend the night. I was getting a little worried that you'd thrown in the towel and decided to become an old maid at twenty-eight."

I bark out a laugh. "It was a close call." I'm not really keen on the idea of talking to my grandmother about my night, so I change the subject. "How are my parents?" I realize it's been a long while since I've talked to them, which is far from unusual. They obviously don't need me to take care of anything for them, so why would they want to talk to me?

"They're fine. Asked if I could talk to you about you reaching out to your brother."

And there it is.

"Of course they did," I say, letting out a huff of annoyance.

My grandmother knows why I kicked Nolan out of my apartment and why I quit talking to him. She also knows that I made my parents aware, and they didn't do anything except tell me that they were no longer going to pay his half of the rent. If they want to believe there's nothing amiss with their son, I can't do jack shit about it.

"I told them if they want *you* to reach out to him, then they need to call *you* themselves."

"Thank you," I say as I load my plate with the food in front of me.

"I know what you had to deal with when you were growing up. Granted, not to the full extent, but it didn't take a genius to realize they were gone all the time and you kept everything running. It wasn't like Nolan was capable. I also didn't interfere because I thought if you needed help, you would have reached out."

"I was fine, really. If anything, it made me capable at a young age. At least I'll never be the one anyone needs to worry about."

"That's not true," she says with a softness in her gaze. "I worry about you. I worry that you're going to spend your life cleaning up other people's messes and not concentrate on your own life."

I scoff. "Jeez, Grandma. I think I deserve a little more credit than that."

"Of course you do. That's why I'm talking to you about this. Knox has never struck me as the type to spend the night at a woman's house, and you certainly don't strike me as someone who would invite a casual fling to stay overnight, either. Not that there would be anything wrong with that. I don't judge."

"Thank you for that," I say with a smile.

"What I'm saying is he's a good man and was a good kid who seemed to have a rough start in life. And that's nothing to be ashamed of. There's going to be talk, and most likely it's going to get back to your parents. We both know they're snobby assholes who put far too much importance on optics."

I nod. "I already know this."

"I just want to make sure you're following your heart instead of your head on this one. You've always been so pragmatic and in control. It's time for you to let loose a little and go with the flow, as the kids say."

"Look at you, Grandma, getting hip with the lingo."

"Smart-ass," she says and sticks out her tongue at me.

"I see I didn't inherit my maturity from you."

"No, just your fabulous ass."

My eyes widen in shock. "Grandma!"

"What. It was your grandfather's favorite attribute."

"Jesus Christ," I say, shaking my head, fighting the urge to cover my ears and hum loudly.

"Okay, okay," she tsks. "Really, Mia, I never took you to be a prude."

I open my mouth to argue but decide to let her have this one.

"I love you," I say instead, and she beams.

"Well, I love you too, dear. I think when we're done with dinner, you should take a plate over to your new beau. I'm sure he'll appreciate a nice home-cooked meal."

The way this woman can go from talking about asses to referring to Knox as my beau as though this is the 1800s is astonishing.

"Okay, Grandma. I will."

CHAPTER FOURTEEN
KNOX

I t's been a shit day. As soon as it seemed things were finally cooling off for us, some asshole decided to fuck with my bike. There's no proof this has something to do with the Italians or the Russians, but there's no proof that it doesn't, and I'm not leaving anything off the table. Ozzy went over the security footage to have another set of eyes on it, but he was just as stumped as me. As far as we know, the threats against the club have been eliminated. It could be assumed that this might have something to do with the Bone Breakers, but that's not really their style, at least not from what we've seen in the past.

I got home from the clubhouse about an hour ago after putting new tires on my bike and helping one of our prospects out with his. I'm tired, irritated, and confused as fuck about what happened earlier. Instead of hanging out with everyone, I decided I needed some peace and quiet and a whiskey in the comfort of my own home.

With my feet propped on the coffee table, I turn the TV on, ready to turn my brain off, when headlights reflect off the wall. My head swivels toward the large window in the front of my house, and I spot Mia's car in the driveway. A smile immediately spreads across my face at the unexpected but very welcome surprise.

Standing from the couch, I head to the front door to let her in but notice she hasn't gotten out of her car yet. I open my front door and lean against the doorway with my arms folded over my chest as I watch her looking down at her lap. Her lips are moving, and it looks as though she's having some sort of argument with herself. She hasn't noticed me, so I slip my feet into my boots and walk down to meet her. My hand taps against her window, and she jumps in her seat, looking up at me. Mia closes her eyes briefly, then shoots me a tentative smile. She reaches over and grabs a plate that's sitting on her passenger seat before I step aside so she can open her door.

"Hi," she breathes out. "Sorry, I should have called. I don't know why I didn't, but I had dinner with my grandmother, and she made too much food because she thought you might be joining us. She knows you spent the night, by the way. Anyways, she suggested I bring you a plate. So after dinner, she handed this to me and shooed me out of the house after I promised to come by with it." Mia holds the plate up to me in offering. Her cheeks are bright red when she finishes speaking, and I'm not sure if it's from embarrassment or from having not taken a breath while she rushed out her reasoning for being here.

"You don't have to call, sweetheart," I say, taking the plate from her hands and kissing her sweet lips. When I pull away, she smiles softly. It's a lot better than the uncertainty that was pouring from her only moments before.

"Sorry." She shrugs. "I guess I'm not clear what the rules are here."

I take her hand and lead her into the house, shutting the door behind me before I take off my boots, all the while keeping a hold of her. We walk into the kitchen, and I set the plate she brought on the counter, then motion for her to have a seat on one of the stools.

"The rules are, if you want to stop by unannounced for any reason whatsoever, you do. Another rule is if you bring me food, you have to hang out with me while I eat it. Oh, and you have to do it with your shirt off."

Mia tilts her head to the side and purses her lips.

Laughter bursts from me as I remove the foil over the plate. "Okay. We'll work on that one." I grab a bottle of wine that I bought yesterday and a bottle of whiskey, holding both up. "Wine or whiskey?"

"Whiskey, please."

I turn and grab a glass, tossing in a few ice cubes from my freezer before splashing a healthy amount into the glass.

"How was your day?" Mia asks when I take my first bite from the plate she brought.

"Don't get me started. I'd rather enjoy my meal and seeing you in my house than talk about the shit from today."

"I'm making a rule, too," she says, arching her brow. "You have to share everything with me. Good or bad. If your day was shit, I want to know. If it was the best day you've ever had, I want to know."

I smile and nod my head. "You're right. Guess I'm not sure what the rules are here, either." I walk around to the other side of the breakfast bar and have a seat next to Mia, taking a sip from her whiskey. "Someone fucked with my bike while I was at Midnight Rose. We aren't sure who it was since they hid themselves pretty fucking well from the camera."

"Who the hell would be that stupid, though? Is that why Wyatt had Maizie watching Pepper for him?"

I bark out a laugh and shake my head. "I'm sure there was more to it than that, but yeah, he had to go in and play security guard tonight."

"You don't have to go back?"

A smile spreads across my face as I lean closer to Mia. "Nope, I have the rest of the night to do whatever I want."

"I can go and let you get some rest." Her gaze darts between my eyes and my lips.

"The hell you will." I close the small gap between us and take her mouth in a searing kiss. Mia responds as she always does when I kiss her—enthusiastically and with every ounce of passion inside of her.

My lips break away from hers, and I begin trailing my lips over the soft skin of her neck, licking and tasting her as I swipe my tongue over her throat. I give her a little love bite, and she groans in pleasure, so I do it again.

"You know, we spent a lot of time last night discovering what I like. I want to know what *you* like."

My mind plays back to the conversation I had with Sylvie earlier today. If this woman is going to be in my life, be my partner, then she needs to know every part of me.

I sit back and run a fingertip over the freckles of her nose. She's told me that she hates those freckles because they make her look so young. I always thought they made her look innocent and sweet. I'm finding that my little librarian is quite sweet but not as innocent as I would've expected. A part of me is scared she'll run screaming when I tell her, but a bigger part of me is excited to see her tied up as she gives the control of her pleasure over to me and trusts me with it.

"I like using restraints," I say, searching her eyes for a reaction.

Her brows furrow. "Come again?"

I smile at her confused look. I'm sure it's not the first thing she thought my answer would be when she asked me that question.

"I enjoy it when a woman trusts me enough to be in charge of her pleasure. And I like the way it takes me out of my head."

"What do you mean?"

She's asking questions—not screaming. This is good.

"When I'm in a scene with a woman, I'm solely focused on her and her reactions. It sort of quiets all the shit in my brain for a while. Plus, I think a woman looks sexy as fuck when she's tied in ropes."

I run my finger down the center of Mia's chest, imagining a series of intricate knots running across her naked skin.

"You want to tie me up?"

"Yes," I breathe out without hesitation.

"I've never done that—been tied up. Have you?"

"I have, actually. It was part of my training. I would never expect a partner to allow me to do anything I haven't experienced myself."

Curiosity and hesitation with a touch of, dare I say, excitement flit through her light-brown eyes. "Did you like it?"

I consider her question so I can answer her as honestly as possible. "My pleasure doesn't come from being bound. It comes from doing the binding. Though I didn't dislike it, I'm not suited to be a rope bottom."

"What do you think the rope bottom gets out of the experience?"

"I think it varies from person to person. The most common thing I hear is that they find power and pleasure in giving up control. There's a certain feeling of release when you make the decision to give that control to someone you trust."

She nods in understanding. "That actually...sounds really good."

I smile before leaning in to give her a soft kiss on the mouth. There was something about her that told me she would be perfect for me, and this just proves that further.

"Would you want to try something tonight? Not a full scene with ropes, but maybe wrist restraints?"

She bites her lower lip as she considers my question. "I think I would."

"That's not enthusiastic consent, sweetheart." Going into this clearheaded and wholeheartedly is absolutely paramount to me.

She nods and sits a little straighter on the stool. "I want to try. I'm just nervous. What if I do it wrong? Or what if I don't like it?"

"Trust me when I say you won't do it wrong. We'll have open and clear communication the entire time. And if you don't like it, we'll stop immediately."

Mia lifts her glass to her lips, but I stop her before she takes a sip. "If you want to try this, neither of us can be drunk or impaired in any way. That's not how I operate."

"Not even to take the edge off a little?" she asks, her gaze flitting between me and the glass.

"If you're on edge that much, we won't play. But there're other ways I can think of that work a hell of a lot better than whiskey."

I grin and slide my palm around her neck, pulling her in for a kiss.

When we separate, her eyes are slightly glazed. "Okay," she whispers against my lips.

"We need a safe word," I say.

"You're the expert here," Mia replies with a smile.

"I've always found it best to use the traffic light system. Green means we're good, yellow means slow down or you want to change something, and red means stop completely."

She nods and the corner of her lips tilt upward. "I can do that."

I stand from my stool and hold my hand toward Mia. When she slides hers into mine, I turn it over and kiss her palm, keeping our gazes locked. "What color?"

She looks up at me with hooded eyes. "Green."

I pull her from the stool into my chest. When I kiss her this time, I bend slightly and lift her up so she can wrap her legs around my waist. My hands knead her delicious ass as she moves against me, rubbing her center over my quickly hardening length. Tonight, I'm not going to take it slow. I plan to sink myself into her and have her come on my cock over and over.

I walk us toward the back of my house, where my large bedroom is located. Gently laying her down on my king-sized bed, I stand and take in the way her auburn hair spreads across my dark-blue comforter. Stepping back, I reach behind me and grab the collar of my T-shirt, pulling it over my head before dropping it on the floor next to me. Mia lifts on her elbows, her gaze trailing over every inch of my naked chest. I love the appreciation in her gaze, love seeing the pupils in her eyes dilate because she's so turned on.

I lean forward, resting my fists on the bed but keeping my arms straight as my upper body pushes Mia flat on her back while I take her mouth in a deep kiss. Her warm hands slide up my sides, then down my chest as a shudder runs through me. When her hands reach the waist of my jeans, I lift my head and look her in the eye, both of us breathing hard as her fingers undo the button. She bites her lip, and the corner of my mouth kicks up in a small grin.

"Are you going to let me taste you tonight?" she asks.

The breath stalls in my chest and my cock nearly punches out of my jeans.

"I'm going to let you do anything you want to me, sweetheart."

Her grin widens as her hand pulls down the zipper of my jeans. When she reaches in, her hand touches my cock for the first time.

"*Fuck*," I groan as she pulls me out and strokes me up and down in her tight fist. "I need you naked. Now."

Mia releases me and pulls her shirt over her head. My hands immediately find the clasp of her bra, and I undo it, letting her full tits spill from the white cotton. I smile when I see her bra. So sweet and unassuming. And, like last night, I get a thrill from the idea of dirtying her up a little.

She undoes the button of her jeans before I yank the fabric, along with her panties, off in one swift motion.

"Better," I say, spreading her legs wide. Her cunt is bare and so fucking wet. My mouth waters at the sight, remembering how delicious she tasted when she came on my tongue over and over again last night.

Stepping back again, I push my jeans and boxer briefs down my legs, leaving me completely naked. My hand grips the base of my cock, and I stroke myself as I walk closer to Mia, sitting up on the edge of the bed. Her chest rises and falls as her gaze darts from my eyes to the way I'm pleasuring myself.

"Open," I demand. She parts her lips and I smile. "You're going to have to go wider than that, sweetheart." Mia stretches her mouth and sticks out her tongue without me asking. Seeing her like this, hungry for me...fuck, I can't even explain.

When I slide my cock over her wet tongue and into her hot mouth, I let out a long moan. "Fuck, baby. Your mouth feels so good."

She hums in response and the feel of the vibration shoots straight to my balls. My length slides in and out, going a little deeper each time.

"Do you think you can take the whole thing, Mia?"

She does her best to nod with my cock still in her mouth, and I pull almost the entire way out. When I slide back in, my tip touches the back of her throat. She gags slightly, and I remove myself completely this time.

"What color?" Though this isn't a scene with any sort of restraints yet, I want her to be comfortable and to openly communicate with everything we do.

"Green," she says.

"Do you want to take more?" I ask, running my thumb along her bottom lip.

"Yes, please."

"When I hit the back of your throat, I want you to swallow. Do you think you can do that for me?"

She answers by opening her mouth again for me.

This time when the tip of my cock hits the back of her throat, I press farther, and she relaxes, then swallows around me.

"Goddamn," I groan out. "You take me so well in your mouth, sweetheart."

I pull out again, giving her the chance to take a full breath. Then, I repeat the motion. Her throat tightening has me ready to shoot down her throat. But that's not where I want to come the first time with her.

"I need to taste you," I say through gritted teeth after I pull myself free from her mouth.

The corners of her mouth turn down in an adorable pout. "But I wasn't done."

"That may be true." I chuckle. "But I will be if we keep this up. Besides, I think this was about taking the edge off for you, and the best way I can think of is by eating your sweet cunt."

The directness of my words—or maybe it's the antic-ipation of it—has my girl's eyes blazing with lust.

My arms band around Mia's waist, and I lift her as I kneel on the mattress and position her head toward the top of my bed. This is the first time I've felt her, skin to skin, across my entire naked body. Though last night I was naked—except for my boxers—this feels different. Her flesh is silken and smooth against every rough part of me when her legs glide over mine as I lie on top of her and press my mouth to hers. It's as if this is always where I was meant to be. With her naked in my bed, and showing her how I feel with my body, if not my words.

Her knees are pressed against my hips, and in one simple move, I could bury myself in her without a second thought. I'm tempted to do just that, but Mia wants to experience something I've never shared with a woman I care about the way I do about her. Honestly, I'm so fucking excited to be here with her I can hardly contain myself. These feelings are like nothing I've ever had for another woman.

I begin my descent down her body, kissing and licking the perfect flesh beneath my touch. My gaze travels up her body the lower I get. Her breaths are coming in hard pants, her chest rising and falling with each inhale and exhale.

"What color?" I ask when my lips brush across her pubic bone.

"Green. So fucking green," she pants out, and I grin as my tongue dips between her legs to taste her for the first time today. This is a real fucking tragedy because she's become my new favorite flavor, and I feel a little deprived.

Mia's eyes are rolled toward the ceiling as my tongue flicks against her clit.

That won't do.

"Eyes on me," I command

Her hooded gaze shoots to me, and I hold her stare as I double my efforts, adding two fingers and curving them just the right way so I can massage her G-spot as my tongue laps at her clit. Her hips roll almost violently between the bed and my mouth while her hands fist around the pillow she has her head resting on.

"Oh my God, Knox. Keep going."

It's not as though she needs to tell me. By now, I recognize all the signs that she's about to come. Her brows tighten, and her lips part as though she's preparing for the inevitable onslaught of sensation. When her body stiffens beneath me and her breath stalls, I know I'm seconds away from tasting her release. Mia comes on a long moan, the walls of her pussy pulsating and tightening around my fingers. Each lick, each press of my fingers against the spot inside her, makes her body quake with pleasure as her orgasm rolls through her.

I prowl back up her body, kissing her damp skin. I make my way to her breast, licking around her nipple before pulling it into my mouth, then giving it a light bite. My tongue runs over her throat until I reach her mouth and plunge inside. Mia's tongue tangles with mine, her fingers running up and down the tight muscles of my back.

"How do you feel now?" I ask.

"So fucking good."

"Are you ready for more?"

"Yes," she answers without hesitation. I hold her gaze a few moments before she continues. "I trust you, Knox, and I know without a shadow of a doubt that anything you do will make me feel fucking amazing."

That's exactly what I need to hear. To know she trusts me implicitly means everything to me. My chest is cracking open with the sincerity in her eyes. The years of keeping my heart locked tight in chains are falling away. When Mia looks at me, there's no doubt she trusts me with more than just her body, and there's no doubt that she's it for me. This is about more than her willingness to explore something with me. This is about her acceptance of me. Fuck, I'm falling for her deeper than I was at all prepared for. It should scare me, but it doesn't. With her, it never will.

I lean down and kiss her again. There's never a time I don't want my lips on Mia. When I pull myself away, I stand and walk over to my dresser, opening the drawer that contains my ropes and a few other things, including soft leather cuffs. I grab four and close the drawer before walking back over to the bed. My hand reaches under my mattress to pull out the leather strap I have hidden underneath at the top and bottom of my bed.

"To think you had this all set up the first time you brought me here. I never would have guessed," Mia says when I lay the end of the strap on the mattress and walk to the other side of my bed to do the same.

I see the excitement in her eyes as her gaze darts to the straps on either side of her.

"To think my little librarian is so excited to be tied up while I fuck her that she can't stop rubbing her thighs together," I say, pointedly looking at the way she's squirming on my bed. I don't even think she realizes she's doing it, but I make damn sure to observe every reaction she has as I prepare her.

When I run a finger through her center, her eyelids flutter.

"You're so wet thinking about all the things I'm going to do to you, aren't you? How you're going to be spread out for me to enjoy."

"Yes," she hisses as I flick her clit several times in quick succession.

A satisfied grin spreads across my mouth. I bring my finger to my lips and wipe her wetness over them before putting the digit in my mouth and sucking her taste off me.

"Fuck," she whispers. "You're going to be the death of me."

I can't help the low chuckle that escapes me. "No, baby. Quite the opposite, actually."

There's nothing I want more than for Mia to finally live her life for herself. To have the things she wants. To let go of the things that she's carried like a lead weight across her shoulders.

I grab one of the cuffs and secure her right wrist in it, then attach it to the strap on the bed. I walk over to the other side and do the same.

"Color?" I ask.

"Green."

I walk to the end of the bed and spread her legs. The second my eyes make contact with her perfect cunt, I lean forward and run my tongue through her center. I can't fucking help myself when it comes to tasting her. Her hips pop off the bed in surprise as she lets out a hiss.

When I have her ankles spread apart and each one in a cuff, I stand back and look at the goddess sprawled out on my bed.

"What color?" I ask again, this time my voice thick with emotion. Lust being the most prominent, but there's something else lying just underneath that. Something that feels too soon to feel but so right.

"Green."

"You look fucking beautiful spread out for me. I want to make you come over and over. And when you think you can't possibly come one more time, I'm going to prove you wrong. Are you ready?"

Mia locks her eyes with mine. "Yes."

CHAPTER FIFTEEN
MIA

The feral grin on Knox's face makes me want to rub my thighs together while he stands at the foot of the bed and looks me over, splayed in front of him. But I can't. I won't get any satisfaction from the ache inside of me until Knox deems it so. And to be honest, the anticipation is ramping up the desire I feel for him higher than I ever thought possible. It's a heady thing to give over control of your pleasure to someone. To give control of anything to another person. Any time with another partner, I had to constantly tell them what to do, how to do it, and sometimes just do it my damn self.

It's not that I'm not opposed to communication. I think it's key. But looking at Knox, seeing the lust in his eyes, it makes me realize that it was never about my pleasure with other men. It was about theirs. And that is the exact opposite of the man standing in front of me, very naked and very turned on. Goddamn, I want to taste him again. I've never felt such an overwhelming need to do that in my entire life. I want him to come undone for me, to bring him to his knees like he did to me over and over again.

Seeing the way he's studying me so intently as though he's trying to figure out where to start, though? The excitement burning in his eyes? Well, that's another thing altogether. Knowing that wringing every last drop of pleasure from me is what he craves, that's a way of bringing him to his knees in an entirely different and unexpected way.

"I want to see my cock in your mouth again, sweetheart."

"Yes, please."

Knox climbs up my body and rests his knees against the mattress on either side of my shoulders. His gaze is searing as he stares down at me, sending shivers through my entire body.

"One blink for green. Two blinks if you need me to stop."

I nod and open my mouth wide.

He gently slides in, testing like he did before. This is a completely different position than I've ever been in, and though it's a touch awkward at first, Knox repositions himself above me, making it easier for me to accommodate his thick length. His hand strokes my cheek as he pumps in and out of my mouth with an intense look in his eyes.

"Looking at you taking me like this, Mia? Fuck, I want to come down your throat right now."

I let out a low moan, and he grits his teeth. "You would like that, wouldn't you?" he practically growls at me.

Another moan vibrates through me, and he shakes his head. "Oh, you know exactly what you're doing to me, don't you, baby?"

If I could smirk at him, I would, because yes, I do. And I fucking love having that kind of power over him.

"Your throat isn't where I'm going to come for the first time with you. Not by a long fucking shot."

He pumps inside of my mouth a few more times, the sweat gathering at his brow as though it's physically strenuous for him not to do what he so obviously wants. But if I know anything, it's that Knox exudes control in every aspect of his life.

When he pulls out, I take a deep breath through my mouth. He wipes the spit from the sides of my cheeks, seeing as my hands are restricted by the cuffs wrapped around my wrists. His fingers lightly trail over my neck before he swirls his fingertips over my nipple and pinches. My hips shift on the bed. Fuck, I need some relief, and having him pull and gently twist my nipples is nearly enough to make me come right now.

"Has anyone ever made you come from nipple stimulation alone?"

"It's rare any man has ever made me come, period."

Knox shakes his head. "That's a fucking tragedy."

He lowers his mouth and exhales, his hot breath making contact with the sensitive point. His fingers lightly trace around my other nipple as he breathes across my skin, then his tongue laves at me before blowing cold air over my wet flesh. My hips jerk with the change in sensation.

"Holy shit," I breathe out, shocked at the tingles racing through my body and heading straight to my center.

Knox gives me a devilish smirk, and I see a plan forming behind his eyes. I'm not exactly sure what it is, but I have every faith that I'm going to thoroughly enjoy it.

He repeats the action on the same side, and every time he blows a cooling breath, the sensations become more intense. Sweat gathers on my forehead, and it's as though he's turned up the temperature in his bedroom by twenty degrees. I feel myself becoming wetter and wetter, and I know if he were to even gently brush my clit, I would shoot off like a damn firework. He switches to my other nipple and does the same thing over and over. Each lick and each breath over my skin takes me right to the edge, ready to fall. Finally, with him scraping his teeth against one nipple while he twists the other, I detonate. Crying out, the orgasm rips through me, sending what feels like tiny electric shocks down to my toes. Knox releases me from his mouth and twists my overly sensitive peak while watching my face as pure pleasure sizzles through every part of me.

When my breathing evens out, Knox gets the widest, most self-satisfied grin on his face. "That's one."

Holy shit.

He begins kissing me along my shoulder and over my clavicle as his lips travel down the center of my chest.

He stops when he reaches my pussy, then looks up at me as he takes a long lick.

"I want the taste of you on my tongue every day, Mia. You're fucking delicious." He licks. "And beautiful." He licks. "And mine." He growls those last two words before doubling his efforts against my clit, adding two fingers. I'm so far beyond stimulated from the orgasm I had only a minute before. When he rubs against my G-spot, I explode again, shattering under his mouth.

"There's two," he says before dipping his head again and gently kissing my swollen clit.

Knox lifts himself from the mattress, walks over to his bedside table, opens the drawer, and pulls out a box of condoms. My eyes follow his every move. Knox has always carried himself with quiet confidence, but right now, he exudes the strong, centering confidence of a man who knows exactly what he's doing. My gaze trails over every inch of naked skin, from the defined planes of his chest to the six—no, eight—pack to that insanely hot band of muscles that point directly to his very hard and very impressive cock. Knox notices my eyes linger there as he strokes himself a few times. God, how is that so fucking sexy?

"Are you ready for me to sink into you, Mia? I can't wait to feel your pussy strangle me," he says before leaning down and running his tongue from the hollow of my neck, over my chin, then plunging his tongue inside my mouth. Instinctively, I try to move my hands so I can run my fingers through his thick hair as he kisses me breathless, but the cuffs stop me. This man takes me out of my mind. And I fucking love it.

When Knox breaks the kiss, he walks to the chest at the end of his bed. Opening it, he pulls out a wedge pillow and sets it next to my hip. He runs his hands from my feet to my restrained ankles, then up my calves, trailing his touch back down to the cuffs.

"What color?"

"Green," I say with a smile.

"No discomfort from being tied to my bed like this?"

"Definitely not." Discomfort is the last thing I'm feeling.

He stares at me from the end of his bed. My arms are stretched out on either side of me and my legs are spread wide. And Knox has never looked at me with such a hungry and reverent expression in his blue eyes that are darkened with lust.

"Lift your hips, baby," he says before sliding the wedge underneath me. The position is completely foreign to me but not uncomfortable.

Knox runs one finger through my center, gathering my wetness and rubbing it over my clit.

"Stop teasing me," I groan.

"Look at you," he says as I wiggle my hips. "So needy for me."

"God, yes, I am." I'm not the least bit ashamed to be begging at this point. I need him to fill me. I need to come again. I need him to do *something* and stop fucking tormenting me.

After he sheathes himself in latex, he crawls over me, holding his weight on his arms. When he lines up exactly where I need him, Knox finally sinks inside of me. His movements are slow and steady. Each thrust forward goes deeper than the one before, as though he's making sure I'm adjusting to him. His cock is definitely bigger than his two fingers, and while I appreciate him taking his time, I want to feel him buried deep inside of me.

When he pulls out, I beg, "Please, Knox. Give me everything."

His gaze bores into me, and with one thrust of his hips, he seats himself fully. I let out a cry, and Knox groans as he begins pumping into me with long, deep strokes. I've never felt so full. It's heaven. It's overwhelming. It's everything I thought sex with this man would be—and so much more. My entire body is overcome with a euphoria I've never experienced with each and every thrust.

"Fuck, Mia. Do you feel that?"

"Yes, yes, yes," I chant. I feel it all. Every emotion, the rightness, the connection I've never had before. I feel it all with him.

His hips continue to rock against mine at a pace meant to draw out the orgasm quickly building inside of me. There's nothing I can do, nowhere I can move, and there's a freedom in that I never would have expected. The only thing for me to do is feel every inch of him sliding in and out of me, taking me higher and higher.

Until I break.

My body shakes with the ecstasy that ricochets through me at lightning speed. I cry out over and over, feeling every pulse of my pussy around Knox's cock, feeling so full and so grounded while, at the same time, it's as though I'm flying through the ether on a high I've never experienced.

"Oh, God. Knox," I scream between the moans falling from my lips.

Knox throws his head back as sweat drips down his temples. His jaw is tight before he opens his mouth and lets out an animalistic roar.

"Fuck, Mia," he yells as his cock jerks inside of me while he empties himself into the condom. His hips slow as we both ease down. When his eyes meet mine, there's a look of awe in them.

"Holy shit, baby, I've never..." his voice trails off, but I don't need him to tell me. I've never experienced something like that, either.

He lowers his head to my face, still keeping his weight off me, and peppers kisses along my forehead and down my nose before reaching my lips.

"You are exquisite," he says, holding my gaze.

I smile because, honestly, I'm so overcome with emotion, I'm not sure where to begin. There are a million things that want to fall from my mouth, words that could change everything, but now's not the time to say any of them.

Carefully, Knox sits back and removes himself from my body. He stands from the bed and walks to where my hands are bound. He removes the soft leather and brings my wrist to his lips, kissing me there without breaking eye contact. He moves to the wedge under me and slides it free before moving to the end of the bed. He holds my ankles and does the same thing, unstraps me, then places an adoring kiss where the cuff was before moving on. When he releases my last binding, he grabs a tissue and removes his condom, as though he wants to make sure I'm released before he pays any mind to himself.

He leans over me and cups my cheek in his large palm, then places a light kiss on my lips.

"I'll be right back," he says softly, then heads into his en suite bathroom. I hear water running moments later, then Knox comes back into the room, sweeping me up in his arms.

"I can walk, you know," I say, giggling as he carries me into the bathroom.

"You can, but I like taking care of you."

Well, if that isn't one of the sweetest damn things he could say to me right now.

He sits on the edge of his large marble tub that looks like it should be in a fancy hotel or something before placing me on his lap. His hand tests the water while the tub fills. All the while, he peppers light kisses over my shoulder, then sweeps my hair up while his lips travel across the back of my neck to my other shoulder. It's not rushed. Hell, it's not even meant to excite me and get me ready for another round with him. His kisses are worshipful and sweet, as though he's thanking me without saying the words.

When the bathtub is full enough for him, he stands and places me on my feet before holding out his hand. I take it and allow him to help me into the large tub, holding on as I sit down near the middle. A long sigh escapes me as the warm water washes over my skin.

Knox climbs in next and lowers himself behind me. When he pulls my back against his broad chest, I relax into him. He begins running his hands up and down my arms as he places more kisses against my shoulders.

"Sore?" he asks as his hands slip from my arms to the tops of my thighs. "I don't imagine you're used to staying in that position for as long as you were."

"I'm good," I assure him. "Actually, I'm more than good," I say, tilting my head toward him with a small smile on my lips.

"Mia, I can't tell you what it means to me that you trusted me with your body. You are absolutely breathtaking."

"That was...I can't even explain."

"Try," he says, imploring me with his eyes.

"I never knew it could be like that. Like I could let go of everything and be so in the moment that nothing else exists apart from the things you were doing and the way it made me feel. It was as though you saw inside of me and knew what I needed without me having to tell you. And I trusted you to take care of me. I knew if something happened that I wasn't on board with, you would stop.

But I also had every faith that you wouldn't do anything I didn't like. There was a connection I've never felt."

"That's exactly how you should always feel with me, sweetheart. And I felt it too, Mia. God, watching the way you lit up for me and the way you looked at me, I could feel that trust, that passion. It was...everything."

I rest my head against his shoulder as my fingertips glide along his strong thighs bracketed against my own. There was never a moment when I thought this would actually be a reality, but as we sit here, I can't imagine ever *not* having this.

Knox grabs a beige sponge and pours some bodywash into it before dipping it in the water and squeezing the sponge until he creates a thick lather. It smells like him, woodsy and citrusy.

"Sorry, this is all I have. I'll make sure to stock up on yours tomorrow."

I smile as he runs the sponge up and down my arms, over my breasts, and down my stomach.

"That's okay. I don't mind smelling like you," I say, turning toward him in time to see the corner of his mouth tip in a small grin. "Besides, how do you know what kind of bodywash I use?"

"I may have taken a peek when you were passed out in your bed the other night."

Jesus, that was only a few nights ago. It feels like a lifetime.

"Is it strange to you that, until four days ago, we'd barely spoken?"

Knox tilts his head back and forth. "Yes and no." His hand reaches for my chin and he swivels my head so I'm facing him, making sure I really see and hear him. "Make no mistake, I knew I wanted you long before that night. I wanted you from the first time I saw you at Thorn and Thistle when you swept in, pissed off about something, and ordered a whiskey seven. I wanted you when I saw you at my brother's the night Lucy's house was broken into. In fact, after that night, I told all my brothers you were off limits when I caught Braxton staring at your ass before I followed you home." He bends and places a kiss on my damp lips. "I knew I wanted you the night your car got a flat tire—and the night of my birthday party. I decided I wasn't going to stand in my own way anymore. So no, Mia, it's not strange for me. Everyone else? Maybe. But I don't give a shit. This is me and you. No one else gets a vote."

Jesus *fucking* Christ. For a man who, until a few days ago, didn't say much in my presence, he's sure as shit making up for it now.

"Does that scare you?" he asks.

Just like I thought, Knox is an incredibly confident man. Nothing much seems to rattle him. But when he asks me that question, I detect a tiny bit of the insecurity that he's trying to cover up.

"There's a part of me that feels like I should be scared, that we should be taking things slow because that's how I've always done it."

"Slow went out the window right about the time you pulled into my driveway tonight, sweetheart."

He leans in for another kiss and resumes running his sponge over my body.

"And I don't regret that decision for a single second," I say.

"No regrets, baby. I don't give a shit about timelines. We're here now, and that's all that I care about." Knox sets the sponge aside and uses his hands to cup the water and rinse my shoulders. "Spend the night?"

I was so unsure about this part. Do I stay? Do I go? There's no controlling the smile that lights up my face. "Of course."

"Good, because I wasn't kidding about wanting your taste on my tongue every day."

"I do have to work tomorrow, so I'll have to take off in the morning."

"That's fine. I'll set my alarm and wake you up with my tongue between your legs."

This man is literally trying to kill me, I swear. My heart rate picks up speed, and my already warm body heats further, making my skin a darker crimson than it was moments ago from being in the bath.

"I could get behind that," I say as Knox's fingers travel to my center.

"You know, I hear an orgasm before bed is a great way to help you fall asleep."

"Really?" I breathe out as his finger begins circling my clit.

He hums in affirmation. "Care to test the theory?"

"Absolutely."

So we do. And wouldn't you know, after two more orgasms, one with his mouth and another while he's buried inside of me, I have the best sleep of my entire life.

Chapter Sixteen
Mia

Knox was true to his word and woke me up this morning with his head between my thighs. Good thing, too, because I slept through the alarm he set after a night of five, count them, *five* orgasms. That was certainly a first for me. I didn't even think it was possible. He held me in his arms and told me how beautiful and perfect I was for him every single time he made me fall apart.

Which leads us to this moment. After he brought both of us to another earth-shattering orgasm with his fingers and cock, thrusting into me from behind while we lay on our sides, he disposed of the condom. He then hauled me over his damp chest and began drawing lazy circles on my back with his fingertips.

"I really have to go," I say with a tired groan.

"I know."

Neither of us moves, though.

"You gonna make me breakfast?" I ask, running my fingers through the soft hair on his chest.

"And coffee," he answers.

"I was just kidding. I can grab something on the way to work."

"Absolutely not. You're in my house and let me into your body. The least I can do is make you a plate of eggs and brew a pot of coffee."

Knox kisses the top of my head and rolls off the bed. He looks down at me, and the salacious grin on his face as he takes in my naked form is enough to make me squirm.

"Baby, you better get out of bed now; otherwise, no one is leaving this room today," he says when he sees the way my thighs rub together.

Knox walks over and pulls a pair of boxer briefs from the tall armoire on the other side of his room. When he pulls them over his ass and turns toward me, he catches me staring.

"Like what you see, sweetheart?"

"Fuck yes, I do."

A bellowing laugh escapes him as he walks over to the bed, giving me a kiss before walking out of the room.

As I dress, it hits me even harder than it did yesterday. Knox Turner spent the night in my bed, or rather, I spent the night in his. Every touch, every kiss, every word spoken of devotion and him claiming me actually happened. Things like that don't happen to me. My friends are lucky enough to have men like that in their lives. It's never been me.

But it is now.

My smile is wide when I walk out of Knox's room in the clothes I was wearing last night. The sun is barely in the sky since it's so early, but waking up at this hour didn't bother Knox in the least. He wanted me to stay the night, to sleep next to him. Though admittedly, neither of us got that much sleep.

For a few moments, I stand on the other side of his kitchen island and take in the man, in his underwear, cooking me breakfast. He doesn't notice me right away, so I have a clear and uninterrupted opportunity to stare at him. His muscular back flexes with every move as he mixes the eggs and pours them into a heated pan. He pops a few pieces of bread into the toaster and uses a spatula to stir the eggs around the pan.

"You might as well take a picture," Knox says without turning around.

I laugh, then walk behind him, raising myself on my tiptoes before kissing the space between his shoulder blades. "Sorry, I like looking at you."

He turns his head and smiles down at me, our height difference more pronounced since I'm not wearing any sort of heel.

"You don't ever apologize for staring at your man. I like when you openly ogle me." He winks and turns back to his task as I walk over to where a cup of coffee sits waiting for me. "I bought some sort of caramel creamer stuff. It's in the fridge if you want it."

"I thought you liked your coffee black?"

"I do, but you like that frou-frou shit, so when I stopped at the store the other day, I grabbed a bottle."

After all the orgasms, after all the sweet words...that's the thing that has my eyes filling with tears. He thought of me when he was at the store. He knew my preference for coffee and grabbed a bottle of creamer. No one's ever done that for me. No one's ever thought of me when I wasn't right in front of them—not enough to remember something so seemingly trivial and go out of their way to brighten my day with a thoughtful gesture like that.

Walking back over to him, I wrap my arms around his waist from behind and press my forehead against his back. Knox has no idea that he has me about to cry into my caramel-flavored coffee. He simply places one of his strong hands over mine and continues scrambling the eggs.

I clear my throat and walk over to the fridge, grabbing the creamer and pouring a healthy amount into it before I notice Knox watching how I prepare my coffee.

When I take a sip, a long moan escapes. "This is perfect. Thank you."

He smiles and walks in front of me, opening the cabinet behind me to grab a couple plates. He leans down and places a kiss on my lips, finishing it with a teasing bite to my lower lip.

"Careful of those sounds that come out of your mouth, sweetheart. Unless you want me to say fuck the eggs and eat you on the counter instead."

"If I didn't have to work today, I'd say that sounds like the best idea you've had so far this morning."

He tilts his head to the side. "Really? That's my best idea today?" His knowing smirk puts a smile on my face.

"Well, I guess you had some pretty good ones earlier."

His chest rumbles with laughter as he walks back over to his stove and dishes scrambled eggs onto plates before sprinkling both servings with a little cheese. The toast pops up, and when I attempt to grab a knife to butter it, Knox takes the knife from my hands and nods toward the kitchen island. "Sit."

"Yes, sir," I say, and Knox growls.

"Careful. I've never been particularly interested in having my woman call me sir, but you might have me rethinking that particular kink."

Knox finishes with the toast before setting both plates down and coming around to sit next to me. We eat in companionable silence, his hand on my knee and my fingers laced through his. That's one thing that I've come to love about Knox in the last few days. He's so tactile. Some touches are meant to elicit a response, but ones like these—or when we were on his bike or having dinner—are simply about connection. I never considered myself a touchy person, but as with most things involving Knox, I'm learning something new about myself.

When I finish, he takes the plate and sets it in the sink as I grab my purse and keys before slipping into my shoes. Knox puts on his boots, still only in his underwear and walks me to my car.

"So this is why you live on so much property. You can walk around in your underwear without the prying eyes of neighbors," I joke.

He laughs and grabs me around the waist before I can get in my car. "No, but it's an added benefit." He dips his head and presses his mouth against mine. God, if I didn't have to go to work, this would lead to so much more.

"Do you have plans tonight?" he asks when he pulls away.

"I was going to hang with Charlie for a bit at the bar. Lucy's working, which means Jude will probably be there..."

"I don't give a shit where Jude is. If you're going to be there, then I want to be there, too. If that's okay. I don't want to interrupt any 'girl gang time' or whatever you guys call it."

I laugh, thinking of all the stupid names Lucy's given our group of friends—and the fact that they've all been vetoed. Thankfully.

"I'd love to see you tonight," I say, kissing him one more time before he opens the car door, and I sit down.

"Drive safe. I'll see you later, sweetheart." Knox closes the door, and I pull away, looking back in my rearview mirror at the man still standing in his driveway before I turn onto the main road.

And the goofy smile stays on my face the entire drive back to my house.

Walking into the library, I feel as though I'm floating. The day goes by in a blur of paperwork, ordering a few things for the teachers and assisting three honors classes with their research projects. All in all, a normal day, but I'm happier than I've been in a long time. I'm finishing up finalizing a book order when Leonard, or *Mr. Miller*, as he apparently prefers to be called, walks into my office.

"I just wanted to let you know the board has received your proposal and they'll be reviewing it next week," he says, having a seat in front of my desk—without being invited.

Obviously I already knew this, considering I'm the one who turned it in.

"Thank you, Mr. Miller," I reply and watch as he looks around my office. The man hasn't gotten up from his seat, so that makes me think he has something else to say. What that is, I have no idea. I really don't understand why he's in here at the end of the day when everyone is on their way out like I should be.

"Is there something else I can help you with?" I'm excited to leave, go home and change, then head to

Thorn and Thistle to see Charlie. And Knox. And this asshole is standing in the way of it.

"You know, your contract is up for renewal as well," he finally says.

"I'm aware."

I was hired here because the last librarian who held my position retired. It just so happened to coincide with moving back to Shine, but I was only offered a two-year contract at the time. I've done a damn good job, so there wouldn't be any reason not to renew my contract. As far as I know, not many people are graduating with a degree in library science and moving to Shine in the hopes of becoming the only high school's librarian.

"The district takes my recommendation into consideration when they renew contracts. Did you know that?" His tone is becoming a little hostile, and quite frankly, it's making me uncomfortable.

"I would assume so, yes."

"So, if I had an employee who seemed to spend all her free time hanging out with a criminal organization and those associated with that organization, how do you expect me in good conscience to recommend her for a position that puts her in the company of children?"

Is this guy fucking kidding me right now?

I lean back in my seat, considering how I'm going to approach this professionally because my instinct is to tell him to get the fuck out of my office or for him to take his Napolean complex and shove it straight up his ass. Or both.

"I'm not exactly sure which organization you are referring to, seeing as there isn't one in Shine that has been accused or convicted by a court of law of being one."

"Don't play stupid with me, Mia. I know exactly who and what the Black Roses are."

"A group of men who own several local businesses and like to ride motorcycles?" My head tilts to the side as I give him a blank expression. His stare is anything but blank though. It's filled with simmering rage, which is strange considering as far as I know, he has zero ties to the MC. He's not even from here. In fact, he hasn't been at the school much longer than me.

He blinks slowly and when Leonard opens his eyes again, the rage has turned into the normal look of annoyance he usually has on his face. How this man was hired in this position is beyond me.

"I'm going to give you some friendly advice, Mia." *Oh, this is going to be fucking good.* "You may want to think about who you spend your time with outside of school. People are watching, and if they see things that don't align with our values, there may be consequences."

"I can assure you, Mr. Miller, there is nothing that I do outside of school hours that could ever be called into question. My family has a long history in this town. In fact, my grandmother used to be on that very school board that you seem to be threatening me with. She's still active in this community, as well. She'll be at the Spring Fling. Maybe it would be in your best interest to introduce yourself to the matriarch of one of the oldest families in Shine." Man, I can really pull off that entitled rich-bitch attitude when I want.

Leonard stands from his seat abruptly and heads to the door. "I was coming to you as a courtesy, Mia. Remember that." He walks out of my office and shuts the door behind him, leaving me absolutely fuming.

Because I'm a mature adult, I hold up both my middle fingers at the closed door and mouth *fuck you, fuck you, fuck you*. Does my silent tirade at the asshole who has consistently pissed me off since I came to this school make me feel better? Yes, yes it does.

I pack my bag up with fast and angry movements, shoving my computer and files into my briefcase. Grabbing my phone and the rest of my things, I stomp toward the door and slam my palm against the light switch to turn it off.

When I get to the parking lot, Leonard's car is still there. The man obviously has no life, considering it's well after school hours, and he's still sitting in his stupid office behind his stupid desk while the rest of the world actually goes out and lives their lives.

Okay, so maybe my angry outburst didn't help as much as I was hoping.

CHAPTER SEVENTEEN
MIA

When I get home, I unload everything on my kitchen table. The fifteen-minute drive did me good, and I'm a touch less irritated than when I left the school.

Charlie said she was going to be at the bar around six, so I have about an hour to kill before I need to leave.

Deciding to check on my grandmother and say hello, I trek across the expansive lawn separating our two houses. Maybe this will be the year I buy a little golf cart to go between our houses. It's not that it's a ridiculously long walk, but it would be fun to cross the couple of acres in a golf cart. Now that I think about it, my grandmother would probably have a ball riding around in it.

I enter through the kitchen door and walk through the house, finding my grandmother in the living room with a book in her hand.

"What is it this time?" I look at the cover of the novel she's lowered to her lap as I come to sit next to her. "*The Rake and His Lady*. Is this another novel about Scottish history?" I ask with a smirk.

"No, dear. This one is about British aristocracy. Very educational." It never ceases to amaze me how my grandma can say half the things that come out of her mouth with a straight face—and this is no exception. "Are you hungry? I can heat something up for you."

I give her a small smile. "No, thanks. I just wanted to say hi before I left for the night."

"Spending the night with your beau?" she asks while arching an eyebrow.

"Maybe," I say through a yawn.

"Looks like that plate of food worked a little too well. You seem to be quite tired today, my dear."

"Grandma!"

"What? I'm just saying it looks like you may have lost a few hours of sleep last night. I'm not judging you."

"I'm not discussing my *sleeping* habits with you."

"Trust me, I don't need to know the details. As long as you're happy, that's all I care about."

"I'm very happy." Blissfully, actually. What's also surprising to me is this very unaccustomed feeling of security and comfort I've found with Knox. In past relationships, I never felt like I fit or like my partner was making an effort to integrate our lives, even after months of dating. But Knox is the complete opposite. It's the small things, like making sure my bath products are in his house or a creamer that he thought I would like is in his fridge. Those little things mean the world to me.

"I had no doubt you would be, dear."

A light laugh tumbles out of me. "You just know everything, don't you," I say in a teasing tone.

"Most things, yes. But I wouldn't be so bold as to say *everything*." My grandmother chuckles and shoots me a wink.

"I love you," I say on a laugh and stand from her couch. "I'll see you tomorrow morning."

"If Knox spends the night, bring him for coffee."

"Okay, Grandma."

I bend and give her a kiss on the cheek before leaving.

Lucy is pouring drinks for a few regulars as I step inside Thorn and Thistle. I recognize one of them as the man who tried to buy me a drink last time I was here, otherwise known as the night I drank way too much vodka and made a complete ass out of myself in front of Knox. All's well that ends well, I guess.

Lucy smiles when she sees me sit and comes bounding over. "A little birdy told me you spent the night at a certain someone's house last night. What's that make it? Three nights this week?"

"Technically. But I'm counting it as two, considering I wasn't exactly in a coherent state the first time."

Her smile is so wide she looks like a damn shark showing off all their teeth. "What do you want to drink tonight?"

"Whiskey seven."

She makes the drink and walks back over, leaning her elbows on the bar top. "So, you and Knox have finally figured your shit out."

"I guess, though I don't know how much shit there really was."

"Trust me, my amazing friend who never thought she was enough for the lumberjack biker who thought you were too good for him, there was shit."

"I love the way you simplify our history," I say, shaking my head with a laugh.

"I just call it like I see it, sister."

"How on earth did you find out I spent the night at his house last night? Did you talk to my grandma or something?" Come to think of it, the last thing I need is those two getting together. I can only imagine the shenanigans that would ensue.

Lucy blows out a breath and her excitement seems to dim a bit. "Cece was going through something last night. Didn't sleep again, and we woke up this morning to two dozen loaves of bread in our kitchen. Jude dropped some off to Linc and Charlie, then the guys took a few over to Knox's. Apparently, Knox hadn't cleaned up the breakfast dishes yet, and Jude asked him about who was over. Then he promptly texted to give me the tea."

I bark out a laugh. "Jesus, I never pegged him for a gossip."

"I've learned a lot about these guys that I never would have imagined."

That's certainly becoming more clear to me after the conversations I've had with Knox. I never would have thought the man was so sweet. Sure, I always thought he was gorgeous, even when I was way too young to do anything about it, but I never realized he was thoughtful and kind, at least not to the extent I've seen in the last couple of days. He's an open book once you get through his tough layers. Or once he deems you worthy. There's a sense of happiness and satisfaction that fills me knowing that now includes me.

"How was work today?" Lucy asks, leaning against the bar.

It wasn't that long ago Lucy and Charlie listened to my rant about the weird interaction with Leonard as I was getting into my car a few weeks ago. "My asshole VP is back at it again. This time it's not about my lack of focus because I have a life outside of work that's the issue. It's *whom* I spend my time with when I'm not at work."

"What the fuck does that mean?" Lucy asks, scrunching her brows together.

The door to the bar opens, and Charlie rushes in. "Okay, the guys are right behind me, but I just wanted to squeal for a minute about how excited I am about you and Knox," she says as she comes to sit next to me. "I figured I'd do it before they walk in so I don't make a big deal of it in front of them and it becomes a whole thing." And squeal she does.

One of the things I love about Charlie is her unabashed excitement for other people's happiness. She had a shitty few years before leaving her hometown, but she never lost the kindness in her heart.

Linc opens the door, and Jude and Knox walk in after him.

"Why did you jump off the bike and run in here like your hair was on fire, Charlie Bear?"

"I had to pee," she answers with a completely straight face.

Linc cocks a brow but doesn't call her out. I'm pretty sure he knows she's full of shit, especially considering she's terrible at lying.

Knox walks over to me and plants a kiss on my lips. "Missed you," he whispers against my mouth before pulling away.

When I pull myself out of my momentary stupor that usually happens when Knox is around, or when he says sweet things that I'm still not used to, Charlie's eyes dart between us with her mouth hanging open. A peanut hits her on the side of her cheek, and she whirls around toward Lucy.

"What the hell was that for?" she asks, swiping the salt from her skin.

"I was gonna see if I could make it in. I think I need to work on my aim."

"You're an asshole," Charlie says.

Lucy shrugs before turning and grabbing three beers for the guys. Knox takes a seat next to me with Jude on his other side and Linc sits next to his girlfriend, throwing an arm on the back of her stool.

"Mia was just telling me another story about her asshole vice principal," she says, and Knox turns his head toward me.

"What's going on with him now?" he asks.

Knox has heard all kinds of stories about the man since he was usually here when I'd come in after work complaining about what a dick the guy is. He never really said anything, but that was a different time, and things have changed.

I take a sip of my cocktail and lean back in my chair. "He was saying I need to be careful about who I spend my time with, and it shouldn't include criminals in a motorcycle gang. I asked him what the club had been convicted of. Then made sure he understood how deep my roots are in this town after he threatened to give a bad review to the school district because my contract is up for renewal."

Knox's jaw is tense, and his eyes dart to Linc, then back to me. "I'll take care of it."

In all the times he's overheard me bitching about work stuff, he's never had this kind of reaction.

"No," I say, shaking my head. "He can't actually do anything. I mean, he could, but I think my reputation speaks for itself. Plus, if he tries, I'm sure there are several tenured teachers who would have a fit." They love me at that school, not only because of how I stay on top of making sure they have the materials they need to teach but also because of my interactions and the help I provide their students.

"I don't like it, Mia. He has no right to talk to you like that," Knox says.

"I completely agree. I think I made my point clear, but if anything else comes out of his stupid mouth, I'll file a complaint or something." The problem with this guy, though, is he skirts the boundaries. Not to mention, there may be people in the district who agree with him. It's a can of worms I'd rather not open.

Knox doesn't say anything else, but he still looks far from happy.

"Can we drop it now? The guy's an asshole, so there's nothing new there, and what I definitely don't want to do on my time off is talk about him or worry about his bullshit," I say, leaning in to press my lips against Knox's. "I appreciate you wanting to protect me, but I've dealt with guys like this before. It'll blow over."

"But before, I wasn't there to put punks like that in their place," he says.

"Which is why I'm so good at it now. I've always done it myself." I smile, and this time he returns it. "My grandmother wants you to come over in the morning for coffee."

"Yeah? Is that an invitation to spend the night?" he asks, the corner of his lips tipping up in a smirk.

"Absolutely."

This has been one of the best, most exhausting weeks of my life. My body isn't used to going without sleep as much as it has, but I'll never be upset over why I'm losing sleep. I've decided I'd rather adjust to getting a little less sleep and a lot more orgasms than the other way around. Knox and I have spent every night together, either at his place or mine.

He kept true to his word and bought me my preferred bodywash, shampoo and conditioner for his place. He's even gone out of his way and got everything I use to get ready, including a hairdryer, a flat iron, and a curling iron. I would have loved to be a fly on the wall when he walked up to check out with all of that. He tried to get me all the makeup I wear, not that it's a lot, but I told him that was too much. I can throw my makeup bag in my overnight bag. He's doing more than trying to make space for me; he's filling that space with things to make my life easier when I stay the night at his place.

I had a feeling being in a relationship with a man like him was going to be different, I just didn't realize how much I wanted different. To have someone care so much about saving me an hour in the morning or go out of their way to make life easier for me without needing a pat on the back is the complete opposite of anything

I'm used to. But to Knox, it's not going out of his way. It's simply something he does.

When Tanya shows up at the high school gymnasium to help put things together for the spring festival happening tomorrow, she walks in with several bags hanging from her arms and two cups with labels from Cool Beans.

"One of these is for you, honey," she says, handing me the coffees so she can set the bags down. "Knox said you like caramel lattes."

"Thank you so much," I say, taking a drink from the cup with my name on it. "That's exactly what I needed."

Tanya puts the bags on a table and begins unloading several things that we're going to use for carnival game prizes for the kids. "Don't mention it. I needed a little pick-me-up, and I figured you probably would, too."

"You're amazing for volunteering to help with all this, especially on a Friday night."

"I've always loved helping out with this one. Trick and Arthur are around here somewhere setting up booths and whatever else. Which basically means they're directing everyone else how to do it."

We both laugh, knowing exactly what their "help" entails.

A small, familiar shiver runs up my spine as I'm sorting carnival prizes into piles. I look up to see Knox walking across the gym, his focus locked on me.

"Hey, sweetheart," he says when he wraps his arm around my waist and leans down for a kiss.

"Hey, yourself." I have to remind myself that not only am I at work, but I'm in front of his mother. That doesn't stop the blush from creeping up my neck with Knox so close. It also doesn't stop my mouth from watering while I take in the way his jeans fit over his strong thighs or the way the blue flannel he's wearing under his cut makes his eyes more piercing than normal.

"Hi, son," Tanya says, and Knox releases me and gives his mom a hug. "Where's your brother?"

"I'm right here," Linc says, walking up behind her with Ozzy and Barrett.

"Perfect. Have you seen Gramps and Trick? They're supposed to be coordinating the booth setup."

"We're going to go find them now. I wanted to say hi first," Knox says.

"I'm sure you did," Tanya says with a knowing grin.

Knox turns to me and winks. "Haven't seen my girl since this morning. Can you blame me?" he asks without taking his gaze from mine.

He really needs to stop being so damn perfect.

"No, son, I can't. But the booths and carnival games aren't going to set themselves up. Ozzy, make sure your dad doesn't try to do too much. He'll act like he's fine, but I'd rather him not work so damn hard that he can't hold a coffee cup tomorrow."

"I thought his new medication was helping the arthritis," Ozzy says with a furrow in his brow.

"It is, which makes him think he can do more than he's supposed to."

Ozzy nods and clasps Linc on the back. "Let's go."

The three bikers begin to walk across the gym, and it doesn't escape my attention the thirsty looks they get from some of the women they pass.

"Can I take you out for dinner after we're done here?" Knox asks.

"Of course." My lips tilt in a small smile.

"Okay, text me when you're done." Knox leans down and kisses me before kissing his mom on the cheek and heading in the direction that Ozzy, Linc and Barrett went.

"That boy is smitten with you, girl," Tanya says, smiling in my direction.

"The feeling's mutual," I say, returning her grin.

"You know, when I called him to talk to him about helping Trick and Arthur and asked if he knew what you liked from Cool Beans, I didn't expect him to know. And I certainly didn't expect him to send me the money to buy both of us coffee." Tanya stops sorting and turns to me. "I don't think that boy has ever remembered a coffee order, and he certainly never thought to send me money to buy a girl coffee. Hell, he never even brought a girl home in high school."

That reminds me of the conversation we had about Knox and the girls he was with in high school. How he was their dirty little secret.

"Yeah, he mentioned he didn't date a lot in high school."

"Dated, no. He hasn't done any of that. I also know that he wouldn't have made it a point to come in here so he could see you just because he wanted to kiss you if he wasn't serious about where this is going between you two."

I don't necessarily need the validation from Tanya because Knox has done a spectacular job at making sure I know how he feels every day, but it sure as hell doesn't hurt.

"It's so different from what I'm used to. I've never been with someone who knows exactly what I need or want without me having to tell them a hundred times. I mean, the first time I spent the night at his house, he bought me the creamer I like. He had no idea when I was going to be there, but he made sure to have it for me." My face scrunches up, and I shoot her an apologetic look. "I'm sorry. I probably shouldn't have said anything about spending the night at your son's house."

Tanya throws her head back in laughter for a moment before collecting herself. "Honey, I am well aware of what my boys get up to. I'm also well aware of how they usually act around the women they get up to those things with. He's different with you, just like I knew the moment Charlie came around—she was it for Linc. My boys don't open their hearts easily. They're guarded. Maybe that was my fault for having a broken picker when it came to their fathers." She shrugs and looks off into the distance for several beats before her focus is directed back to me. "They went through a lot, and they don't give their hearts away easily—or ever. But I see the same thing with Knox as I saw with Linc. When they go in, they go *all* in. And I want you to know how happy I am. Not that you need my approval, but you have it."

"That honestly means more to me than you think. I didn't grow up with parents who cared enough about me to ever have this kind of conversation with the person I was dating. Knox is lucky to have you."

Tanya smiles and tilts her head as she studies me. "I'm well versed in having parents that aren't particularly interested in actually being parents, shall we say." Tanya reaches over and touches my arm. "And you have me now, too. Family means something different in the club. We protect our own, and you're one of ours now, honey. Remember that."

I clear my throat, holding back the tears. It's not that I didn't think the club or Tanya didn't care about me. But hearing her say that, say that I was part of a bigger family now, it fills a part of me that I'd long ago accepted I didn't have. I thought I didn't need it. Obviously, my reaction is proving that wrong.

"What are you doing just standing around?" I hear a familiar voice call.

I turn and see my grandmother, along with Maizie and Colby, walking up to us.

"What are you doing here?" I ask as I give my grandmother a hug.

"You didn't think I was going to let you have all the fun, did you? We're here to help," she says, smiling broadly.

"Hi, Elaine," Tanya says, also giving my grandmother a hug. "I thought maybe you were going to sit this one out."

My grandmother waves her hand. "Nonsense. I've been a part of this festival since you've been in diapers. This old lady is far from throwing in the towel."

"If this is what old looks like, I can only be so lucky," Tanya says.

"You and me both," Maizie agrees as I lean in to hug my friend.

We watch my grandmother set her large designer bag under the table so it's out of the way, and she starts going over what we've been doing, adding to the pile with everything she brought.

"How did this happen?" I quietly ask Maizie as Tanya explains the plan for the prizes.

Maizie shrugs. "She called and asked if I could give her a ride over here because she didn't want to pester you. When we picked her up, she had us take her to the party store in Ayre. She practically bought out the whole place. Even had Colby helping her. She said he would know what the kids want. I honestly didn't think she still had my phone number."

I knew they talked when Maizie's grandmother passed since our grandparents were friends, and Maizie needed help with arranging the funeral, but I had no idea my grandmother still had her number, either.

"Okay, you two. These bags aren't going to fill themselves. Colby, come sit by me and show me how you think we should put all this together."

Maizie's son bounds over to my grandma and studies what's on the table.

My friend smiles at the scene in front of her and clears her throat much in the same way I had to earlier.

I link my arm through hers and squeeze. "You miss your grandma, huh?"

"So much," she says in a rough whisper. "Family is so important, and you don't realize how much until you don't have it anymore." She smiles at me, then moves to stand next to my grandma and her son.

"Get on over here, girl," my grandmother tells me.

"Yes, ma'am."

Chapter Eighteen
Knox

Being with Mia has given me a new appreciation for being an early riser. Normally, I'd roll out of bed whenever I felt like it and go about my business. Unless I had to be somewhere early for the club. But mornings look a little different when you date the school librarian. I make sure to send her on her way to work with a wide smile on her face by waking her up with either my tongue or cock. Sometimes both if we have time. I was serious when I told her I didn't want a day to go by without her taste on my lips. I'm a glutton for the woman, and that's not changing anytime soon. I was hoping to have a chance to leisurely wake up next to her so I could take my time this morning, but apparently, she volunteered to help with the parade staging that starts at the high school.

Does that mean I'm going to let her out of her bed without making her come? Fuck no.

After she screams my name while I'm buried deep inside of her—and I let out the roar of my own release—we get in the shower. The last two nights have been spent at my house, so Mia wanted to make sure we were at hers this morning so we could have morning coffee with her grandmother. It's a little tradition they have, and her spending time away from her own house has cut into that. Of course, Mrs. Dawson, or Elaine as she's insisted I call her time and time again, doesn't seem to mind. I think the woman sees how badly she needs someone of her own to take care of her the way she deserves. It's obvious that Mia has always been the one doing that for other people. I've caught her staring at us a couple of times, and the smile she wears tells me she's happy her granddaughter finally has that.

After quickly getting dressed and ready for the day, we walk hand in hand to her grandmother's house. Mia knocks, then lets herself in the back door before her grandmother answers.

"Good morning," she calls into the house.

Elaine comes around the corner, already dressed as though she's about to leave. "Oh, I thought you'd be getting an early start this morning," she says, smiling. "I have a pot of coffee ready if you'd like, but I'm leaving in a few minutes."

"I didn't realize you had plans this morning. Are you helping with the parade?"

There's a knock at the front door, and Mia looks to where the sound came from, then back to her grandmother with confusion.

"Knox, be a dear and get the door for me. Tell him I'm almost ready."

I nod and head through the hall toward the front of the house and pull the door open. Gramps is standing on the other side with a small bouquet of flowers in his hand.

"Good morning, Knox. I'm here for Elaine."

"Hey, Gramps," I say with an amused grin on my face. "Come on in. Elaine will be right out."

"Didn't know you were going to be here," he says.

"Didn't know you were, either."

"Elaine and I have known each other for years. I'm taking her out to breakfast before the festival gets underway."

"You don't owe me an explanation. I'm not her keeper."

"Good morning, Arthur," Elaine says, coming from the kitchen, followed by Mia.

"Elaine, you look beautiful today," Gramps says.

She smiles at him and, if I'm not mistaken, has the same blush that covers Mia's neck and cheeks when I pay her a compliment.

Gramps holds out the flowers to Elaine and she accepts them, taking a long whiff of the fragrant buds. "Thank you so much, Arthur. I love fresh flowers."

Gramps stands with a proud smile on his face and Elaine hands the bouquet to Mia. "Would you mind putting these in water for me, dear?"

Mia takes the flowers and smiles. "Of course not. We'll see you at the festival."

Gramps opens the door for Elaine and offers his arm as they walk to his truck.

"Is he courting my grandmother?" Mia asks, watching Gramps help her grandmother into his truck.

"Looks like," I reply.

She giggles and walks back toward the kitchen. "Come on," she calls. "Let's have some coffee, then I need to get going."

Apparently, I'm not the only man who has been taken in by the Dawson women's irresistible charm.

After dropping Mia at the high school, I head to my brother's place. When I walk in, Linc is sitting on his couch with coffee in hand, and Jude is in one of the chairs on the opposite side of the room.

"Hey, grab a cup," Linc says, holding up his mug.

I pour myself some coffee, then head back into the living room and have a seat.

"Where's Charlie?" I ask.

"Over at my place," Jude answers.

"I have a feeling the two of you living next door is a smoke screen for the girls to basically still live together." I swear, anytime I come visit, one of the girls is at the other's house while either Jude or Linc is hanging out in the other house.

Both my brother and Jude shrug, completely non-plussed.

"You coming to help today?" I ask Jude.

"Of course. Tanya would have my arse if I skipped out."

"What about Charlie and Lucy?" I ask.

"Lucy is working so Maizie can take Colby to the festival," Jude says.

"Charlie is meeting us there later. She needs to work on her psych paper for a few hours." Linc says.

My phone vibrates with a text. When I pull it out and open my messages, there's a picture of Mia standing in front of a dunk tank with a wide smile on her face.

Mia: *What would I have to do to get you to be the dunkee today?*

Me: *No way in hell am I getting in there, sweetheart. I'll freeze my balls off, which would be a travesty for the both of us.*

I turn to Jude. "Have you had a chance to talk to your brother about the dead girl they found?" A couple weeks ago, the mutilated body of a woman was found in a shallow grave outside of Boston. It looked like there were ties to the women found in New York last year. Seeing as Liam has had some dealings with the now-dead skin traders who worked out of New York, Ozzy is worried that this shit is back in Massachu-setts—and way too fucking close to home again.

"He hasn't found anything that could be linked back to anyone defying Petrov and getting back in the skin trade after they were explicitly told it's off the table," Jude answers.

Nikolai Petrov runs the New York Bratva, and it was his father who was dealing in women.

Key word being *was*.

My phone dings again, and it's another picture, this time of Mia in front of a kissing booth.

Mia: *Fine. But I'm going to volunteer in this one then.*

Me: *Over my dead body, or rather the dead body of any man who attempts to claim that particular prize. Those lips are for me alone, Mia.*

Mia: *Touchy this morning, aren't you?*

Me: *Not as touchy as I'd like to have been.*

Mia: *Ugh. I walked right into that one.*

Me: *Sorry, sweetheart. That was too easy.*

Mia: *Your mom's here and asking quote "where the hell are Knox and Linc?" It's safe to say you guys should get here soon.*

Me: *On our way.*

"Mia texted. We need to go," I say as I stand from my chair.

"Oh, the little woman is already calling the shots?" Jude asks while laughing.

Like this fucking guy has any room to talk.

"One," I say, holding up a finger. "Yes, and don't act like your woman doesn't one-hundred-percent wear the pants in your relationship. And two," I hold up another finger. "My mom is looking for us."

Jude and Linc's eyebrows shoot up, and they both stand from their seats, all of us filing into the kitchen to empty our cups.

I chuckle at the fact that all it takes is mentioning my mom and even the toughest bikers I know jump to attention.

The three of us park our bikes next to where the rest of the Black Roses have parked theirs in the lot at the school. Since the main road was closed for the parade, we had to take the back way in. I spot a man in the parking lot, eyeing us as we get off our bikes. I don't like the stern look he has on his face, but I'm accustomed to guys who aren't in the club giving us that type of angry scowl. I could really care less that some punk bitches are intimidated by me and my brothers. They know damn well all they can do is sit there with pissed-off looks on their faces. None of them actually have the balls to say anything. But because I'm me, I look right at the guy and give him a little chin lift. He turns on his heels and stomps away being followed by Jude and Linc's laughter.

"Who the fuck was that asshole?" Jude asks.

"No clue," I respond and head in to find my woman.

The parade has ended, and now all the kids are running around to get in line for the face painting or one of the many game booths that are still being set up.

"You're late," my mother scolds, coming from behind me.

"It's Knox's fault," Linc tells her with a shit-eating grin on his face.

"Lincoln Anderson, you have two feet and a head of your own. Don't try to blame your brother for not being here on time."

Jude snickers next to him, but all that does is redirect my mom's focus to him. "Same goes for you, Jude."

The Englishman looks sufficiently chided, not that it takes more than a few words from my mom to do the trick, and apologizes.

"I need you to help with setting up the goldfish toss," she says to my brother. "Jude, you go help set up the dessert raffle, and Knox, go find Mia. I think she's over at the fish pool."

Every year, we have a giant catch-and-release pool set up for the kids to try their hand at fishing. It was one of my favorite things to do when I came here with my brother when we were kids.

I find Mia next to the pool, talking with one of the guys who runs it for the kids. Lo and behold, it's the same guy who wanted to buy Mia a drink the other night at Thorn and Thistle.

"Hey, sweetheart," I say, coming up to her and grabbing her around the waist, placing a hard kiss on her mouth. Mia instantly melts into the kiss as she always does.

When we separate, she turns to the man and introduces us. "Will, Knox. Knox, Will," she says, waving her hand between us.

"Nice to meet you," I say, shaking the man's hand a little more forcefully than necessary.

I catch the way he stretches his fingers at his side when I release him, and I can't help the small smirk on my face.

"Mia, I'm going to go grab the rest of the fish while one of my guys sets up the poles."

Mia turns to me before Will walks away. "How are you with a fishing pole?" she asks.

"I can hold my own," I reply, and she turns to Rusty.

"Knox is going to help with poles, too. These kids are about to swarm us."

Will nods and walks away before Mia turns her attention back to me. "Was that necessary?"

"Yes," I reply, not caring if I come across as a caveman.

"Are you going to piss a circle around any man who has ever been kind to me or even shown the smallest amount of interest?"

"That's not really my thing," I say, and she looks at me with slight irritation but smiles nonetheless.

"What am I going to do with you?"

"Give me another kiss?" I suggest with a shrug.

Mia rolls her eyes but perches on her tiptoes and plants a sweet, albeit brief, kiss on my lips.

"There, now get to work," she says, pointing at the row of fishing poles.

"Yes, ma'am," I say and salute her.

She laughs and walks away, writing something on the clipboard in her hands. I watch the way her hips sway in her tight jeans, not giving a flying fuck that I'm ogling my girl before I turn and get to work.

A few hours later, the festival is in full swing. Kids are running around on sugar highs from the sweet treats, and parents are laughing and cheering on their kids playing carnival games. I've stayed at the catch-and-release pool for most of the morning and early afternoon to help with the crowd, show the kids how to cast, and to restring the poles when needed. Since the crowd around the fish pool has cleared a bit, I tell Will I'm going to see if Mia needs help anywhere else.

As I walk through the crowd, I spot my mom talking with Trick.

"Hey, Mom, have you seen Mia?"

"Yeah, she needed to grab something out of her office."

"Thanks," I reply, walking toward the school.

I know exactly where the library is, but I'm not too sure where her office is. I walk to the front doors of the library, which are locked. Obviously, no one has been coming through this way then. Walking around to the side of the brick building, I spot Mia talking to a man whose back is to me. He looks familiar. Mia doesn't see me right away. Her gaze is focused on the man in front of her, and she looks pissed.

"You allowed that biker to kiss you in front of students and parents alike while you were performing your duties as a school librarian," the man says.

"First of all, Leonard, I am volunteering my time as a resident of Shine. The only reason the school is involved in the festival is because, as with years past, it allows the town to use this property for the festival. Second, it is highly inappropriate for you to be commenting on my private life in any capacity at any time."

"You're going to lose your job with the school. Then what? Take your clothes off for money at that perverted club they own?"

"Hey!" I holler, quickening my steps. Grabbing the man by the back of his collar, I spin him around and slam him against the wall. Well, would you look at that. It's the punk-bitch from the parking lot.

"Knox, stop," Mia says, putting her hand on my arm.

"Is this your vice principal? The one who's been giving you a bunch of shit?" I ask through gritted teeth.

"I have it under control," she says, but I'm too pissed to listen to her after what I just heard him say to my woman.

"Let me make something very clear to you, *Leonard*. No one talks to my woman like that. You have a problem with my club; you come talk to me like a fucking man. But a guy like you is too much of a pussy to confront a man like me, aren't you? You think you can tell my woman what she can and can't do? Who she can and can't spend her time with? You think you have some sort of authority over her? You threaten her job?"

"Knox!" Mia yells, this time pulling at my arm as I keep Leonard pinned against the wall.

I release the prick and take a step back.

He straightens himself and pulls at his rumpled shirt. He doesn't say anything, but he gives Mia a scathing look and turns, scurrying away like the little weasel he is. I watch him until he rounds the corner, heading the same direction I came from.

"Jesus Christ, Knox. I had it handled," Mia says.

I look at her and see the anger in her gaze is directed at me. "Are you serious?"

"Yes, I'm serious. I told you before to let me handle him. This isn't something that's going to be resolved with brute force. You putting your hands on him gives him ammunition. And until you did that, I had the upper hand."

"Yeah? And what were you doing with it?"

"I was handling it!"

Mia turns toward the door and grabs the handle, throwing it open so she can stomp away. I follow her angry steps into what I can tell is her office. Her sweet scent surrounds me, and I see a couple pictures on her desk of her and her grandmother and another one of her, Lucy and Charlie, at a color run they did last year to raise money for the women's shelter.

"You think you have everything handled all the time. That you're the one who has to manage everything and everyone. Jesus, I do the bare minimum—which is stand up for you—and you jump down my throat about it. Mia, I never said you can't take care of yourself, but I'm not going to stand back and allow that."

"You can't fight my battles for me."

"Not all of them, no. But that one?" I point toward the door that leads outside. "I sure as shit can."

"You don't understand," she shouts, holding her hands up in frustration.

"I understand better than anyone. You're so in your head all the time about taking care of everything yourself because you don't trust anyone else to do it. I understand that, for the entirety of your life, it's been your responsibility. I also understand you don't know what the hell to do with someone who wants to take that pressure off you. To be the person you can turn to. To take care of all the shit that's been resting on your shoulders for far too long. I understand because I feel the same way about you. It's fucking scary to allow another person to be the soft place for you to land and trust that they can deal with it. But I'm here, Mia." I walk over to her and lean down, taking her cheeks in my palms. "No one is going to say those kinds of things to you and walk away unscathed. No one is going to make you feel inferior because you follow your heart. No one gets to tell you how to live your life. If I see it, I'm putting a stop to it. Period. No one is allowed to treat the person I love like that."

Mia's eyes widen, and her mouth parts on a gasp. "You love me?"

"Yeah, sweetheart. I do."

I don't wait for her to say it back. My lips find hers, and I kiss her with all the emotion swelling inside of me. I love this woman. Her soul, her heart, her unending loyalty and the kindness she shows to the people she cares about. I love every inch of her. It would be impossible to spend any amount of time with the woman in my arms and not fall for her.

Her arms clutch my waist as she pulls me closer, pressing her curves against me. When her hips begin moving as she rubs herself against me, trying to find purchase, I yank my mouth away and stare into her bright eyes.

"Don't start something we can't finish," I say in a low whisper before moving my lips to the soft skin on her neck.

Mia lets out a groan, and my tongue reaches out to taste the skin below her ear as my teeth scrape her delicate earlobe.

When her fingernails scrape up the back of my neck and tangle in my hair, I decide *fuck it*—we're going to finish this right here.

I grab her by the hips and turn her quickly to face her desk, taking her hands in mine and placing them in front of her.

"Stay," I say as I walk to her office door and shut it, locking it for good measure. I doubt anyone will be coming to the library, but I like the added security that there's no chance for anyone else to see my woman's face when I make her come.

Mia's hands rest on the desk, and I notice the tips of her fingers digging into the faux wood finish. A thought runs through my mind—her wrists tied in beautiful knots with a dark-blue rope that would look perfect against her fair skin. My cock pulses against my zipper. Then all thoughts escape me when I catch the way Mia's eyes beg me to take care of the ache building inside both of us.

"I want to taste your perfect cunt, Mia, but my cock is feeling particularly greedy right now." I rip the jeans she's wearing down her legs and clasp the back of each of her thighs, gripping hard as my hands run up to her ass, where I squeeze the ample flesh there. I fucking love the way Mia's ass bounces when I pound into her from behind. My lips connect with each smooth cheek.

"You're teasing me," Mia groans.

"Yes, I am."

"Well, stop," she pleads.

A dark chuckle escapes me as I run my hands under her shirt and over the taught muscles of her stomach that are tight with anticipation to the cups of her bra. Pulling the material under her breasts, my hands knead her perfect fucking tits while my fingers twist her already hardened nipples.

"You don't have a say in that do you, sweetheart? The only thing I want you to do is try not to scream while I sink so far into you that when we leave this office, your jaw hurts from how hard you've had to clamp that pretty mouth shut."

I grab my wallet from my pocket and pull out a condom, tossing the leather on the desk next to her. With shaky hands, I roll the condom over my stiff length. I'm so fucking excited to be inside her that the anticipation is strumming through me with each beat of my heart.

I line my cock up with her entrance, and when I sink into her, we both let out a groan as her head falls backward. The same intoxicating feeling that rushes through me every time I enter Mia is back in full force. It's like coming home and feeling like I could explode at any second, coupled with the rightness of our connection, all rolled up into one.

My hips begin moving, and I thrust in and out of her at a fast pace with my hand around her throat. Not enough to cut off her air, but enough to hold her steady, to make her understand there is no escaping me—escaping us. We don't have much time, but I need to feel her, to claim her as mine. To show her what that means. Sweat drips down my brow as I continue my furious pace, trying desperately to bring us both the release we crave. When I adjust my stance behind her, my cock finds the spot inside of her that has her crying out.

"Shh," I say, leaning over her so my front is flush with her back. "You can't scream, remember?"

I don't stop. At this point, I don't think I could—not even if the walls were caving in around us. Mia is mine, and every time I sink deep inside of her, I'm claiming her over and over.

"I'm going to come," she says in a harsh whisper.

"I know."

The walls of her pussy have begun fluttering around my hard cock. I feel the vibration of a hum in the back of her throat against my fingers, that telltale sign that she's going to scream out her release. My hand moves to her mouth, and Mia lets out a cry into my palm, not as loud as usual when we're at either of our houses and don't run the risk of being overheard, but loud enough that it needs to be muffled.

Her pussy grips me like a fucking vice, and there's no way I can hold back. With my forehead pressed against the back of her head, I release myself into the condom.

"You're mine, Mia," I whisper, still pumping into her, feeling wave after wave of her orgasm as I'm tumbling through mine. "Mine to take care of, mine to protect, and mine to love."

"Yes, yes, yes," she chants as we both ride out the last of our releases.

I'm still inside of her, my hands on either side of hers as I hold myself up as we try to catch our breaths. My face tangles in her hair, and I kiss the back of her head before pulling out. Her jeans are still around her ankles, so I bend and pull them up, putting her panties back in place before tugging the denim over her glorious ass.

Mia straightens and turns toward me as I find a tissue on her desk and pull the condom off, disposing of it in the trash can at the side of her desk.

"I love you too, you know," she says while I'm putting my own pants back in place.

"I know."

"Oh, really?" she asks with her hand on her hip.

"Baby, I can read you like an open book." I swipe her hair away from her face and cup the side of her neck as I press myself against her. "And I'm so fucking happy you feel safe enough with me to finally admit it."

I'm not sure she would've had I not said it first, but if she needed me to take the lead on that, then, of course, that's what I'm going to do. No matter what, Mia comes first in every way, shape, and form—even if that means protecting her from her own insecurities.

CHAPTER NINETEEN
Mia

A couple of weeks have passed since the festival. I won't lie and say it's all been wine and roses, though. I was beyond nervous about going to work on the Monday after the Spring Fling because of the confrontation between Knox and Leonard, but so far, he's avoided me pretty much every day, not that we would have much of a reason to interact. I thought about going to the principal and the district about his behavior, but he seems to understand that it's in his best interest to stay the hell away from me. It's not as though having him fired would be an easy process, and honestly, I'd rather not have to deal with the headache and gossip that would ensue if I were to take that action. It wouldn't look good for me or the club, considering Knox threatened him.

Last week, Knox brought up the idea of going into Boston tonight to check out the club he's a member of. A couple that he's friends with is going to be showcasing shibari techniques. They're the ones he met years ago who actually trained him in the art of shibari.

He and I haven't experimented with that yet. Knox let me know it can be very intense, more so than the scenes we've already done. He wants me to be fully educated like he was before engaging in it. I've been doing a lot of online research, and I'm more than a little intrigued. I've loved everything Knox and I have done so far. There's something incredibly freeing about being restrained, which seems like such an oxymoron. Every time he pulls out the restraints, I know I'm in for a night completely centered around my pleasure.

Through my research, I've come to learn Knox is a bit of what's referred to as a *pleasure dom*. He finds his pleasure in making me come over and over while denying himself a release until I'm so wrung out, I can barely form a coherent thought. Then, and only then, will he allow himself his release. I don't know that I would consider myself a brat, though, which is a common dynamic. But I'm all for lying back and allowing him to make my body quake with desire and unbelievable pleasure any damn time he wants.

When I agreed to go with him tonight, the way his face lit up was like he was a kid at Christmas, and I was his present. It never occurred to me that he's never introduced anyone to this type of thing, but he told me his previous scene partners had all been in this lifestyle just as long, if not longer, than him. Then I asked him what would have happened if I'd told him I wasn't interested. He assured me he could sense the part of me that needed the release of letting go and letting him be in charge. He explained that it was almost instinctual, just that he'd never cared enough for anyone else who wasn't already a part of this life to introduce them into it.

There's a lot of trust involved on both ends for it to work, and seeing as I'm pretty much the only committed relationship he's ever been in, he hasn't ever broached the subject with another woman. From what I know of Knox before he and I were together, his reasoning behind it is clear. I've never been one to go to all the club parties, but I've known him to be unattached, and he never seemed to want to change that. I never saw him look at a woman the way Linc looks at Charlie or the way Jude looks at Lucy—until me.

My phone buzzes with an incoming call, and I look down, expecting to see Knox's name. Instead, it's another *Unknown Caller*. I've been getting so many of these calls in the last week, I'm just about ready to change my damn number. For the life of me, I can't think of what I signed up for that someone would have gotten my information. I answer the call and immediately tell whoever is on the other line that I'm not interested in anything they're selling. It's so incredibly annoying. I resume putting on my makeup and my phone vibrates again.

I grab the phone, irritated that in less than a minute they're trying to call again. "Hello?" I say into the phone.

Silence.

"For the millionth time, I'm not interested in anything. Take me off your call list," I tell the person on the other end, then hang up. Thankfully, my phone stays silent as I finish getting ready to go to Boston.

A knock sounds at my door, and Knox calls my name as he enters.

"In here," I call back, walking out of my bathroom into the bedroom to slide my feet into my heels.

Knox is standing in my bedroom doorway, and I take in the gorgeous man before me. I've never seen this look on Knox before. His blond hair is slicked back, not with a ton of gel or anything, but it's more styled than usual. He's wearing a fitted black dress shirt and black slacks that show off his long, muscular legs, paired with black boots that look nearly new. I love this man when he comes in from working on his bike, dirty and rumpled. I love this man when he's dressed casually to take me to dinner or hang out with our friends. But holy hell, this is a whole new side that I've yet to see, and I'm starting to think we may not be making it out to Boston tonight.

"You look beautiful," Knox says, startling me out of my silent appraisal.

I went with simple tonight. A black formfitting dress that hits just above the knee with high slits on both sides. It has a square neckline that accentuates my cleavage beautifully if I do say so myself. I opted for something without long sleeves, seeing as I'm assuming they keep these kinds of places on the warmer side if people are walking around barely dressed like the pictures I've seen. Knox said the main floor of the club is tamer than the other levels, which is where we'll be. If I want to check out the rest, I'm sure we could, but the only thing he's interested in tonight is seeing his friends and sharing the beauty of shibari with me.

Knox reaches into his pocket and pulls out a small velvet box. "I've been meaning to give this to you," he says and opens the box. A beautiful pair of earrings are nestled inside. They're a deep red and match the necklace I always wear.

"Thank you," I say, taking the box from his hand and walking over to my dresser with a mirror attached. Setting the box on the dresser, I take out each stud and put them in my ears. "They're perfect."

Knox comes to stand behind me and wraps his arms around my middle. "I saw them a few weeks ago on a run we did to Michigan."

Knox has told me while he was on that trip he had a lot of time to think, and that's when he decided he was done trying to convince himself that I was too good for him or whatever nonsense kept him from me. Knowing that story makes the earrings even more special. He was thinking of me, already making plans to give them to me even though he had no idea if I felt the same. Well, he probably had *some* idea. It's not like I've ever been particularly skilled at hiding my feelings.

He leans down and presses a kiss to my bare shoulder. "Ready?"

"As I'll ever be."

Knox parks his truck in a private parking garage an hour later. We head to an elevator where there's a large man in a suit waiting in front of the doors. Knox hands him his ID and a membership card. The man scans the cards and hands them back to him. "Good evening, Mr. Turner."

I have never heard him referred to as Mr. Turner. It's almost as though this is an entirely different life than the one he has back in Shine. I hand the man my ID, and he scans it and smiles, pressing the button for the elevator doors, which open immediately.

"Have a good night," the security guard says, closing the door.

"Fancy," I say to Knox's reflection in the mirrored walls of the elevator.

"They take security and privacy seriously. That's something I like about it. It's not necessarily the most exclusive club or anything like that, but they treat everyone with respect. Even a biker like me."

"You don't exactly scream *biker* tonight."

He shrugs but doesn't say anything before the doors open again. We step into an alcove with a pretty blonde woman in a dark-green dress standing in front of a dimly lit podium.

"Good evening. May I have your phones, please?"

Knox is reaching into his pocket before the woman finishes her sentence, obviously already accustomed to the rules. We hand ours over, and she gives Knox a card with a number on it.

"Thank you," he says and slips the ticket into his pocket. Then we walk through a deep cherrywood door carved with beautiful filigree and into a large room filled with people.

This is my first time at a club like this, and from the looks of it, it seems like any high-end lounge. My eyes adjust to the dim lighting, and I notice a few differences—one being several women and men wearing collars attached to leashes held by, I assume, their partners. There's a large main stage that's empty and two smaller stages with girls in cages dancing to the sultry music playing through the speakers. Couples and groups of people sit in the booths lining the perimeter. Swaths of deep-purple fabric hang against the walls, which give the space a dark and sexy feel. My eyes travel to the ceiling where intricate black and white crystal chandeliers hang, casting a low, warm glow over the space.

"Wow," I breathe out as I take in my surroundings.

"Come on," Knox says, leading me to the bar. "There's a two-drink maximum, but they have pretty much anything you can think of."

I look around at all the bottles lined on the glass shelves behind the bar, illuminated by muted, soft lighting.

"I'll have a glass of champagne please," I say to the bartender and Knox orders a water.

"You don't want anything?"

"Not tonight," he says, leaning down to kiss me.

"Knox," I hear a slightly accented feminine voice call from behind me.

Knox lifts his head and smiles just before I turn to see a woman with long black hair and a rich tan complexion walking toward us. She's accompanied by a man nearly as tall as Knox, with a head of curly black hair and dark eyes. Both are wearing matching smiles as they approach us.

"Camila," Knox says in greeting and leans into the woman, giving her a brief kiss on both cheeks. When he straightens, he shakes the man's hand. "Andrés, good to see you."

This is the couple that Knox told me about. The ones who he studied under when learning about rope bondage.

"This is Mia," he introduces, and Camila and Andrés both shake my hand.

Andrés is dressed much like Knox, except his shirt is a dark blue, and Camila is wearing a light-pink silk robe.

"We wanted to come say hello before our show. We reserved a table for you." Andrés points to one of the tables closer to the stage with a small sign sitting atop, then turns to me. "Knox has told us this is your first time at a shibari show. I can't wait to hear what you think."

"I'm excited to watch," I reply with a smile.

"Wait until you try it," Camila says. "There's nothing quite like it." She shares a loving smile with Andrés before he checks his watch.

"We need to head backstage, my love," he says, lifting her hand to his lips and kissing her palm. "Are you ready?"

"Yes," she says with a smile meant for only him on her face.

"See you after the show," Andrés says, and Camila gives us both a small wave before they disappear back into the crowd, then behind a curtain to the side of the stage.

Knox grasps my hand and turns it over, bringing it to his lips and places a gentle kiss on my palm. "Let's go to our table."

"They seem really nice," I say to Knox. "Did you...did you practice on Camila?"

I'm not sure where my insecurity is coming from all of a sudden. Oh, yeah, she's absolutely stunning and knows this entirely different side of Knox that I'm just learning about.

"With Andrés, yes. He was there every step of the way. But it was never sexual between us, Mia. Camila may be willing to help train people learning the art, but Andrés is far too possessive of her to ever share her for anything else."

I'm well aware that Knox has had partners before me. I mean, look at Heather, beautiful and sweet. Did it suck to learn that Knox and Heather played with ropes? Yes. But he was honest and forthcoming with the entire conversation and assured me that it was a purely physical relationship. Knox is many things, but a liar isn't one of them. However, I'd be lying if I said it didn't sting to know she was the only person he had done this with who didn't belong to this club.

"Hey," Knox says, leaning toward me. His hand palms the side of my neck. I've noticed he does that when I start freaking out about something in my head. And I've also noticed the calming effect that connection has on me. Obviously, Knox has noticed it, too.

"Take a breath. I love you."

I exhale the ball of tension that was forming in my chest and Knox smiles.

"Good girl."

And just like that, with his hands on me and his gaze boring into me, my body relaxes into him.

"I love you, too," I say, and Knox leans in and kisses me tenderly on the mouth.

The overhead lights in the room dim as the stage lights illuminate. Soft music plays in the background as Camila and Andrés walk on the stage. Camila has rid herself of the pink robe and is wearing a retro-style bra and panty set. Black lace covers her full breasts, and she's wearing a cheeky pair of panties with ruffles on the back. It's absolutely adorable and sexy at the same time.

Andrés walks to the side of the stage and grabs a bundle of black rope. When he walks back over to Camila, he whispers something to her. It's too quiet for me to hear what he's saying, but I read her lips when she agrees.

"Andrés checks in with her at every stage when they do their shows," Knox whispers to me.

"Like you do with me."

He nods, then turns his attention back to the stage.

Andrés undoes the bundle, and several feet of rope pile at his feet while he holds the middle in his hands. He steps behind Camila and begins wrapping the rope around her. He forms knots around her breasts and down to her navel before he loops the length around her thighs, pulling one leg up, then tucking it behind her. He attaches another rope hanging from the ceiling and lifts her tied form, slowly spinning her so the audience can see the knot artwork on her back. She swings slightly as though he's showing off his work of art, which, I suppose, is exactly what he's doing.

Camila's face is serene and relaxed while Andrés continues his work, putting her in different positions and showing the crowd different styles of knots. The entire time, I'm watching every position he puts her in, and my heart rate is increasing with each new display. My skin tingles against the hand that Knox keeps on my upper thigh. I thought we were coming for a demonstration, but it's turning into so much more for me. I want to be the woman being tied. I want to feel what Camila is feeling.

The show only takes about thirty minutes, but it bare-ly feels like it's been five. I am completely enraptured by the scene in front of me. The look on Camila's face. The control and precision that Andrés exudes. It's over too quickly, and when Andrés is finished and unties Camila, he carries her off the stage. She looks like she's in a completely different stratosphere when she rests her cheek on his shoulder, and he tenderly kisses the crown of her head.

"Wow," I say on an exhale.

Knox is staring at me, studying my face. "What did you think?"

"I think...I think I can't wait to get home."

He smiles and stands, taking my hand in his. "As you wish."

When we step through Knox's doorway, I can't seem to keep my hands off him. The ride home was filled with tension, unlike anything I've ever felt. I was a bit nervous that we would offend Camila and Andrés by leaving without saying goodbye, but Knox assured me that it would be an hour or so before they emerged from whatever room they were in. Camila was feeling the effects of shibari subspace, and there was no way they would be leaving that room until Andrés was confident that she was taken care of.

The moment we're inside the house, Knox bends at the waist and takes my mouth is a hard kiss before lifting me in his arms. I immediately wrap my legs around him, once again thankful for the slits in my dress. Honestly, I probably would have ended up ripping my dress at this point had they not been there.

He walks us into his room and gently sets me on my feet next to the bed, then takes a step back.

"Take your dress off," he says in that growly voice that makes me wet.

I slip the straps from my shoulders, then peel the dress from my body. When it pools at my feet, I kick it away with one of my heeled shoes. Knox's eyes devour the sight in front of him. I'm left in nothing but a see-through lace bra with matching panties, a garter belt that's attached to silk stockings, and my black patent leather heels.

"Holy shit," he breathes, the hungry look in his eyes making his pupils darken with desire. "We would've never left your house tonight had I known what was on underneath that sexy-as-fuck dress."

"Funny, I was thinking almost the same thing when you walked through my door."

Knox takes a step toward me, his knuckles brushing the soft skin of my stomach, making my muscles clench. His hand strokes up and down my belly as he stands, allowing his eyes to drink in their fill. I love having his eyes on me like this, appreciating the woman standing in front of him with his worshipping stare and reverent touches. He slowly walks behind me, studying every inch of skin on display while his knuckles trail along my stomach and over my side to my back. He moves his hand up and down my spine, eliciting another shiver.

"You looked absolutely stunning in your dress tonight, sweetheart. And you look just as beautiful out of it." He leans down, his breath warm against my ear as he whispers, "But fuck, I'm ready to see what you look like in my ropes."

"Please." I lean against his chest and feel the silky, cool fabric of his shirt caressing my heated skin.

Knox's fingers move under the straps of my bra so he can slide them off my shoulders before his fingers deftly unhook it from the back. When the lace falls from my arms, his hands cup both breasts while he stands behind me, softly running his palms against my hardened nipples over and over. It reminds me of the night he played with them until I came just from that. The tingling between my legs makes it hard not to rub my thighs together to try to ease the ache quickly building there.

He walks in front of me and brushes his mouth against mine, then trails his lips down, leaving light kisses in his wake. Down between the hollow of my throat, between my breasts and over my stomach until he's on his knees in front of me.

When he looks up at me, there is so much love and gratitude in his gaze it almost brings a tear to my eyes. There, he kneels in front of me, worshipping me as though I'm vital to his existence. It strikes me at this moment that that's exactly what he's become to me. Vital in every way I could have imagined.

He places my hands on his shoulders and removes one shoe, then the other, as I use him for balance. His fingertips trail lightly to the tops of my stocking, where he undoes the first clasp, kissing the top of my thigh before rolling the silk down my legs and removing it completely. He does the same to the other, his motions slow and precise as he takes his time unwrapping me.

Meanwhile, my panties are completely soaked, and I'm about to beg him to touch me where I need it most. As difficult as it is for me to stand straight and not melt into a puddle of goo on the floor before him, I allow him to do this his way, in his time. As much as he makes me the center of pleasure, allowing him to have this his way brings him his own gratification.

He slips the garter from my hips, brushing his lips against each bone before sliding it off me. My hands are still on his shoulders, my fingers holding onto the tight muscles under his shirt like my life depends on it. When he reaches my panties, he kisses me between my thighs, and I cry out. His molten stare meets mine, and the man winks at me, holds my gaze, then leans in, licking me over my panties.

"Fuck," I moan, and he does it again. "Harder," I plead, wanting to come this second. It would only take a few more brushes of his tongue, lips, or fingers. Fuck, if he breathes on me the right way, I'm liable to explode like a fucking cannon.

Instead of doing any of that, Knox chuckles as he kisses my pubic bone and stands.

"On the bed," he says, nodding toward the mattress.

I crawl over his comforter and look back. His bottom lip is in his mouth as he bites down, staring at the way my ass sways.

"Temptress," he says through gritted teeth.

"Absolutely," I reply with a smile.

Knox returns my smile and walks over to his tall dresser, where he keeps his restraints. He opens the drawer and pulls out a thick bundle of rope.

"Are you ready?" he asks, walking back toward me and standing at the edge of the bed.

I nod and sit straight on the bed with my ankles tucked under me as he undoes the long length of the rope. He holds it in his hand while running it up my arm, then over my shoulder. I tilt my head to the side, and he runs the rope across my neck and past my shoulder, down my other arm.

"It's a lot softer than I thought it would be," I say.

"It's not supposed to hurt. But if it does, make sure you tell me right away."

"I trust you."

"I appreciate that. But make sure you tell me if there's something you don't like. I'd like to think I'm trained well enough that it wouldn't happen but remember, none of this should hurt. If it does, use our safe word."

I nod and he leans in to kiss me. "This is as much for you as it is for me, and if you aren't ready to jump out of your skin from being so completely filled with pleasure, then I'm not doing it right, got it?"

"Yes, sir," I reply cheekily.

"I fucking love that mouth of yours, Mia. I can't wait to have it wrapped around my cock."

When Knox talks to me like that, I swear to God my mouth waters with how bad I want to lick him from root to tip.

He walks in front of me and kneels on the bed, sitting back slightly on his haunches. "Put your hands on my thighs."

I place a hand on each thigh, and he trails the rope over my wrists, looping it through each one. In one meaningful motion, he tightens the loops, forming a knot that ties my wrists together.

Knox's eyes flare as he studies the first knot before he meets my gaze. "What color?"

"Green."

He nods and begins tying me much the same way we saw before. He wraps the length through my thighs, and on each side, he tightens it on the crease between my pussy and thigh. I let out a low moan when I feel the pressure there. My eyelids droop as Knox begins wrapping the rope around my arms and waist, making a row of knots over my stomach. With each pull and tug, my body sways as though I'm being gently rocked by waves. His eyes are zeroed in on every spot he's working, and I look down, seeing the effect this is having on him. His hard length is pressing against his slacks as he continues his work.

"Color?" he asks as he reaches my breasts.

"Green," I reply in a rough whisper.

I've never felt anything like this. It's as though I'm being cocooned and bound at the same time. My mind is quiet, but every nerve ending is shooting off with the delicious feel of the soft fibers of the rope.

He ties the rope under, then over my breasts, before reaching behind me and making his final knot.

Knox steps from the bed and looks over my body, bound in a beautiful design of his making.

"You are breathtaking," he says as he unbuttons his shirt. He rips the material from his body and immediately removes his pants and boxer briefs, standing naked and proud before me.

His hand goes to his cock, and he strokes it up and down. "How do you feel?"

"Like...I'm floating," I respond, my words coming out slightly slurred.

He steps toward the bed and gently moves my legs, guiding me to lie back.

Spreading my thighs, he eyes the wetness dripping from me. I'm so turned on it feels almost out of body at this point.

"You're so fucking gorgeous," Knox growls before he drops to his knees and looks at me from between my spread thighs. His first lick has my hips jerking, which moves the rope across my skin, and I cry out in pleasure at the sensation. Then he eats at me like he's absolutely starving for my taste. Lick after lick, savoring every drop of wetness, Knox never stops, never slows. The orgasm starts between my thighs, but moments later, it's as though my entire body is on fire as I cry out in pleasure. And Knox keeps licking. His hand presses on the knot on my lower abdomen and then he adds two fingers, immediately stroking over my G-spot. The pleasure is indescribable and so beyond powerful that there needs to be another word to describe it. For the first time in my life, I gush, the wetness squirting onto his face and into his mouth. I scream louder, never having felt anything like this before, as my pussy pulses so intensely that my vision goes hazy around the edges.

"Fuck, baby," Knox says, lifting his head from between my thighs with a look of awe in his heated blue eyes. He jumps up from his kneeled position and kisses my mouth with such force that it takes my breath away for a moment when he shoves his tongue inside of my mouth. "That was the most beautiful thing I've ever seen," he says when he pulls away. "I need to be inside of you right now."

"God, yes."

Knox reaches over to the nightstand and yanks the drawer open, grabbing a condom before straightening himself. I watch him roll the condom on his hard length between my thighs, then he sits back on his heels and drapes my legs across him. His hand grips the rope under my breasts, and he pulls me toward him. It doesn't hurt in the least. It's almost as though I'm swaying in a hammock when he presses his lips to mine again.

"I love you," he whispers against my lips.

"I love you, too."

Before I finish my sentence, he enters me in one thrust. I let out a loud exhale, and Knox moans as he begins pumping into me, still holding me off the bed. Sweat beads and drips down his chest as Knox fucks me, his eyes darting between where we're connected, then to my face over and over.

"Goddamn, baby, you take my cock so fucking good. Look at you, so beautiful, tied up and letting me fuck you."

"Oh, my God, I'm about to come again," I cry out, my belly tightening in anticipation.

Knox repositions me on the bed and takes my hips in his hands, pulling them off the mattress as he pumps into me so hard my entire body jerks with each thrust. The orgasm washes over me, making every part of me tremble as Knox roars into the room, his cock twitching as he releases himself inside of me. His eyes stay locked on mine as he slows his movements, allowing both of us to catch our breaths. Knox leans over and kisses my mouth again, his tongue languidly stroking in and out of my mouth as he pulls himself out of me. He lifts up and balances himself on one arm, reaching over to grab a tissue, then uses it to remove the condom.

"How do you feel?" he asks.

"Like I'm glowing," I reply dreamily.

Knox kisses me again, then settles me into a sitting position. He begins untying the rope, starting at my back. As he removes the bindings, he kisses every part of me that was tied. His lips trail over the pink lines across my skin. It doesn't hurt in the least. There was never any pinching or feeling of rope burn anywhere. As I look at where the lines are, I actually think it's kind of beautiful to see the marks they left, kind of like a lovely afterglow of sorts.

When the rope is completely gone, Knox tosses it on the side of the bed and gathers me in his arms.

"You were perfect, Mia. Fuck..." He shakes his head like he's at a loss for words. "I've never seen anything like it."

I hum into his chest, my eyelids becoming heavy as I'm being lulled by the strong beat of Knox's heart. His hands slowly trail up and down my back, his touch calming and soothing after one of the most intense experiences of my entire life.

"We should clean up," he says, and I hum in agreement. "How does a bath sound?"

"Like heaven."

Knox chuckles and gently rolls me off him. He disappears into the bathroom and starts the bath before coming back and holding out his hand to help me up.

"I'll be right in. I'm going to change the bedding real quick."

My nose scrunches and I dip my chin, remembering why he has to change his sheets. "Sorry about that. If I would have known that was a possibility, I would have warned you."

"Is that the first time you've ever squirted, baby?" he asks as his finger tilts my face back up to his.

"Pretty sure we established that this"—I wave my hand toward the bed behind me—"is all new territory for me."

"First of all, never, ever apologize to me for that. That was fucking hot and will be my mission every time I eat you out from now on. Secondly, the fact that never happened before is making me feel on top of the fucking world right now, so there's no way in hell you're allowed to feel any embarrassment over that. Got it?"

"Yes, sir."

Knox laughs. He's already told me he doesn't have that particular kink and that's not the kind of relationship we have, but it makes him smile, and I love that, so...

He spins me around and lightly smacks my ass. "Go get in the bath, and when I'm done in here, be prepared for me to stick my cock in that sassy mouth of yours."

That shouldn't have the effect on me that it does, should it? *Oh fucking well.* It does, and I'm done questioning and second-guessing my happiness.

CHAPTER TWENTY
KNOX

It's been a week since Mia and I went to the club—a week since the first night I used my ropes on her. But it wasn't the only time this week. Last night, I had her legs and torso tied in a beautiful array as I positioned her on her side and fucked her so deep she came three times before I was finished. Fuck, I'm getting hard just thinking about it as I pack an overnight bag.

We're headed to Michigan again for a run to the Iron Disciples clubhouse. The Monaghans dropped another shipment to us yesterday and Linc, Jude, Wyatt, and I are taking a load to them. I hate the thought of not sleeping next to my woman tonight, but duty calls and all that shit.

There's a knock on my door, and I check my phone to see what time it is. Mia left about thirty minutes ago for work, and I doubt any of my brothers who aren't going on this trip are awake yet.

I walk to my foyer and look out the window, seeing my mom's car.

When I open the door, my mom is standing on the other side with a plate of something in her hand.

"Hi, Son. You going to let me in?"

"Shit, sorry, Mom." I step aside, giving her room to move past me after she places a kiss on my cheek.

"I know you're heading out. I just wanted to drop off a plate of breakfast to you before you left," she says, looking around the house.

"Mia isn't here."

My mom walks into the kitchen and sets the plate on the counter. "Just checking," she says with a smile.

"Breakfast, huh?" I walk into the kitchen and remove the aluminum foil she has covering the plate. "Wow, chicken-fried steak, even. My favorite."

"I make it every once in a while for Trick. It's kind of a pain in the ass." My mom grabs a couple of paper towels from the roll next to the sink and a fork from the drawer, setting them next to the plate. "Do you mind?" she asks, pointing to the half-full coffeepot.

"Help yourself. And while you're at it, maybe tell me what you're really doing here." My lips tip up in a half smile, and my mom laughs.

"I'm that obvious?"

"Not usually, no."

I grab my fork and start with the eggs before my mom hands me a knife to cut the steak with.

"I wanted to check in with you. We haven't seen a lot of you lately, and I want to know where your head's at."

"With what?"

"With Mia. Where you see this going. You know, all the stuff that moms worry about."

"Did you have this conversation with Linc when he met Charlie?" I ask around the mouthful of food.

My mom smiles and sits next to me with her coffee in hand. "You and Linc are different, honey. Things with Charlie happened at Mach speed—like most things with your brother."

That's the fucking truth. I'm pretty sure when he showed up at the clubhouse with Charlie in tow, he'd claimed her before he'd even touched her. After she got here, we were almost immediately thrown into the Mob bullshit we barely got finished with.

"You've always taken things slower and more methodically. Ever since you were a kid you would weigh out every decision before you made it. But when you picked your path, you went full force. So, I'm wondering where your head's at. I know you, son, and I know how deeply you care and how fiercely protective you are of the people you care about."

"I love her. She's...it."

A wide smile spreads across my mom's face. "You have no idea how happy that makes me." My mom looks out my glass patio doors for a few moments, then back to me. "When we left Nebraska, hell, even before that, you had to deal with more than anyone your age should have. I think it closed something off in you. Your life became about protecting me and your brother, then it was about your club."

"Of course it did. That's what family does."

She reaches over and places her hand on my fore-arm. "I know. And I know how seriously you take the responsibility you have as an older brother and the club's VP. Sometimes I'd worry that you were so busy looking after everyone else that you didn't take time for yourself. Or take the time to find someone who would be willing to be there for you the way you're always there for the people you care about."

"Are you checking on me or making sure Mia is happy?" I ask only half-jokingly.

My mom laughs. "Maybe a bit of both," she answers and shrugs one shoulder. "I really like her. And the way she looks at you is every mother's wish for her kids."

"Yeah, how's that?"

"Like the sun rises and sets on you. And you look at her the same. Maybe I just want to make sure you aren't letting anything stand in the way of the happiness you both deserve."

"Mia makes me forget all the shit I went through," I start, then shake my head. "No, that's not right. She's the balm for everything. Everything I thought about myself, feeling like I wasn't good enough for someone like her. She makes me realize I never felt this way about another person because the only person right for me is her. That's why I've always guarded myself. Because I hadn't met her yet. Does that make sense?"

My mother looks at me with a sheen in her eyes. "It makes perfect sense, son." She takes a sip of coffee and nods toward the plate. "Now finish your food."

"Yes, ma'am."

Mom starts to leave a few minutes later, and I let her know I'd like to have a big family dinner over here with her, Trick, and Mia's grandmother.

She looks at me with a happy smile on her face and affectionately pats my cheek like she used to do when I was a kid. "I'd love that."

When I get to the clubhouse, Linc and Jude's bikes are parked next to the van. Walking inside, I find Ozzy drinking a cup of coffee, sitting at the bar with a newspaper in hand.

"Hey, Oz," I say in greeting.

"Hey." He sets the paper on the bar, and I read the headline.

"Still no clue who killed that girl, huh?"

Ozzy shakes his head. "No. I realize this kind of thing can happen without ties to all the shit we dealt with last year, but it makes me nervous, especially considering it's so close to home, know what I mean?"

"Yeah. Maybe Jude can have Liam look past any possible Petrov ties and see if we can't get some answers." I pick up the paper and begin reading the article. Whoever did this to these girls is one sick fuck.

"Liam's out of the country with Cillian and Nova for the next few weeks. But this isn't club business, so I don't feel right about asking him to make it a priority. Nik assured Finn that the Russians had nothing to do with it, and Finn said there was no way that any of Farina's men who he let live would defy him. They were just as disgusted with what Farina was doing as the rest of us."

"Guess the Italians have some morals after all."

"The ones who are still alive seem to."

Our club has never had the best relationship with the Italians who were absorbed into the Monaghan organization, but I suppose that was before the Monaghans—and us—took out the heads of their organizations. Now, they answer to Finn, and the man is practically family at this point, thanks to his lieutenant being engaged to Cooper's little sister. Cooper might be gone, but Nova is still family, and by extension, so are the Monaghans.

Jude and Linc walk out of the kitchen, each carrying a rolled-up pancake with sausage inside.

"Your women don't cook you breakfast?" Ozzy says.

"Have you met Lucy?" Jude remarks with a smirk.

"I didn't want to wake up Charlie banging around in the kitchen. She was up late studying last night."

Wyatt emerges from the hallway, freshly showered and looking like he's ready to get out of here.

"Who's in the van?" I ask.

Jude and Linc raise their hands.

"We'll take the van there if you take it back," Linc says.

"Sounds good," Wyatt replies. "I'm going to grab some breakfast before we go."

As the guys finish eating, I speak with Braxton about security over at Midnight Rose. He'll be the point of contact while I'm gone.

"Everything still quiet over there?" I ask.

We never figured out who put a knife in my tires, but so far, there haven't been any other incidents.

Braxton nods. "I don't know, man. Maybe it was a pissed-off boyfriend or customer or something."

He could be right, but something doesn't sit well with me. Maybe because this is our town, and I'll be damned if any asshole off the street thinks he can get away with fucking with our shit. But in all the years the club's been active in Shine, the town has pretty much left us alone, minus the shitty stares and the occasional attitude we've had to deal with. But to outright vandalize our property? That's never happened.

"Check in with Sylvie and make sure she got the delivery today. But otherwise, everything should be good on that end. I hired an extra security guard over there so we don't have to have a brother there every night."

"Not gonna lie, I didn't mind my security detail," he says, wearing a smirk.

"You better not be harassing the girls, fucker."

"Define *harass*."

I shake my head, my eyes rolling toward the ceiling. "Shut the fuck up."

Braxton laughs and Linc walks over. "Ready, brother?"

"Yup, let's get on the road." We file out the door and put Jude and Linc's bikes in the back of the van before Wyatt and I get on ours. The prospect opens the gate for us, and we head out. It's a beautiful day for a ride. Although I'd prefer to have my woman on the back of my bike, having this time with my brothers settles the same thing in me that it always has. This brotherhood gave me a place before I found mine with Mia, and I appreciate every second we get to do what we want on our terms and at each other's sides.

About six hours later, we stop at a little roadside diner. It marks our halfway point before we get to the Iron Disciples' clubhouse. We all need to stretch our legs for a bit and grab some dinner since we'll be on our bikes for another six hours. All I know is we'd better leave a hell of a lot earlier tomorrow morning than we did today because I plan on falling asleep with my woman tomorrow night.

The waitress has just dropped off our food when my phone rings.

Charlie's name flashes on the screen, and my brows furrow. "Hey Charlie, what's up?" I ask, and Linc meets my gaze with a surprised look on his face.

"Have you heard from Mia? She was supposed to meet Lucy and me at Thorn and Thistle, and I can't get a hold of her."

"No. I didn't know she was going over there."

"It was a last-minute thing. But she was supposed to be here over an hour ago, and she isn't answering her phone or text messages."

"When was the last time you talked to her?"

"When I called to see if she wanted to meet us. Nice job on the flowers, by the way. She was gushing about them on the phone."

I stiffen and stare my brother in the eye. "Charlie, I didn't send her any flowers." A thought comes to my mind about the newspaper article this morning. Something about the women last year and the one they just found being buried holding a bouquet of white tulips. "Did she say what kind of flowers they were?"

"White tulips."

Anxiety grips my throat. "Charlie, I want you to stay at the bar. I'm sending Cash and Barrett over there."

"Why?"

"I have a bad feeling, and I'd rather be safe than sorry."

"Okay. Is Linc with you?" she asks, nerves apparent in her voice.

"Yeah, call him."

I hang up, and a second later, Linc is pulling his phone from his pocket and answering Charlie's call while I dial Mia.

No answer.

I try again and the same thing happens. There's no answer. My next call is to Braxton.

"Hey, man," he says when he answers my call.

"Where are you?"

"At the clubhouse."

"Are Cash and Barrett with you?"

"Yeah...what's going on?" he asks, confusion lacing his words.

"I'm not sure, but I need Cash and Barrett to head to Thorn and Thistle to hang out with the girls, and I need you to look for Mia. She was supposed to meet the girls there and never showed," I say, trying to keep the alarm out of my voice.

"Where am I looking?"

"Try Main between the bar and the high school. If you don't see her car, make your way to her place. Do you know where it is?"

Braxton calls out to Barrett and Cash before answering, "Yeah, Tanya had me pick some shit up from her grandmother a few months ago."

"Call me and tell me what you find."

Linc hangs up with Charlie at the same time I disconnect the call with Braxton.

"Charlie's a little freaked out, man," he tells me.

"She's not the only one," I reply.

"What do you want to do?" Jude asks me.

"Wait here until we know something."

"I'll call Silas," Wyatt says.

"Not yet. If it's nothing, then there's nothing to tell him." And I hope like hell I'm overreacting.

I flag the waitress down and we pay for our food, though we've only eaten about half. We head outside, and Jude lights a cigarette, something he does when he's stressed out.

About fifteen tense minutes later, my phone rings. I look at the name and am disappointed to see Braxton's and not Mia's.

"No sign of her car at the school or between there and the bar. I'm going to drive to her place now."

"Okay, thanks, man."

"Yup." He hangs up, and the rest of the guys look at me expectantly. I shake my head because there's nothing for me to report, and I don't know if I can form words past the lump in my throat.

There's this thing that happens when you grow up around someone who is violent and unpredictable. It's almost as though you feel a disturbance in the universe before everything goes to hell. I became adept at reading that feeling, and it's served me well in my life. It's as though I'm drowning in it now, but it's coupled with a helplessness that hasn't been there in years, considering I'm hours away from my woman.

Then it happens.

I answer the phone when I see his name light up the screen.

It only takes ten minutes between my last call with Braxton and this one for my world to crash around me.

"I went to her house. The door was wide open and everything in her purse was all over the floor. A bunch of shit was knocked over on her kitchen counter, too."

"Fuck!" I scream into the night.

"There's more. There's blood on the corner of one of the counters. She's gone, man."

CHAPTER TWENTY-ONE
MIA

Two hours earlier

"I'll be there in an hour. I'm just finishing up some work here, then I'm going to run home if I have time and change." I'm exhausted and wearing my *librarian uniform* feels restricting. I really want a pair of jeans and a big cozy sweater instead of the skirt and heels I'm currently in.

"Okay, can't wait to hear everything," Charlie says.

I won't be sharing *everything*, like the life-altering orgasms I've been having and the waterworks that accompany them. I'd rather not make my friends jealous. I still can't believe my body can do that, let alone repeatedly.

"Did I tell you about the flowers Knox sent me?"

Charlie chuckles into the phone. "Only about a million times today."

I laugh as I stare at the bouquet of white tulips on my desk.

"Well, consider this a million and one then," I say with a wide smile on my face.

"Who knew Knox was such a romantic?"

"Right? I'm one lucky girl." For more reasons than one. "See you in a bit."

I disconnect the call and finish up some ordering and a couple other things before checking the time. I'll have just enough to get home, change, and meet the girls for a drink.

Knox and a few of the guys are going on a run today, and while I'll miss him, it's a good time to hang out with the girls without our men crashing the party. Not that they aren't always welcome, but it'll still be a nice distraction from missing Knox since we're still in what Charlie calls the honeymoon phase. I asked her if it's worn off with Linc, and she laughed and told me no. I have a feeling it's not so much a phase as it is a new way of life for me, and I can't say I'm the least bit mad about it.

Gathering my things, I head to my car, making sure to buckle the vase of flowers so they don't topple over. He left a note this time saying see you soon. I love that he was thinking of me before he left this morning.

Pulling my phone out of my purse, I dial my grandmother's number.

"Hello, dear," she answers.

"Hey, Grandma, I'm heading home to change, then I'm going to meet the girls for a drink. Do you need anything before I get home?"

Knox and I split our time between our houses. Even though I don't need to live on my grandma's property, she and I have fallen into a routine, and I don't want to upset that too much. Plus, I like spending time with my grandmother, and she likes "having a man around" as she puts it.

"No, I'm about to leave myself. Arthur is taking me to dinner."

"Hi, Mia," I hear him call.

"Tell him I said hello." I smile, liking that she's found someone to spend time with even if she insists they're only friends. That could very well be the case, but I notice the way she brightens when he's around. "Okay, Grandma. I'll see you tomorrow for coffee."

I hang up and start my car, pulling out of the parking lot to head home. It's the perfect spring evening, not too cold, which means summer is right around the corner. This is my favorite time of year because summer vacation is almost here. It'll be nice to have weekday mornings to myself for a bit and not have to rush out to head to work.

I pull up to my house and turn the car off before reaching over and grabbing the vase of flowers and my purse.

"I see you got my flowers," I hear behind me, the voice making me jump so suddenly that I nearly drop them.

When I whirl around, Leonard steps out from the shadows.

"What the hell are you doing here?" I'm so stunned by the last person I ever expected showing up in my driveway that all I can do is stand there and stare as he approaches.

"I just want to talk to you. Don't be scared," Leonard says, holding out his hands.

That knocks me out of my stupor, but fear isn't the first emotion that comes rushing in. It's fucking anger.

"I don't know who the fuck you think you are, but lying in wait for me to get home is beyond inappropriate, Leonard."

"I know you think that, but really…I'm here to help."

I start backing up toward my house as I feel around my key ring for my house key. I just need to get inside and call the police. This has gone too far, and it's about damn time I file charges—not only with the school board but the authorities as well.

"I don't need any help from you, and you need to leave right now. Knox is on his way, and if you don't get off my property, that little scene at the festival is going to be child's play."

I saw the fear in his eyes when Knox had him pinned against the wall, and while I was pissed as hell at Knox for getting involved, I think I should have let him do a lot more than just rough him up a bit.

Leonard shakes his head back and forth slowly as he continues to approach me with an eerie look in his soulless eyes. "I know he's not here. And I know your grandmother is gone, too. I watched her leave with that old man. It's just us, and you need to listen to me, girl. What you've been doing, who you've been spending your time with, it's evil and wretched."

What in the actual hell?

"He's leading you down a path of sin. He's not the man to show you the true way—the true light."

When my heel reaches the first step of my porch, I throw the flowers at him and race up the stairs, shoving my key into my lock. I swing my door open, but before I can shut it, Leonard reaches in and makes a grab for me. He snatches the strap of my purse and tries to pull me back, but he yanks the purse off my shoulder instead, sending everything inside scattering around my floor. I try to slam the door on his arm, but he's too quick and slams his body against the wood. He steps through as I make a run to the kitchen, more specifically to the butcher block sitting on the counter.

My hand reaches for the biggest knife there. Just as I grasp the handle, my knee is kicked from behind, and I collapse to the ground, smacking my head against the corner of my counter as I fall. I'm only stunned for a moment, but red tints my vision almost immediately. Just when I turn around, still sitting on the floor but ready to kick, scratch, or bite anyone who comes near me, a fist connects with the side of my head—and it's lights out.

The first thing that registers is the pounding headache when I try to open my eyes. The second is what happened to give me the headache, and the third is the rope cutting into my wrists when I try to move my arms and hands. This isn't the soft rope that I've become accustomed to. This rope is thick, and the fibers feel like tiny needles shredding my skin.

I'm tied to a bed in a dingy room. The rope is knotted around my waist and looped around my arms and up to my wrists, where it's connected to a metal bed frame. My legs are tied in a similar fashion. Basically, I can't fucking move.

From the looks of it, this house or wherever I am, has seen better days. There's paper over the windows, so it's dark in here but not pitch black. From what I can see and smell, the place I'm in is old. The walls are stained wooden panels. When my eyes travel to the ceiling, I see the source of the damaged walls and probably the dank smell that accompanies it. Huge brown water stains cover the lighter wood of the ceiling as though the roof has been leaking for ages. My head moves from side to side as my eyes adjust to the dimly lit space. In front of me is a splintered door that leads to God knows where, and to the right is a closet with its doors leaning against the wall. I spy a few shirts hanging on old wire hangers and shoes haphazardly strewn inside the bottom of the closet. I can't see much else since I'm tied down to this fucking bed by my arms and legs.

Tears sting my eyes when I realize the likelihood of me getting out of here alive is fucking slim. I have no idea where I am or who else is here. I try to move my arms and legs, but the rope is so damn tight, and it's not budging. Even if I could get free, I have no idea what lies on the other side of that door.

Stop it, Mia. This is not the way it ends for you.

I take several deep breaths, trying to calm my racing heart. Panicking never did anyone any good. There has to be something somewhere that I can...what? Reach? Yeah, that shit isn't happening anytime soon.

The door creaks open, and in walks the man responsible for me being here.

"Hello, Mia," he says, walking to the edge of the bed with something in his hands. "I brought you something to eat."

"Where am I?" I croak out, still groggy from being unconscious.

"At our cabin. I really think you're going to like it here."

My eyes dart around the room and I try to get a look at what's beyond the door. "How long have I been here?"

Leonard tilts his head back and forth. "It's about six in the morning."

Oh my God. I've been here overnight? That hit to the head really did a number on me.

Leonard must see the shocked expression on my face. "I was surprised you slept so long, too. When I shot you up with my little concoction, it worked better on you than it had the others."

My eyes widen. "You have other women here?"

Leonard shakes his head and runs a finger over the cut on my forehead. It stings like a bitch, but I try my damndest not to wince. "No, they left. They weren't up to the task of cleansing themselves from the sin that they'd allowed to ruin their soul. It takes a strong woman to be able to handle such a trial, but I have a feeling you'll have what it takes." The creepy smile he wears sends chills down my spine.

"What...what do you mean? What trial?"

"Shh, shh. There'll be time for that. You must be hungry. You're going to need your strength for later."

Leonard sits down and grabs the spoon out of a can. "Here, have a little soup. I know the drugs I gave you can make it hard to eat at first, so I've found broth to be the best thing when you wake up." He holds a spoonful in front of my mouth. "I hope you liked the tulips. I have to admit, I was a little disappointed that you never said thank you."

Oh my God. It was Leonard, not Knox, who sent me those beautiful bouquets? He's been planning this for months, and I had no idea I was in the presence of a madman this entire time. An asshole? Sure. But this man is certifiably insane and has been walking around without a care in the world. Working with children, for

God's sake. And now he's kidnapped me, and no one has any idea who I'm with or where I am.

Leonard waves the spoon in front of my face. "Come on, Mia. It's good for you."

I consider not eating it, or maybe taking it in my mouth, then spitting it at him, but then another idea forms in my mind. This isn't going to be my end. It can't be. But that means I'm going to have to fight. I open my mouth, and the chicken broth tastes like the most vile thing that's ever touched my tongue. Then I pretend to choke and the broth dribbles down my chin.

"I can't eat like this. I need to sit up a little," I say, pleading with him with what I hope is a pathetic look in my eyes. If he thinks I've resigned myself to my fate, maybe he won't think I'm a threat.

Leonard considers my request and sets the can next to him. "No trying to get away, hear me? Right now, the devil is still inside of you, so you're going to want to run." He pulls a large hunting knife from his belt that I hadn't noticed before and sets it on my stomach. "But if you do, I'll have to start bleeding him from your body before you're ready."

I nod, terrified of what will happen if I try to escape but just as terrified of what will happen if I don't. Leonard unties my wrists and helps me sit up on the bed. I rub at the raw skin there as he settles back down next to me with the soup and leaves the knife on my lap.

"There. That's better," he says as he brings another spoonful to my mouth."

"I can do it."

"No, no. I want to take care of you."

While his eyes are on the spoon to ensure that he doesn't spill the broth, I rear my head back and crash my forehead on his nose. He falls from the bed and groans.

I grab the knife and slice at the rope on my ankle, cutting myself in the process. The rope comes undone and I get to work on the other. Thank God the hunting knife is sharp as hell.

"You fucking bitch!" Leonard cries as he lifts himself from the floor with blood pouring down his face. I swing the knife in his direction but miss my target, which is pretty much any part of his body. When I swing again, Leonard grabs my wrist. I struggle with all of my might, kicking, screaming, and flailing my body. Anything to make it hard for him to keep hold of me.

But it's no use. Leonard rips the knife from my hand. I continue to scream and thrash until I feel a sharp pain in the side of my neck.

"It's the devil inside of you, Mia. Don't fight me. I'm going to save you."

My world tilts on its axis as I fall back against the mattress. Before my eyes close, the last thing I see is Leonard's bloody face leaning over mine as I'm swallowed by blackness once again.

CHAPTER TWENTY-TWO
KNOX

"**H**ave you heard from Liam yet?" I ask Jude for the hundredth time in the last couple of hours. "No. He told me he would be hard to reach."

When we got back to Shine late last night or, fuck, maybe it was early this morning, we went directly to Mia's. I looked around her house, seeing if there was anything I could glean about what happened. But other than what Braxton had already told me, there wasn't anything else that stood out to me. Which pisses me the fuck off. Someone has my woman. I have no idea who, how they got her, or why. The only lead we have are the tulips. But that does little to ease my fears considering the girls who were found with them were already dead, and the cops didn't have a single fucking lead. At least nothing they're sharing with the general public.

Ozzy has called Cillian and left messages with him and also Finn to see if he would have more luck getting in contact with him since Cillian could probably hack into the police records. But so far, no dice. I'm going crazy sitting in this clubhouse.

Last night after checking Mia's house, we looked around her property to see if there were tire marks or any clues that would give us a lead on who took her, but that didn't give us answers, either.

Jude and Linc brought their women to the clubhouse along with Freya. The one thing we learned in the last couple of years is whoever our enemies are, they have no problem going after our women. But I have this sinking feeling in my gut that we aren't dealing with the usual type of enemy we're used to.

It's the damn flowers. I never sent her any.

When I picked her up for our first date and she had a bouquet of white tulips, I didn't think anything of it. But now I realize I should have. Maybe if I had asked where she got them, if she bought them herself or if they were sent to her, I would've been able to prevent this. Maybe I could have tracked down who sent them to her, if anyone, and prevented the entire thing. I was so excited about finally getting to take her out that I didn't think twice about them. But the memory of those flowers is taunting me now. It's all connected, and that scares me more than anything else.

"Knox," Maizie calls as she barrels into the clubhouse. It's early, not quite nine in the morning. "I think I have something."

I jump from my seat as she comes to stand in front of me, out of breath and with wild eyes.

"I dropped Colby off at school and realized he forgot his lunch in the car when I got home, so I went back to the school to drop it off in the office. The women were talking about the high school's vice principal not showing up for work and Mia not being in there either." She stops and takes a few breaths. "One of them said her sister-in-law works at the high school and saw him carrying a bouquet of white tulips into the library yesterday before anyone was supposed to be there. But the woman's sister-in-law got there early and saw him walking through the back door of the library with them. They were gossiping about them having an affair or something."

"Knox," Jude calls from the other side of the room. "My brother's on the phone."

In four quick strides, I'm in front of Jude, grabbing the phone from his hand. "Liam, I need you to find me an address and anything else you can for Leonard Miller in Shine. And I need it yesterday."

"Got it. I'll call you back."

He hangs up without saying goodbye, and I clutch the phone, waiting for it to ring. When it does, about fifteen minutes later, I answer right away.

"Leonard Miller, age thirty-seven. No living parents. Transferred from a private school in New York to Shine High School a little over a year ago. I'll text you the address and his DMV information."

"He's from New York?" I ask with a lump in my throat.

"Yeah, a little town outside of Albany."

That's within a hundred-mile radius of where the other bodies were found last year.

"Thanks, Liam."

"Aye. Sending the text now."

He hangs up, and three seconds later, Jude's phone dings with a text.

"Let's go," I say to my six brothers standing at the ready.

We take the van to the address Liam sent Jude. It's about two miles from the school in a quiet, unassuming neighborhood. A couple cars are in the driveways of the other houses, but otherwise, the street is empty, seeing as it's a workday. Jude parks the van a few houses down from the house where Liam sent us. I can't help neighbors seeing us enter the house if they look out their windows, but I pray to whoever is listening that if they do, they don't call the cops. Most everyone in this town, especially in a working-class neighborhood like this, would see our cuts and turn a blind eye. I would've rammed the van through this fucker's house if I wasn't worried about either it hurting Mia if she's here or it giving him a head's up that the cavalry has arrived and given him a chance to escape.

We walk around the side of Leonard's house. Thankfully, his next-door neighbor appears to be gone. I peek through the windows but don't see anything. His TV is off, as well as all the lights. When we get to the backyard, I look in the windows at the back of the house but don't see any movement inside.

Jude walks up to the back door and pulls a lock-picking kit from his pocket. The man spent several years in the Royal Marines and has numerous skills that come in handy in these types of situations. When the door opens, we all file into the house with our guns drawn. It's small from the looks of it. I wasn't going to wait for Liam to find the plans for the house, so we're going in blind. It's pretty amazing that seven big-ass bikers can be as quiet as we are, though.

Ozzy and I silently creep into the hallway while Jude and Linc head toward the front of the house. Barrett and Wyatt walk toward the garage, and Braxton positions himself so he can cover both exits just in case Leonard's hiding somewhere and tries to run.

Quietly, I open the first door on my right. It's an empty bathroom. I close the door and head to the next closed door when Ozzy steps out of the room at the end of the hall. He shakes his head, signaling no one is in there, either. When I open the door to the last room, I can tell it's the primary bedroom. The bed looks like it was recently slept in and is still unmade. I walk over to the dresser and find only a few pairs of men's underwear and socks. There are several empty hangers in his closet like maybe he's skipped town or he doesn't have a lot of clothes to begin with. Regardless, the room is empty.

We walk back into the small kitchen where my brothers have gathered, obviously not having found any signs of Leonard or Mia. Next to the refrigerator is another door.

"Basement," I mouth to my brothers.

Ozzy nods and stands in front of the door to open it. I clasp him on the shoulder. When he turns to me, I shake my head, stepping in front of him. This is about my woman, and I'll be damned if Ozzy takes the lead. My prez nods and steps aside. I slowly raise my gloved hand to the knob and twist, opening the door. Holding my gun in front of me, I begin walking down the stairs without turning the light on. I'm focused on listening for any movement as I carefully take each step, but there's no noise coming from the darkness. When I reach the bottom, the rest of my brothers file down behind me.

The basement is dark, with only a small amount of light coming through the rectangular windows at the tops of the cement wall. I look around for any other door that may lead to another room or any place this fucker could be hiding, but there's nothing except the water heater, a washer and dryer, and a large cabinet against the far wall.

"No one's here," Wyatt says at the bottom of the stairs.

"Let's check the house and see if we can find anything that might be useful," Barrett suggests.

Ozzy nods, and Barrett, Wyatt, and Braxton make their way back up the narrow wooden staircase. Linc flips the light switch at the bottom of the stairs, and the basement is illuminated with a dim yellow glow from the single bulb hanging from the ceiling. I walk over to the cabinet and try the handle, but it's locked.

"Why would he have a locked cabinet in his basement?" Jude asks.

With the butt of my gun, I hammer at the handle. When it clatters to the cement floor, the door swings open. What I find inside chills me to my bones.

Displayed on four shelves are pictures of women tied to a bed with a metal frame. Each one is in a different state of undress, some wearing their clothes while others are stripped down to their underwear. The one thing they all have in common, though, is the look of terror in their eyes. Next to the pictures are small mementos. A pair of earrings, a necklace, and a bracelet. On the bottom shelf sits a watch next to a picture I recognize. It's the one the news showed when they identified the woman they found outside of Boston.

"Fuck. It's him," I say on an exhale.

And he has Mia.

"Knox, we found something," Braxton calls from the doorway at the top of the stairs. I haul ass up the stairs and into the kitchen, where Braxton is holding a paper that looks like a property tax statement.

"It's for a cabin about thirty miles outside of town," he says, holding up his phone to show me the map. I take the paper from him. The name isn't Leonard's, but if this is all we have to go on, we'll be making a drive out there.

"Let's go."

The cabin is in the middle of the woods. There's a fire access road near the clearing, so we take that to get us as close as possible without alerting anyone that we're here. We pile out of the van, and all of us check our weapons before heading into the thicket of trees. It takes less than five minutes for us to meet in the open space where a small, dilapidated cabin sits.

And out front is an old station wagon that looks like the same make and model as the one owned by Leonard Miller. Liam was very thorough in the text he sent when he gave us the address.

"Jude, Linc, Wyatt—you three head around back. The rest of us are going in through the front," Ozzy says as he starts walking toward the house.

There's no cover between the trees and the cabin, so the only thing we can do is haul ass and pray he doesn't see us coming. The four of us quietly make our way up the steps, guns raised and ready to fire. There aren't any windows in the front of the house, and I have no idea if the man is inside or not.

Until I open the door and nearly get my arm shot off with buckshot.

"Motherfucker!" I yell.

"If you take a step closer, I'll put a bullet in her before you can make it inside," Leonard calls out.

"Mia!" I yell into the cabin.

"Knox," she calls back. "I'm tied up."

"Shut up, whore," Leonard hollers, and I peek my head quickly around the corner.

He fires another shot at me.

"That's two," I say and step around the corner with my gun raised.

I see Leonard jump through a doorway, and Mia screams in terror.

In three long strides, I'm standing in the doorway of a bedroom. On the bed lies Mia, tied much like I saw the women in the photos. Standing next to her is Leonard, and in his hand is a gas can. The smell of gasoline instantly assaults my senses, making my eyes burn.

He throws the can at me, and I duck to miss getting hit with the metal container. Next thing I know, he has a lighter in his hand.

"You're too late," he says and drops the lighter on the floor.

The gasoline instantly ignites in front of the door and the fire quickly spreads up the wall. I watch in horror as Leonard raises both of his arms over his head with a long hunting knife in his hands. He squeezes his eyes shut and says a few words as though he's praying or some insane shit. Before he plunges the knife into Mia, I fire three shots. Two in the chest and one between his eyes. The piece of shit collapses to the floor. Mia screams as blood splatters across her face.

I don't think twice and jump over the flames in front of the door. Instantly, my brain registers the searing pain on my calves and the smell of burning denim, but my body refuses to stop. Pulling a knife from the holster on my belt, I cut into the ropes, trying like hell not to let the blade score Mia's flesh while also trying to hurry the fuck up. This place is old as fuck, and there's no doubt in my mind that it won't take long for the fire to destroy the cabin. I have her wrists free in moments, then get to work on her ankles. The rope is thick and tough to cut through, but fortunately, I keep my blade pretty damn sharp, so it doesn't take too long. Scooping Mia into my arms, I turn, knowing I'm going to have to make another jump for it, and it's going to hurt like hell. Before I take a step toward the doorway, the ceiling comes crashing down, blocking our exit.

"Fuck!" I bellow as Mia clings to me.

"Window," she coughs out, and I turn to see a window on the other side of the room that's covered with old newspaper. Thankfully, the fire hasn't spread to that side, but it's only a matter of seconds. The smoke is thick, making it hard to breathe. When I reach the window, I lift my leg and kick through the glass, shards cutting into my already burned calves.

"Over here," I yell to anyone outside.

"Holy shit, stand back," Ozzy shouts, and I see him pick up a fallen branch to knock off the large pieces of glass around the window frame. Ozzy reaches in carefully because the frame isn't completely clear. I maneuver Mia out of the window while the scorching heat from the fire licks at my back. He takes her in his arms, and Braxton comes to stand in front of the window, grabbing my forearm to help me through as well. As soon as I'm on steady ground, I grab Mia from Ozzy's arms and we take off toward the tree line. When we reach it, we turn and see the entire cabin engulfed in bright orange and red flames.

"Where is he?" Linc asks.

"Dead."

Mia clings to me, crying into my chest as I hold her tightly against me.

"Shh. I got you, baby." I try to comfort her, but she continues to cry. Fuck, it's not like I can blame her. God only knows what she's been through in the fifteen hours she's been gone.

"You need a hospital," my brother says, pointing to my calves.

"How the fuck am I going to explain how I got my injuries?"

"I'll make a call," Jude says, pulling his phone from his pocket. "But we need to get the hell out of here before someone sees the smoke and calls the fire department."

We begin making the trek back to the truck as Jude talks on the phone.

"Liam will have a doctor at the clubhouse in an hour," he says.

"You can let me down," Mia says into my chest. "I can walk."

"Not a chance, sweetheart."

At this point, I don't think I'll ever let her out of my arms.

It takes about forty-five minutes to get back to the clubhouse, and I keep Mia in my lap the entire time. She doesn't tell me to let her down again. I think she senses that I need to hold her right now. If she's in my arms, then nothing bad can touch her. I need the warmth of her body, the reassuring feel of her breathing against me right now. I need the physical evidence that we got to her in time and that sick fuck didn't murder her in front of me like he was planning.

We walk through the door—me still carrying Mia—past Lucy, Maizie, and Charlie. I take her straight to my room, not stopping until I'm inside and I lay her on the bed.

"Brother, at least let me look at your legs," Ozzy says.

"I'm fine. Can you get me a couple washcloths?"

I nod toward my bathroom and hear the water running before Ozzy comes out with two warm, wet washcloths and hands them to me.

The first one I use to wipe Leonard's blood from her face. She doesn't need a single piece of that man touching her. The second is for Mia's forehead, where there's a nasty gash. She winces when I gently brush against the bruising cut but doesn't pull her head away.

"I know, baby. The doctor will be here soon and have you fixed up."

"What about you?" she asks me with a worried look in her eyes.

"She'll fix me up, too."

There's a knock on the door, and I turn my head to find Lucy standing next to Ozzy.

"Doc's here," she says, and a small blonde woman walks into the room carrying what looks like a paramedic bag.

"I'm Dr. Lasher," the woman says, introducing herself. "What do we have?"

"She has a head wound," I say as the doctor steps around to the other side of the bed. She sets her bag down and grabs a pair of gloves from the inside pocket.

"Any other wounds that I can't see?" Her gaze locks with Mia's, a meaningful look passing between them.

"No," Mia replies, and the doc nods.

"He has burns on his legs and probably a few chunks of glass stuck in there as well," Ozzy says from the doorway.

Fucking snitch.

"I'll take a look when I'm done here," the doctor says as she takes out a penlight and shines it in Mia's eyes.

Dr. Lasher goes through a series of questions as she checks my woman's vitals. Mia tells her she was drugged twice as far as she knows but isn't sure with what. My hand tightens in hers, and she tries to give me a reassuring smile. Of course she's the one trying to reassure me that she's fine. And I can see that she is, but nothing about what happened to her is fine, and it never will be.

After listening to Mia's lungs, the doctor nods. "I'm going to clean her head wound, then give her a few stitches to be safe. But all in all, everything checks out."

When she's finished with Mia, she turns to me. "You can either go in the bathroom and change into a pair of shorts, or you can drop your pants. I don't really care, but I need to see your legs."

I stand from the bed and pull my jeans off, my breath hissing through my teeth when the fabric peels from my calves.

"Figured," the doc says and walks over, bending down to look at my legs. "Okay, lie down next to your woman. This is going to take a while."

After cleaning my wounds, the doctor tells me I have second-degree burns. The cuts aren't deep enough to require stitches, but I'll probably have some nasty scars. She gives me instructions on how to clean the burned skin every day to prevent infection and tells me what to look out for in case they do become infected.

"Thank you, doctor," Mia says, and the woman gives her a small smile.

When she walks out of the bedroom, Ozzy closes the door, leaving Mia and me alone for the first time.

"Can you tell me what happened?" I ask, gathering her in my arms so she can rest her head on me.

"Can we talk about it later? Right now, I need to be here with you and know that I'm safe." She looks at me with tears in her eyes, and I wrap her tighter against my chest.

"Of course, sweetheart. Anything you want."

We lie in silence for several minutes until I feel her breaths even out. When I know she's asleep, I reach over to my nightstand and grab my phone to text Jude since there's no way in hell I'm leaving this bed.

Me: *Cleanup?*

Jude: *Taken care of. Liam made a call to the FBI. A statement will be made tomorrow.*

I set my phone back on the nightstand, and Mia doesn't stir. Though I'm fucking exhausted, sleep doesn't come easy. Thoughts of the fire, the memory of Leonard holding that knife above my woman with every intention of plunging it into her chest, the fact that he got to her period, it all keeps racing through my mind. When I hear her breath hitch, I look down. She hasn't opened her eyes, and she's fine.

She's sleeping and safe.

She's alive and in my arms.

And that is the only reason I can close my own eyes to let sleep take me, too.

Chapter Twenty-Three
Mia

It's been a month since Knox rescued me from the cabin. It took two weeks before I went back to work. I didn't want to go in and have to explain the marks around my wrist or the gash and subsequent bruising on my forehead, so I waited until the raw skin healed and my head wound could be covered with makeup.

I told my principal there was a family emergency that was going to take me out of town for a couple weeks since I didn't want my name associated with what happened at the cabin. It could have implicated the Black Roses. I was surprised to see the news report on the incident. A spokesperson for the FBI came out and said they'd been investigating the murders, and before they could apprehend the suspect, he started a fire and killed himself. It sounds like Jude's brother has more pull in federal law enforcement than I could have imagined.

For the first two weeks of my healing, I stayed with Knox. Honestly, the idea of going back to my house scared me. That's where Leonard kidnapped me from, and the thought of walking in there before I had a chance to process everything was overwhelming. Every day, Arthur would bring my grandmother to visit me. I'm so thankful she wasn't there the night Leonard took me. If she would have heard the commotion and come to check on me...I don't even want to think of what he would have done to her. She held me while I cried the tears I didn't want Knox to see, and she sat with me, reading one of her books when I was quiet. For someone who spent their life taking care of everyone else, it was a stark reminder that it's okay to let the people who love you do the same.

If he could, I think Knox would wrap me in bubble wrap until he felt the world was safe. But there's no way I'm going to live my life under lock and key. I've made concessions, though, because I understand his fear, and I'm willing to work through it with him. Even though the threat to me has been terminated, the fear for Knox is still alive and well. He follows me to school every day and walks me to my office. Then in the afternoon, he meets me at my car. If anyone's thought it odd, they haven't said anything, and his routine also does double duty. The idea that people were making jokes about Leonard and I being a couple still makes my stomach churn with disgust but seeing Knox at the school every day has made it clear that he's the only man I'm with.

When news broke that it was our vice principal who was identified as the serial killer, the town was in an up-roar. How did this happen? How was he living under our noses? How was he allowed around our children? All the questions that scared parents and residents would ask.

And believe me, those questions have run through my head time and time again. He hid his evil well, and I think that scares everyone. It's going to take some time for the town to come to terms with having a sadistic killer who masqueraded as a normal person so well that he was free to walk around this town for more than a year. It's going to take all of us some time.

But that doesn't mean I'm going to stop living my life.

The things he said to me in that cabin were the ramblings of an insane person, nothing more. And I refuse to allow any actions he took to dictate my life. And I refuse to allow my man to suddenly walk on eggshells around me, denying himself and me the life we had before. In particular, the exciting and spectacular exploration of our sex life.

It's not that Knox hasn't wanted to have sex. We've done plenty of that since my injuries have healed. And he's been more than sweet about everything. It was hard for him to see the remaining marks of the rope I was held captive with. Since that day, he hasn't pulled out any sort of restraint and has avoided all conversations surrounding it. But I know him. He's afraid that his ropes are going to bring back memories, and he's terrified of seeing that look on my face. He doesn't trust that I know the difference, which is understandable. But I can't live with him scared, and neither can he.

"Mia," he calls from my living room.

I sent him to my grandmother's to check the leaky faucet I may have had a hand in loosening, needing some time to set up a few things here.

"In here," I say, lying on the bed.

When he walks in, his eyes widen. Instantly, there's lust and heat in those blue depths. And need. The need he's denied himself the last month.

I'm wearing a dark-blue bra and panty set that matches perfectly with the midnight-blue bundle of rope lying next to me.

He squeezes his eyes shut. "Mia," he says in a rough whisper.

"Please listen to me, Knox. I love you, and I want you to hear me. You *need* to hear me."

He peels his eyelids open and nods, but there's still uncertainty in his gaze.

"I know the difference between how I was restrained and how you do it. I'm not afraid of this. Not with you. What...what that man did was to hurt me, Knox. Nothing you've ever done has been to cause me any sort of pain. But not being able to express yourself with me, not allowing me to have the freedom that your ropes bring me, that *is* hurting us."

Knox's jaw tightens, and his Adam's apple bobs slowly as he swallows. "When I saw you like that..." I stay silent, allowing him to gather his thoughts. "To see someone hurting my woman and using the same restraints I do to bring you pleasure, it fucked something up in here." He taps the side of his head.

"Are you afraid I'm going to see you as a monster?"

"I'm afraid I *am* a monster," he whispers.

I jump off the bed and go to him, wrapping my arms around his middle.

"No, Knox, no. You are anything *but*," I emphasize as I stare into his unsure blue eyes. "You know the difference between wanting to cause someone pain and wanting to bring them peace and pleasure. You can't let one person's actions completely derail the years you've spent understanding and reveling in the difference. I would never want that for you. I won't let you do that to yourself."

"Mia, when I first saw a woman being tied, it confused me that it turned me on. I had long conversations about it with Andrés. I thought there was a part of me that enjoyed a woman's pain, and that scared me, especially considering what I saw when I was little. When I talked with Camila about how she felt being in ropes, that cleared up my doubts. I realized it was the pleasure I was giving to another person, that the control I had in giving it was what I craved. But seeing what he did, knowing he was getting some twisted enjoyment from seeing you like that, it brought back all of those questions and doubts. And yeah, it scares the hell out of me that even a small part of you could see me as a monster."

"Don't you see the difference, though? You just said it. You realized that you craved it because you wanted to be the one giving pleasure. That it made sense after you talked to Camila because you understood what it does for the person being tied up. That's as far from being a monster as you can get, Knox. And as for me, I will *never* see you like that. It's not just you who needs this, Knox. It's me too." I take a breath and reach up to kiss him. "If you need more time, I understand, but please don't deny yourself or me because of your misguided fear that I'll see you as anything less than the man who loves me with his whole being and would literally walk through fire to save me. I know your heart." I rest my hand on his thumping chest. "I trust your heart."

I feel him relax into me even further. When he exhales, it's as though all the tension and worry he's been carrying around is expelled in that breath.

He presses his forehead to mine. "Fuck, baby. I don't know what I did in a past life to deserve you, but I hope you know I'm never letting you go."

"Good thing because there's no way you're getting rid of me."

He lifts his head and stares into my eyes as though he's looking for something more than what I just told him.

"You'll tell me if it's too much?"

"I promise," I answer with firm certainty.

In the blink of an eye, he captures my lips in an explosive kiss. This is the Knox I need, the man who has so much passion inside of him he can hardly keep it contained.

His hands run down my back and under my ass before he lifts me from the floor, and I wrap my legs around his hips. Without breaking the kiss, he walks us over to the bed and lays me down, his weight covering me, pinning me to the mattress. I rub my center against him, desperate to relieve the ache he so skillfully creates in me.

"Do you need to come, baby?" he asks, breaking the kiss before moving lower and swiping his tongue and lips over the tops of my breasts.

"Please," I reply in a rough whisper.

Knox continues to taste my skin as he makes his descent down my body. Every kiss, every swipe of his tongue, lights me up inside. When he reaches the apex of my thighs, he looks up, and our gazes stay locked as he gently uses a finger to move my panties from my center. Then he lowers his head and begins licking at me mercilessly. I'm writhing under his tongue, my hands tangling in the soft blanket at my sides.

The way Knox eats my pussy like he's a starving man will never cease to drive me wild with desire. It doesn't take long for the orgasm to build while he flicks his tongue against my swollen clit over and over. He worships me with his mouth, his tongue, and his lips. He moans with satisfaction as I begin to feel the telltale flutters of my fast-approaching orgasm. Two of his fingers enter me, and when he finds that bundle of nerves, my world explodes. I'm robbed of every other sense except the sheer magnitude of the pleasure rolling through my entire body. Knox licks at me through the crest of every wave I fall under, over and over until I'm a satiated mess of sweaty limbs lying limp beneath him.

"I'll never experience anything as beautiful as watching you come undone under my touch, Mia."

His words of love and appreciation always make me feel—no, believe—that I'm the most precious thing to the man kneeling in front of me.

Knox stands from the floor, and with one hand, he grabs the back of his shirt and pulls it over his head. He makes quick work of ridding himself of his jeans and steps out of them, kicking the denim to the side. His hand finds his thick shaft, and he runs his fist over the length. Walking to the side of my bed, he grabs a condom and tosses the packet onto the bed.

I sit up as Knox stands at the foot of the bed and hand him the bundle of rope.

"You're an eager little thing, aren't you?"

"Yes," I say without any shame at showing him how desperate I am.

He kneels on the bed, and I place my hands on his lap. This is how it always starts. It's my way of telling him I'm ready. That I want this. That I'm handing control over to him because I know I can trust him. Knox loops the rope around my wrists, and with a quick tug, I feel the pressure against my skin.

"What color?" he asks.

"Green."

He smiles and begins looping the rope around my middle and up to my breasts in a similar way to the first time we experienced this together. When he finishes, he leans back and examines his work. I'm still on my knees, sitting back on my heels, watching him through hooded eyes.

"What color?"

"Green. Please, Knox," I beg. "I need you inside of me."

Knox reaches for the condom on the bed and tears the package open, his gaze only leaving mine for a brief moment while he rolls the condom on. He pulls my panties off before spreading my thighs. His hand grasps one ankle and lifts my leg straight, resting it against his shoulder while my other leg is bent with his hand on my knee, pressing my thigh into the mattress. I'm spread wide for him as he stares at my wet center and licks his lips.

"God, I don't know if I want to taste you again or fuck you."

"Fuck me, please."

Pulling me to the edge of the bed, he stands with his legs wide and bends at the knees, entering me in one quick thrust.

"Fuck," he bellows as he begins pumping into me at a furious pace. "Your pussy feels so good around me, Mia."

Sweat gathers at his hairline as he watches his cock enter me, then slide out again and again. His hand leaves my knee, and his fingers begin rubbing over my clit with perfect pressure.

"I need you to come, baby. I'm almost there. Fuck, your pussy takes me so good."

His words, his fingers, and his cock make it impossible for me to hold in the torrent of sensation ricocheting through my body. I cry out, the pleasure building faster than ever, and my pussy clamps down around him. Knox never slows his thrusting as his cock jerks inside of me.

"Ahh, fuck," he yells as he thrusts one last time and holds himself inside of me. His breath comes in harsh pants before he slowly pulls out.

"I love you," he says and sinks to his knees, gently kissing my thighs, then my pussy. His kisses aren't meant to excite, though any time his lips touch me, that's exactly what happens. This is his way of worshipping me, of showing me that he loves me and honors the power I willingly hand over to him every time he ties me up.

He stands and helps me into a sitting position so he can untie the knots. And like every time before, his lips caress every line left behind by his ropes.

The idea that I would feel anything other than adored and respected by Knox is so completely beyond anything I could comprehend. The time and care he takes with me has shown me that, and he's proven it many times over.

He lies on his back and gathers me in his arms, running his calloused hands over the soft skin at my waist, then down the thigh I have resting over his leg.

"Thank you," he whispers after a few silent moments as we both relish being in the other's arms.

"For what?"

"For reminding me who I am. For reminding me who we are. I love you, sweetheart. More than I ever thought a man like me could love anyone. More than I ever thought I deserved."

Tears prick my eyes. How many times have I thought the same thing about myself? I always thought it was stupid to think one person could somehow make you whole. That one person could make you look at yourself and your world in an entirely new way. Then Knox Turner kissed me, and I realized I was the stupid one for ever doubting that it was possible.

Or that I deserved it.

"I love you, too."

EPILOGUE
MIA

Summer vacation is finally here. Maizie and I are at the park with Colby, enjoying a warm day and an iced coffee.

"You look good," she says, eyeing me up and down.

"I feel good. The sun is out, I have a delicious beverage, and I'm here with one of my favorite people in the world. What's not to feel good about?"

Maizie leans back and exhales a long breath. "Fuck, I need to get laid. If getting some on the regular has you waxing poetic, I'm definitely missing out."

"Well, there's a certain biker I know who has had his eye on you," I say in a singsong voice.

She shakes her head. "Nope. No bikers. Plus, I work for the club, and that adds in a layer of shit I have zero interest in navigating."

"So you're not the least bit interested?"

"Nope," she replies.

Yeah, she's full of shit, but I don't press her on it.

"Any plans this summer?" she asks.

"Knox is planning a road trip on the bike. I'm not sure what he has in mind, but he told me not to worry about it, that he's taking care of everything."

That's a concept I'm still struggling with—that someone else is taking care of all the details. That I can actually trust someone else to do it. I realized it hasn't always been about no one else willing to pick up the slack. Sometimes, it was about me not allowing them to pick it up. Knox has called me out a couple of times for my tendency to manage everything and everyone, though he may have used the words control freak. It's taken time, but Knox has shown me that a part of letting go is about trusting him. It's easy in the bedroom. Not as easy in real life. But I'm learning, and he's patient.

Colby runs over to us, jumping from foot to foot. "Mommy, I have to peeeee."

Maizie looks at me and laughs. "Let's go," she says and heads with him to the bathroom on the other side of the park.

I sit on the bench and tilt my head toward the sky, letting the sun warm my smiling face.

A shadow falls over me, and I open my eyes, turning my head to the end of the bench.

"Hey, Mia."

Nolan stands in front of me, tall and proud, with a smile on his face that doesn't quite reach his eyes. "Long time."

"What are you doing here?" I ask.

"Business."

My gaze travels over my brother who I haven't laid eyes on in years. He looks the same, maybe a little more filled out, but still holds himself with that cocky attitude he's always had. Girls used to find it attractive, but I always thought he was an asshole who thought more of himself than he had any right to. I take notice of the leather vest he's wearing. It's a cut much like the one Knox wears.

Looking past him, I spot Maizie making her way toward us, holding Colby's hand. Nolan notices that he's no longer the center of my attention and turns around to see what I'm staring at.

That's when I see the large patch on the back of his cut and read the top rocker.

Bone Breakers.

The End

Thank you so much for picking up Mia and Knox's story. I hope you had as good of a time reading them as I did writing them. If you loved them, it would mean the world to me if you left a review where you purchased the book. Reviews are such an amazing way to help out indie authors like myself share their stories with the world.

Do you want to know what it was like for a few of my guys growing up in Shine? Join my newsletter by going to my website www.katerandallauthor.com or scan the QR code to get the free prequel, **Rose Colored Glasses,** when you subscribe. It's an angsty first-love novella featuring Ozzy and Freya. See where they got their start!

<u>Stalk me on my socials!</u>
TikTok
Facebook
Instagram
Goodreads
BookBub
Or you can scan the QR code below for a link to all my socials and to sign up for my newsletter and get your free copy of **Rose Colored Glasses!**

ALSO BY KATE

<u>The Ones Series</u>
The Good One
The Fragile One
The Other One

<u>The Black Roses MC</u>
Linc
Jude
Ozzy
Knox
Wyatt

<u>The Boston Syndicate</u>
Finn
Luca
Eoghan
Cillian

About Kate

Kate is a lover of all things books. It doesn't matter what sub-genre, as long as there's a HEA, she's in. She started reading romance in high school and would hide novels in textbooks to read during class. Becoming an author was always a dream she had and finally decided to put pen to paper (or finger to keyboard) and write what she loves. She grew up in the beautiful upper peninsula of Michigan then became a West Coast girl where she lives with her amazing husband and hilarious son. She would love to hear from readers so check out all her socials and sign up for her newsletter so she can keep you up to date on her books and whatever other ramblings come to mind.

Acknowledgements

I want to start by saying *thank you* for going on Mia and Knox's journey with me. Without you picking up these books and loving my bikers as much as I do, I wouldn't be here writing what I love. MC romance holds a special place in my heart, and I'm thrilled it does for you, too.

Huge thank you to Kiki, Megan and Anna with Next Step PR. They keep me organized and help me immensely with all of this author stuff. And they are all wonderful people who support me and this community in so many different ways. You guys are absolute rockstars!

Thank you to my editor, Victoria. You help me polish my words and make my stories the best they can possibly be. You're never allowed to leave me!

Big thanks to my proofreader, Rose. Oh my gosh, thank the gods for your eagle-eyes!

And as always, thank you to my amazing husband who holds my hand—and oftentimes my sanity—in his. I couldn't do this without you.